Sisters
Ever After

ENDORSEMENTS

From the opening page to the last, Erin S. Quint has crafted a cannot-put-it-down novel. Warning: don't start this book at bedtime!
—**Kathleen Y'Barbo**, Publishers Weekly bestselling author of *New Leash on Life* and *The Bayou Nouvelle Brides*

Erin S. Quint never disappoints with her fun, romantic, and realistic stories.
—**Barbara M. Britton**, author, the Tribes of Israel series and Whispering Creek series

Something you can always expect from an Erin S. Quint novel are real, engaging characters that you fall in love with. And Gianna and Brock are no exception. I'd love to sit down with them and share a cup of coffee and a game of twenty questions. Bravo to Ms. Quint for another captivating story.
—**Carol James**, author, *Streams in the Wasteland*, *Redemptive Romances*

Erin S. Quint does a fine job with her first book for Elk Lake, also the first in the Canadian Meadows series. The spiritual arc in this story is strong, and not tacked on. Faith permeates these characters. This is a good book and a promising series.
—**Kathleen D. Bailey**, author of the Western Dreams series and *Hilltop Christmas*

Sisters

Ever After

Erin S. Quint

ELK LAKE PUBLISHING INC.
PUBLISHING THE POSITIVE
Plymouth, Massachusetts
A Christian Company
ElkLakePublishingInc.com

COPYRIGHT NOTICE

Cover and Interior Design:
Editor(s): Cristel Phelps; Deb Haggerty

PUBLISHED BY: Elk Lake Publishing, Inc., 35 Dogwood Drive, Plymouth, MA 02360, 2024

Library Cataloging Data
Names: Quint, Erin S. (Erin S. Quint)
Sisters Ever After / Erin S. Quint
314 p. 23cm × 15cm (9in × 6 in.)
ISBN-13: 9798891341159 (paperback) | 9798891341166 (trade paperback) | 9798891341173 (e-book)
Key Words: romance; remarriage; mystery; family; faith; trust; blended family
Library of Congress Control Number: 2024xxxxxx Fiction

DEDICATION

This one's for you, Weasel. You know why.

PROLOGUE

Brock Hennessey signed the note, wrapped the message over some folded bills, and stuffed the wad in an envelope. He scrawled a name on the front. A pang of remorse squeezed his heart. He shoved another couple of bills in and laid the envelope on the kitchen counter next to the front door key.

The digital clock on the stove turned from 11:59 to midnight. Brock took one more look around to make sure he hadn't left anything. The day he had moved into the small, furnished duplex five years ago was a distant memory.

But the time had come. He had no other choice. This chapter in their life was over.

Brock walked to the couch and gazed at his sleeping daughter. A wave of fierce protection rolled through his veins, and he bowed his head in a silent plea. He hoped to God he was doing the right thing.

Brock tiptoed to the couch, scooped her into his arms, flipped off the feeble overhead light, and closed the door. He was anxious to get on the road, but he had one last thing to do.

Twenty minutes later, he knelt beside a small headstone. His daughter slept in the idling car mere feet away. A crushing weight settled in Brock's chest, and the heartbreak from the first goodbye flooded his thoughts. A sob escaped as he kissed his fingers and touched them to the name on the cold, engraved marble. *TJ.* Dark hair and dancing eyes swam before his eyes.

He returned to the car without looking back, shifted into gear, and drove away. They needed to be as far away from San Diego as possible before morning.

CHAPTER 1

CANADIAN MEADOWS, MONTANA

Gianna Harper skimmed her feet along the slick, wet sidewalk and concentrated on maintaining her balance. She clutched an umbrella and her keys in one hand, and the straps of her laptop and purse dug into her shoulder. Two plastic bags dangled from her other arm, the hand cradling a bakery box. A foam cup balanced on top, a curl of steam rising from the opening in the lid.

She should have made two trips, but women followed an unwritten rule about getting everything in one trip. Gianna was certain if she didn't, she would let the universal sisterhood down. Mornings were difficult enough without rain and high winds. Now she had to make a decision in order to get the back door to her hair salon unlocked and to open her valued cargo safely inside. Something had to give.

Gianna had washed her hair upon awakening but planned to complete the dry and style at the shop before her first customer arrived, so the decision was easy. The umbrella hit the pavement and bounced away, carried by a gust of wind. She'd retrieve it later.

Her hand shook as she inserted the key into the lock, but Gianna focused on the foam cup. She couldn't wait to take the first long, hot swallow, to feel the ambrosia flushing through her body. Was there any better way to face a Monday?

Door open. Light on. Twelve steps to the counter. Almost there.

Her phone blasted, and Gianna flinched. "For the love of ..." As she grabbed for the cup, everything else tumbled out of her arms onto the floor, and she rummaged in her pocket for the cell.

"Hello?"

"Mrs. Harper?"

Am I even a Mrs. anymore? Gianna ignored the shaft of pain piercing her heart and pushed a piece of dripping hair off her forehead. "Yes?"

"This is Ms. Fleming calling from the school. Paisley forgot her lunch."

Not again. "I'm so sorry. I set the bag next to her backpack." Gianna closed her eyes and lifted the cup to her lips. She took a long drink and nearly sighed out loud. Her daughter was almost ten. Shouldn't she be more responsible? No doubt Paisley was engrossed in a book. Gianna had been rushing around trying to pull her own things together and didn't follow up.

She swallowed. "Can she buy a hot lunch today?"

Ms. Fleming paused. "Yes. But no more until you pay the balance on your account." The woman's voice softened and was laced with pity.

Gianna took another deep drink and rubbed her temple. "I—I'll take care of the payment today." Her resources were drying up. Last week, a check she wrote from her joint account with Greg bounced, and she had no idea why. They had always carried a healthy balance. She swallowed past the lump in her throat. "Thank you, Ms. Fleming."

A beat of uncomfortable silence followed. "I know it's been hard for you, Mrs. Harper. If you want, you can apply for assistance—"

"No," Gianna cut in sharply. She straightened her spine and winced. "The offer isn't necessary. I appreciate your—" She fumbled for her next words. "—concern." The platitude sounded hollow in her ears.

The truth was, Gianna didn't appreciate much of anything from anyone in Canadian Meadows right now. She'd always considered the town of almost seven thousand to be not too small but not too big. The close-knit sense of community and neighborly concern she'd grown to love over the past eight years now mocked her. Greg Harper hadn't been well-liked, but his widow would survive and carry on ... without charity or pity.

Gianna ended the call and tossed her phone on the counter, then gathered her items from the floor. She lifted the lid of the box and breathed a sigh of relief when she saw the two muffins nestled together still intact.

The light caught the large diamond on her wedding ring, and Gianna's heart gave a painful squeeze. She sank onto the stool at the counter and covered her mouth in an effort to hold in a sob. Would these waves of grief ever stop?

Gianna couldn't believe she wasn't even thirty yet and now a widow. She closed her eyes and let her mind go to a place from which she'd desperately tried to keep it for the past thirty-four days—thoughts of Greg. She still couldn't accept she would never see, hear, or touch him again. Never see the appreciative light in his gaze when he arrived home after a trip. Never go on another date night or romantic moonlit walk. Never hear his terrible singing in the shower.

And she would never know what he had been hiding from her for the last few months.

Gianna reached across the counter for a tissue and dried her eyes. She had no idea what she would do.

The back door flew open, and her coworker and best friend, Vanessa, blew in. "Is this your umbrella?"

Gianna coughed and turned away. "Ah, yeah, thanks. You can throw it in the corner."

Vanessa was one of the most intuitive people Gianna had ever known. Vanessa walked over and opened her arms. "Oh, sweets." Gianna loved Van's pet name for her.

No words were needed. Gianna let the tears fall as Van held her. Moments later, she straightened and reached for more tissues. "I brought muffins."

Vanessa closed her eyes and moaned. "Lemon blueberry or chocolate cheesecake?"

Gianna walked over to the counter and flipped a smile over her shoulder. "One of each. You choose."

Van shot her a sly smile. "You know me too well, girlfriend." She hung her jacket on a peg and took a knife from the drawer. "We'll split them."

"Probably the last ones for a while." Gianna lifted her cup. "And my budget can't handle many more of these."

Vanessa's green eyes widened as she stepped to the small coffee maker and put a filter in the basket. "You mean you'll force yourself to drink this swill the rest of us live with?"

Gianna grimaced. "I may not have a choice." She shook her head and sighed.

Vanessa prepared the coffee and flipped the switch on. "I'm so sorry, sweets." She spread her hands out. "If I had any extra at all—"

Gianna waved her off. "You know I wouldn't take your money." She tilted her head. "Your hair turned out great. The color looks even better today."

Van ran her fingers through the long waves falling past her shoulder blades. "Not too much blonde?"

Gianna shook her head. "Not at all. There's so much depth. You can still see the brunette through it. I'm glad we went with two shades of gold instead of one. Look at the sparkle when you turn your head."

Van shimmied her shoulders. "I hope Reid likes my new look."

"Is this getting serious?"

Van folded her hands as if in prayer. "I sure hope so."

Gianna smiled. "I'm so happy for you. He seems like a great guy." *Van's love life is beginning, and mine is over.*

Vanessa stepped to her side and squeezed her shoulder. "Are you getting any answers at all?"

Gianna took a bite of muffin. "Greg's business dealings are so much more complicated than I ever realized."

"I'm sure," Van murmured.

Gianna wasn't willing to share more—for now. She nibbled at her muffin halves and sipped her coffee. "I have an appointment with his accountant in Kalispell on Thursday." Surely by then the man would have discovered why the check bounced. Greg must have moved their money into one of his other accounts. In the past, he'd shuffled some of the funds around, but not all. She shook off a feeling of unease.

"Maybe you can straighten things out enough to get at least part of the insurance money released," Vanessa mused.

Gianna's stomach sank. Not until the detective in charge of the investigation into Greg's accident offered some answers. Fortunately, details about the single-vehicle crash had been withheld from the press, and Gianna had kept things to herself.

"I hope," she said vaguely. Gianna finished the last of her breakfast and dusted the crumbs from her hands. "What's on the schedule for today?" She opened her laptop and stared at the screen. "Two perms this morning, five shampoo and cuts, and a full color."

"Sher Graham?" Vanessa asked around her last bite of muffin.

Gianna nodded, and the two friends exchanged eye rolls. "Maybe we can convince her to tone the color down this time," Gianna said with a laugh. Why sixty-five-year-old Sher thought flame orange complemented her pale skin was beyond them.

Vanessa peered over Gianna's shoulder. "Afternoon's full, too, and we'll get a lot of walk-ins."

Gianna let out a breath. "I don't mind. We need the business." She slapped a high-five on her friend's outstretched hand. Then her optimism turned to dread as she scrolled through her email. "Oh no."

Vanessa's brow wrinkled. "What?"

"The rental on Lake Helena Road. The tenant's father had a heart attack back in Minnesota and isn't expected to survive. He's leaving this morning." The guy was a contract worker and Gianna hadn't expected him to stay long term, but she was counting on the income from the rentals to keep food on the table and the lights on while she waited for Greg's estate to untangle itself.

Vanessa squeezed her arm. "You'll find another renter."

Gianna rubbed a hand over her face and expelled a breath. "Not with the way things have been over the last year." She had a high-level understanding of Greg's property management business even though she'd never been involved in the day-to-day dealings. A couple of the properties had sat empty for months, one after they'd had to go through the eviction process and spend several thousand dollars to repair the damage. Greg had rented the newly fixed house a week before the accident.

Van's expression brightened. "Why don't you sell off a couple of the properties? Fewer hassles, and the funds would tide you over until the insurance money comes through."

Gianna winced. "My name isn't on any of them. I can't do anything until the estate settles."

"I'm sorry."

A wave of helplessness dropped Gianna into her chair. She ground her teeth to bite back a boiling mix of anger, grief, and frustration. At last, she braved a look at Van. "What will I do with these properties? I can't handle all this along with the salon. I don't even know how many there are, and no one at Greg's office seems to know who's doing the maintenance on them." *No one* equated to the woman who answered the phone and shuffled papers. A few others had worked with him, but Gianna didn't know them.

The words came pouring out. "In the last week, one house developed an electrical problem, and I had to pay overtime wages to a plumber to fix a bad leak at another. The front steps on the house over on Sycamore are crumbling, and I'm trying to get bids to replace the concrete before someone falls and sues me for negligence. One of the trees in the backyard of the Apple Valley house is almost dead, and those tenants have been calling nonstop. One strong wind, the tree crashes into the house, and I'll have to replace a roof and who knows what else, but I have no idea what to do."

Vanessa rubbed her arm. "I wish I knew someone who could help."

Gianna inhaled and counted to ten, then exhaled. "Have I told you lately how much I appreciate you? I couldn't—" The lump in her throat made further conversation impossible.

"Hey, girl." Vanessa's arms surrounded her with the comfort only one's best friend could give. "You'll be fine. I'm not going anywhere. We'll get through this together." She patted Gianna's damp hair. "Come on, let's get you dried and combed out."

Gianna squeezed Vanessa's hands. "I'm so thankful for you," she whispered.

CHAPTER 2

"Daddy, why are we in the truck?" A pause. "Where are we?"

Brock rubbed his hand over his stubbly beard and met his daughter's gaze in the rearview mirror as best he could in the predawn darkness.

Piper was resistant to change. Explaining to her wouldn't be easy, and the conversation wouldn't go well with distance between them and the constraint of seatbelts. She would need lots of hugs and squeezes for reassurance. Brock wouldn't have it any other way. He glanced at the clock and winced. They'd been on the road five hours. He had hoped to put more miles behind them before their first stop.

He cleared his throat and tried to insert some enthusiasm into his voice. "We're taking a sort of vacation."

"In the middle of the school year?" Piper's voice was incredulous. "On a *Thursday*?"

This was the problem with his precocious, nine-year-old daughter. Her mind processed everything quickly, and whatever he offered as a simple answer always led to more questions.

Brock scanned the inky darkness beyond the beams of the headlights. According to the GPS on his new burner phone, they were past the Mojave National Preserve and should cross out of California into Nevada any minute. The trip would take close to twenty-four hours if Brock traveled the interstate, which he had no intention of doing. Sticking to back highways would add to their travel time but staying undetectable was more important.

"Let me find a place to pull off. Then we'll have some breakfast and have a little talk."

"Where? I don't see anywhere to eat. There aren't even any lights," she grumbled.

If they were lucky, they wouldn't see a fast-food sign for the next thousand miles. Brock had packed a cooler with all her favorite foods and drinks and had another bag filled with chapter books and puzzles in the back of the truck next to the tent. He hadn't had time to do much other than close his bank account, delete his online footprint, empty out the duplex, and leave.

"I need to go to the bathroom." Brock had made preparations, but she wouldn't be happy. Dawn was about to swallow the darkness, and he saw a stand of scrubby trees ahead. He slowed and eased the vehicle off the deserted road.

"Hold on a minute." He jumped out of the truck, lifted the back hatch, and snatched a roll of toilet paper from the top of one of the boxes. He opened the back door and held out the roll.

"Really?" Piper muttered. Brock couldn't help smiling at her pert little nose scrunching up.

She unhooked her seat belt and climbed out of the truck. Brock patted her shoulder. "Come on, you've done this when we've gone camping."

"Only because I didn't have a choice." She stomped off and disappeared behind the trees. When she returned a few minutes later, fingers of sparkling golden sun peeked over the horizon, beckoning them to grab hold of the new day.

Brock had opened the tailgate and laid out a simple breakfast spread. Cinnamon buns, milk for her, a thermos of coffee for him. He halved an orange and a banana and gave her half of each, their ritual.

Piper climbed onto the tailgate, then exchanged the toilet paper for a bottle of hand sanitizer. She knew the drill. "Do you have my glasses?"

Brock lifted them out of his shirt pocket and handed them over. She slipped them on.

"What's the real story?" As he expected, she wouldn't make things easy.

Brock busied himself opening the carton of milk. How did you tell a nine-year-old her mother's been released from jail and is threatening to come after her? Especially when she's never known her mother was alive?

He aimed for a reassuring smile. "I have a new job. It'll be exciting." He set the bun on a paper towel.

Piper didn't blink. She took a sip of her milk and shot him an even gaze. "Why are we in the desert?" She'd had her glasses on for thirty seconds and had already identified their surroundings in the shadowy darkness.

"My new job isn't in San Diego."

Her chin quivered. "We're moving?"

Brock sighed. "Yeah, honey. We—we have to. Aww, come here." He moved around to her other side and took her in his arms.

For a moment, he held her and watched the rosy golden sunrise give way to buttery yellow. Reveling in the feel of her hair against his jaw, he closed his eyes and drank in her little-girl scent.

"But why, Daddy? Why? I didn't—I won't be able to say goodbye to Miss Carmen. Or my friends. Or Daisy." The tears fell in earnest. "I won't—s-see her—pup-p-p-ies."

Brock's heart splintered as he held his daughter tighter and blinked away the wetness in his own eyes. "I know, Pipe, I know. I'm so sorry." For the past five years, the retired woman who owned the duplex and lived in the other half had been the sole maternal figure Piper had known. Carmen had been so good to them, and the money Brock had stuffed in the envelope couldn't begin to repay her kindness.

Brock drew back and grabbed a napkin, making a clumsy attempt to dry her tears. He took her hands. "You mean more to me than anything in the world. You're my girl." He swallowed. "You have to trust me for now. This is the best way for us."

Another piece of his heart chipped off as her tears-shiny, trusting gaze met his, and she nodded.

He struggled to push out the next words. "I would never, ever take you away from everything and everyone you've ever known and loved if there was any other way." He swallowed around the boulder in his throat. "I love you." The words came out little more than a whisper.

Piper threw her arms around his neck and squeezed harder than he imagined she could. She nodded, and her voice broke. "I love you, too, Daddy. I trust you." She dropped her arms and sat up straighter. "Am I allowed to know where we're going?"

"Yes. A small town called Canadian Meadows, Montana, not far from the border."

Piper loved geography and made the connection quickly. Her mouth formed an O. "The border into Canada?"

Brock smiled and nodded.

"Cool. Maybe we can go." Her lips pursed in concentration. "But we would need passports." Her earlier apprehension regarding the move had evaporated.

Brock had fleetingly thought of this, but there hadn't been time to make the necessary arrangements. The documentation would give him another option if they needed to keep moving.

"What states are we driving through?"

"Nevada, then Utah, Idaho, and Montana. You can be in charge of the road atlas."

Her eyes shone. "Awesome. What are we waiting for?" She threw her arms around him and squeezed.

Brock hugged her back, and the bands circling his chest relaxed. If this was all he ever had, Piper safe in his arms would be enough.

With each mile taking them farther from California, Brock relaxed. He rolled the windows down to let in the cleansing wind. The absence of congestion and city smells was heavenly, as was the pristine sunlight. He cranked up the oldies and belted out his favorites, even though he was pretty sure he sang in a different key most of the time. Piper pretended to complain, but soon she joined him.

"We're in Utah now, right?" she called from the backseat.

"Yes, ma'am. We're coming into some mountains." In an effort to be overly cautious, Brock was keeping to lesser-traveled roads. The beautiful scenery and absence of traffic made for a relaxing trip. He had every intention of driving straight through, but late in the afternoon when they crested a hilltop, his plan came to a screeching halt.

A long, narrow valley lay before them, cocooned between two mountain ranges. Trees hugged the hills, and a rolling river accompanied the winding road. Sunlight sparkled off the crystal water like diamonds.

"Can we stop? Can we camp here tonight?" Piper exclaimed.

Brock opened his mouth to refuse, then saw her hopeful expression in the mirror. He'd ripped his daughter out of their familiar life and spirited her away in the night. A delay wouldn't hurt. The new job would be there waiting for him. His plan was to arrive in Montana over the weekend so Piper could start school Monday morning, but no one was expecting her, so one more day wouldn't matter.

Brock pulled off onto a side road. "Yeah, let's explore." His daughter rewarded him with a smile.

As far as he could tell, the valley was deserted. Piper was disappointed when he said they couldn't have a campfire, but she understood when he explained.

He fixed a simple supper from the provisions he'd packed in the coolers and pulled out a deck of cards when they were finished. They played War, and Piper won. Then, Brock set up the small dome tent, and they climbed into their sleeping bags.

"I love camping." She snuggled into his side. Peace settled on Brock, and for the first time in a day and a half, he had the assurance he'd made the right decision for the two of them.

He didn't set an alarm, and they set out the next morning after enjoying a leisurely breakfast. Brock decided to maintain a comfortable pace for the remainder of the trip. He wanted his daughter to have good memories of this pivotal time in their lives. When they saw something interesting, they stopped. They hiked, and Piper picked wildflowers. One afternoon, they took a nap in a shady spot next to a stream.

They were on a desolate stretch of road in Idaho when Brock sensed a change. Had they crossed into Montana? He looked in vain for a sign, but saw nothing. Some invisible essence seemed to embrace them. Impossibly, the landscape grew more beautiful, the mountains more majestic. The sun glowed brighter, and the sky seemed to swell. Brock took a deep breath, filling his lungs with clean, fresh mountain air.

He met his daughter's gaze in the mirror. "We're in Big Sky Country, little one."

Piper threw her arms open. "Welcome to Montana."

CHAPTER 3

"What do you think, Mrs. Chamberlain?"

The lady turned her head one way, then the other, and smiled at her reflection. "Lovely. You're a miracle worker as always."

The bell on the shop door jingled. Gianna's back was to the door, and even though one jingle couldn't sound different from the rest, somehow this one did.

"Hey, Momma," the most cherished voice in the world sang out.

Gianna's irritation from the morning evaporated under the sunshine of Paisley's smile. "Hey, Curly Girlie." One more cloud of hairspray, and Mrs. Chamberlain was done for this week. Gianna removed the drape and lowered the chair.

"Hello, Mrs. Chamberlain," Paisley said as she hugged her mother.

Gianna glanced between the two and couldn't believe it. Paisley was almost as tall as the woman. True, Mrs. Chamberlain stood an inch or so over five feet, but when had Gianna's little girl sprouted? Soon, she'd be growing out of her jeans, and where would Gianna find the money for new ones? This was a new challenge for her. She pushed the thought out of her mind.

"You look so pretty today, Paisley. Are those new glasses?" Mrs. Chamberlain asked.

"Yes. Momma let me choose them."

The little lady reached out and patted one of the girl's long, shiny, thick curls. "Your hair is such a pretty color."

"Thank you," Paisley said politely, and Gianna's heart swelled.

Mrs. Chamberlain looked at Gianna. "What is this shade called?"

Gianna thought a moment. "Sable brown. Much prettier than mine."

"Yours is lovely too, dear. Black and shiny, with almost a tinge of blue in the light."

"Thank you, Mrs. Chamberlain."

"Can I have a snack, Momma?" Paisley asked.

"*May* I have a snack? Yes, from the fridge." Gianna squeezed Paisley's shoulder. "Twenty minutes of reading or screen time, and then homework." Most fifth graders would choose screen time, but Paisley almost always opted for a book. Gianna was fine with her daughter's choice.

Paisley headed for the back room while Gianna moved to the cash register with Mrs. Chamberlain and completed her transaction. "See you next week."

As the woman exited, a tall man with dark hair stepped into the shop and held the door for her. Gianna had never seen him before. Who was he?

Brock closed the door and stepped to the counter. A tall, slender woman with raven hair and tired eyes greeted him. "May I help you?"

Brock smiled. "You can if you're Mrs. Harper. I'm looking for your husband."

The woman gripped the counter, and her hand turned white. "I'm Mrs. Harper. Who told you to come here?"

"I went to his office, but no one was there. The lady at the insurance agency next door directed me here. All my calls go to voicemail, and he hasn't returned any of them."

Her features tightened, and her eyes turned flinty. "May I ask what this is in regard to?"

Brock pulled some papers from his jacket pocket. "He offered me a job. I planned to come ... later, but things ... my timetable changed, and I'm here now. He said I could come anytime."

"Look, Mr.—"

"Hennessey, Brock Hennessey." He held out his hand.

Mrs. Harper's fingers brushed his before pulling away. "Mr. Hennessey. I'm sorry to have to tell you this, but my husband is ... he's deceased."

"He's—oh, I'm, I'm so sorry, ma'am." He swallowed.

"Thank you," she said curtly. She stepped from behind the counter and turned her attention to a woman and little girl sitting in the corner. "Are you ready, Violet?"

The little girl clapped her hands. "Yes. I love getting my hair cut."

Brock's mind swirled with the implications of this tragic development. He tapped Mrs. Harper on the arm. "Excuse me. I ... um, look, could we talk?"

"About what?"

"I—" he ran a hand through his hair. "He offered me a job, and I drove here from California and I ... I need the work. I can do anything—"

Mrs. Harper straightened. "Mr. Hennessey," she said, enunciating each syllable, "whatever job my husband offered you is no longer available. Did you not hear me say he is dead?" Her voice shuddered with rage.

"I know, and I am so sorry." He pulled some papers out of his back pocket, opened them, and pointed. "Here's my contract."

"Which is, no doubt, null and void now upon his death."

Brock's heart thundered. He was more than a thousand miles from all he had ever known, almost out of resources, and had no idea where to turn. "I need a job."

"The Burger Barn is always hiring," she snapped.

He exhaled loudly. "This contract was my lifeline. I'm not willing to walk away." He tapped the papers. "I want to investigate this to see if I have any legal rights." He probably didn't, but he hadn't read the fine print and needed to buy some time to plan his next steps.

Gianna pointed to the door, willing her hand not to shake. "Get out."

"Excuse me?"

"I'm asking you to leave. Now." She pulled out her phone.

Brock held up his hands, palms out. "I'm going." He didn't know where he and Piper would sleep tonight, but God would provide.

A blonde woman wearing an apron identical to Mrs. Harper's slipped an arm around the indignant woman's shoulder. "Let's talk," she murmured and looked at Brock. "We need a minute. You wait right there."

Gianna followed Van into the back room where Paisley sat at the counter, engrossed in her book. Van lowered her voice to a whisper. "This guy could be the answer to your prayers."

Gianna shook her head in confusion. "What are you talking about?"

"Apparently, he had some kind of deal with Greg. He looks a little desperate, but I'm not getting any weird vibes off him. I think his reaction to the news of Greg's death was real. He said he could do anything. Why don't you ask him to stay around and work on the rental properties while you look into his contract?"

Gianna blew a piece of stray hair off her forehead and crossed her arms. "What an awful idea. We don't know anything about him. What makes you think he could do maintenance work?"

Vanessa looked at her intently. "I have a hunch. With those muscles, he can at least swing a hammer."

Gianna hadn't noticed any muscles. "I—I can't afford to hire someone right now."

"Maybe you can work something out. Maybe you have something he needs."

Gianna shot her friend a dark look.

"I didn't mean ... um, sweets." Van giggled and rubbed Gianna's arm.

Gianna nibbled at her thumbnail and didn't respond.

Van threw up her hands. "You have a better idea? Or do you want him hiring an attorney and bringing another monkey into your circus?"

Gianna sighed. With each passing day, another layer of confusion landed on her shoulders. Could this be God's provision for one of her dilemmas? "I suppose I can talk with him."

"Stay here, I'll bring him to you. I'll finish Henry's haircut and then do Violet's trim." She breezed back into the shop.

Gianna barely had time to pull her jumbled thoughts together when her friend returned with Brock Hennessey, who looked a little wary.

Van took Paisley by the arm. "Come with me, honey," she ordered, and off they went, leaving Gianna and the man alone.

Silence enveloped them, and his presence filled the room, which until now had always seemed adequate. Gianna took note of him. She was five feet nine in flats but came to his shoulder. He was certainly broad. Van was right about the muscles.

Gianna pulled out a stool at the counter and motioned for him to sit on the other one. She still wasn't crazy about having this conversation. She cleared her throat. "Mr. Hennessey—"

He gave her a crooked smile. "Call me Brock."

She ignored the comment. "You believe you had an arrangement with my husband." Gianna swallowed a frisson of unease. The more she dug into Greg's business dealings, combined with the details surrounding his accident, and now the missing money, the more unsettling things became. What if this man was connected? Gianna knew nothing about him, or whether she could even trust him.

He crossed his arms over his broad chest. "I had a signed deal with Greg Harper." His words were firm, his gaze was steady, and he didn't act as if he were trying to hide anything.

"I can't—" Gianna took a fortifying breath. "It's only been a month. I have such a legal mess to wade through, and I'm facing more complications every day." His brown eyes were twin pools of smooth, deep chocolate, and Gianna steeled herself against them. She straightened her spine. "What kind of work were you supposed to do for him?"

"I'm a general contractor." *How did Van know?* "But he said he was working on a big land development project and had something special in mind for me. He would share the details once I arrived."

What? All Greg's work revolved around property management. "I don't know anything about land development, but we—I have a lot of rental properties all over the county, and they're in disarray." She splayed her hands. "I'm not sure if Greg was managing the maintenance, but no one else seems to be. And some of the homes are coming apart at the seams." She summed up the most urgent needs.

"You'll hire me to do this work?"

"I can't pay you right now, but—"

His eyebrows shot up. "You expect me to work for free? Nothing doing, lady." He pulled out the purported contract and flipped to the end. "Look. He promised me a ten-thousand-dollar bonus on arrival and a salary. I banked on his word—and on his signature on this legal document." Brock jammed his finger over what looked like her husband's signature, stood, then stuffed the papers in his back pocket. "I spent everything I had on the trip. I'll sleep in my truck tonight and consult an attorney first thing tomorrow morning."

"No. Stop." Gianna hated the desperation in her voice. Silence throbbed between them. "You need a place to stay?" He nodded.

She still wasn't sure this was the right thing to do, but she would trust her instincts. Van was right. No weird vibe surrounded this guy. But serial killers hid their evil intentions too. *God, help me.*

Gianna reached into her purse and drew out a key. "5810 Helena Valley Road. The tenant left this morning. I haven't had time to hire a cleaning service, but you can stay there for now. I don't believe there's much furniture, but there's a bed and linens." Her mind raced. She still had an account at the local grocers. "Charge your groceries to me at the Food Mart, about a mile west on the left. Tell Charlie to call me if he has any questions. You may need some bathroom cleaner." The former tenant was a bachelor. "Meet me back here tomorrow morning at eight. I'll give you a list of things to start on, and we'll go from there." She looked at him evenly. "I'll find a way to pay you something."

"I can't be here until at least nine o'clock."

Annoyance bubbled inside. "Calling the shots already? You're pretty bold."

Brock sighed softly, and when his eyes met Gianna's, she saw a hint of despair mirroring her own. He was hiding a secret. What was it?

He swallowed. "I'll be here as soon as I can."

"I'll see you tomorrow."

Brock stepped toward her. "Where I come from, a handshake is as legally binding as a contract." His gaze held a clear challenge and didn't flinch as he stuck out his hand.

Gianna drew herself to her full height, lifted her gaze to meet his, and gave his hand a firm, strong shake.

CHAPTER 4

Brock exited the hair salon and approached the bench where Piper sat holding her favorite stuffed animal, a well-loved pink and lavender hippo. He'd been reluctant to leave her but didn't feel comfortable taking her inside. He'd never told Harper he was bringing his daughter with him. Leaving her in the car wasn't an option, and even though he never would have left her alone on a public bench in San Diego, Brock had a good feeling about this town. He'd also taught Piper how to attract attention if anyone bothered her.

He paused and observed his daughter taking in her surroundings. No doubt she would already have some strong opinions about this place, so unlike San Diego.

"Hey, kiddo." Brock plopped beside her and slung his arm over her shoulder.

"Everybody here looks like a cowboy. Are we in the Wild West?"

Hmm ... Brock should buy himself some cowboy boots and plaid to fit in.

His daughter chattered on. "I was studying the atlas. San Diego is more west than Montana." She pushed her glasses on her nose. "I don't understand."

"It is, but California's in the southwest US. We're close to the Rocky Mountains, and everything around us is ranches and cowboys." He ruffled her hair, glittering copper in the late-afternoon sun. "Ready for the next step in our new adventure? First stop, grocery store, then to the place where we're staying."

She clapped her hands. "A hotel? With satellite and a pool?"

Brock shook his head. "Nope, sorry."

Piper squinted at him. "I'm hungry. Can we stop for a burger and fries? And a chocolate shake? Puh-leeze?"

With the turn of events, Brock would have to watch his cash carefully. He was grateful for Mrs. Harper's offer to charge groceries to her account. "Not tonight. You can help me shop." He unlocked the truck and opened the back door.

"Can I sit in front? There's no traffic here." Brock bit back a smile at her astute logic.

"Nope. Into the back seat. The air bag's too dangerous."

"Nobody my age sits in the back."

"Height and weight determines who sits in the front or back." He adored his daughter's petite frame. What she lacked in size, she made up for with intelligence and a sparkling, sassy personality. He kissed the top of her head. "I have to keep you safe."

"Not fair," she grumbled as she climbed into the back and pulled her seat belt in place.

Time to exit the *Life is Unfair* expressway. "What do you want for dinner?"

"I already told you."

"From the store."

"I don't know what kind of food they have at this store. What if Montana food is different than San Diego food?"

"It won't be." Except for the lack of authentic Mexican food, which they would both miss. Miss Carmen was a fantastic cook and had doted on them. Brock had called from the burner phone a couple of days ago when she was at her quilting club and left a voicemail saying they had to leave town unexpectedly and didn't know when they'd be back. His news had probably broken the woman's heart. Miss Carmen was more like a mother—to them both. She'd likely cry when she heard his message. How could he have made this easier on her?

A five-minute drive brought them to a rustic town square, surrounded by quaint shops with window boxes overflowing with fall flowers. Brock slowed the vehicle to a crawl. People sat chatting on benches. Children played on the grass. Babies napped in strollers. American flags stood at attention around the gazebo in the center of the square. Brock hadn't come upon a scene like this in years. Feeling as if they'd stepped back in time, his heart lifted a little.

"Doesn't the town square look fun?"

"What? I don't see anything fun." Piper muttered.

"There's a gazebo and a bandstand."

"What do you mean? They don't have town squares in California."

Not in their part of California, anyway. Brock would enjoy introducing his daughter to small-town life.

They found the Food Mart and made quick work of shopping. Brock was concerned with purchasing enough provisions for the next day or so. Mac and cheese for tonight, and they still had breakfast food for a few days but needed milk. He splurged on a little lunch kit for Piper's first day of school, and they still had fruit in the cooler.

He managed to sneak a carton of chocolate brownie ice cream into the cart when she wasn't looking, a treat for tonight.

Piper looked worried when they arrived back at the truck. "I don't want to go to a new school. I'd rather stay with you."

Brock heard fear in her voice. He rapped her head with his fingers and placed a kiss on her forehead. "Fourth grade is the best. You don't want to miss any more days, and you'll make new friends quickly." His first priority tomorrow morning was to enroll Piper in her new school. If he were on his own traveling around to various properties, he could collect her in the afternoon and take her along. But he wasn't ready for Mrs. Harper to know about Piper yet. He'd rather ask for forgiveness later than permission now.

He needed to survive the next few days until he determined if he had any legal recourse regarding his contract. Then he could figure out what to do next.

As Brock settled the groceries in the back, Piper's arms came around his waist from behind. "I'm scared." He could barely hear the words.

Brock knelt and wrapped his arms around her, his stomach in knots. He'd shattered her world, and he was all she had. "I know, little one," he crooned. "I'm sorry." He drew back and thumbed away her tears. "I know change is scary. To be honest, I'm a little scared too. God will take care of us, and remember, you said you would trust me. We need to be here. So long as you and I are together—" *and safe*, he wanted to add, then changed his mind. He tweaked her nose. "—nothing else matters. Everything will be OK. I promise."

Piper grabbed him around the neck. "I love you, Daddy."

"I love you too." He stood and helped her into the truck. "We need to move along, or a surprise in one of the bags might melt."

"Ice cream?" she squealed.

"Hmm, I don't know," Brock teased. He climbed into the front seat and punched the address for their lodging into his phone. They would need to drive to the west edge of town, about six minutes away. He had no idea what to expect and steeled himself. Mrs. Harper's admonition about bathroom cleaner made him uneasy. If the accommodations were terrible, he could pitch their tent in the backyard and find another solution tomorrow.

The sun still shone when they arrived at the address. Wait. Was this right? A stunning, dark wood A-frame home sat on an oversized lot with a deep, park-like front yard.

His jaw dropped.

"Is this our house?" Piper's voice was filled with awe.

Brock checked the number. Yep, this was the right place. He pulled up the long driveway. "We'll stay for tonight and then see." They hadn't seen the inside yet.

"This is awesome," Piper said.

Brock stepped out of the truck and stood still. Peace and serenity settled around them. Exactly what he and his daughter needed right now. No freeway traffic noise. No blaring music. No rowdy teens. Nothing but the wind in the tall, towering pine trees and an occasional bird call.

Brock removed the key from his pocket and grabbed the groceries. He grinned at Piper, his heart light. "Let's take the food inside. We can come back for the other stuff."

She skipped up the walk ahead of him, held out her hand for the key, and unlocked the front door.

When they stepped over the threshold, the breath left him. The home was small but rustic and charming—and pretty clean, to boot. Piper ran from room to room while Brock put the groceries away. The kitchen and living room were one open area. A stone fireplace soared from floor to ceiling. A bank of tall windows overlooked a deck and a small, wooded backyard with a breathtaking view of the mountains.

Mrs. Harper had been right about the lack of furniture. A counter with two bar stools separated the kitchen from the living area. The only furniture was an upholstered chair with a slipcover, a small end table, and a wooden Adirondack chair facing the fireplace.

Piper had already made the rounds. She came running down a circular staircase. "Your room and the bathroom are to the left," she said, pointing to a short hallway. "My *loft* is upstairs." She pointed up. "It has three walls, and I can look over the railing into the living room." She grabbed his hand. "You have to come see. There's a window with a bench and pillows for a reading nook."

Brock squeezed up the little staircase, ducking when he arrived at the top. The loft was great for Piper, but he wouldn't be spending much time here, unless he wanted a crick in his neck. "There's no bed."

"I'll sleep on the air mattress," she said breezily. "There's a bed in your room. Let's go look at the backyard."

He grinned as his daughter scurried past him. She threw open the sliding door leading to the deck. "Look," she cried, pointing past the small round table accompanied by two weathered chairs. At the bottom of the stairs off the deck was a pretty little stone patio with a bubbling fountain and fishpond. Lush perennials in myriad hues of green spilled throughout the small backyard. Brock's gaze honed in on a corner of the deck

Piper's squeal almost shattered his eardrum. "We have a hot tub." She clapped her hands on her cheeks.

Brock couldn't help but laugh. "Simmer down, Piper. The neighbors will wonder what's happening over here." The last thing he needed was someone calling the cops. He walked toward the covered tub. "The hot tub may not have water, and may not work." But a quick inspection assured him everything was in working order.

Piper launched herself into his arms. "This is so beautiful. I've never seen such an awesome house in my life. I'm really glad you brought us here."

Brock had no idea what tomorrow held, but for now, their first night in Montana, this was enough. More than enough. He picked up his daughter, spun her around, and uttered a prayer over the sweet sound of her laughter. *Thank you, God.*

CHAPTER 5

"I'm sorry for the wait, Mr. Hennessey. Principal Garritsen will be with you as soon as he can. This morning has been busier than usual for a Tuesday." The school secretary, whose badge read Ms. Fleming, gave him and Piper a kind smile.

An image of Mrs. Harper's scowling face swam before him, and Brock forced himself not to glance at his watch. The delay was inevitable. He returned the woman's smile. "No problem."

Ten minutes later, a tall, slim man with reddish-blond hair walked into the waiting area. Brock stood and received the man's firm handshake. "I'm Ben Garritsen, Mr. Hennessey. I apologize for the wait. It's been one of those mornings." His dark blue eyes and easy smile conveyed his sincerity.

"Please, call me Brock."

"Brock." The man smiled at Piper. "And you must be Piper."

"Yes, sir." Piper wasn't her usual bubbly self, and Brock could tell she was nervous.

"Everyone calls me Principal Ben." He turned and beckoned them to follow. "Come into my office."

Ten minutes later, Brock had completed the required paperwork, and Ms. Fleming returned, followed by a young woman with shoulder-length hair almost the exact shade as Piper's.

Principal Ben stood. "Piper, this is your teacher, Ms. Spencer." He made the introduction to Brock.

"I like your hair, Piper." Ms. Spencer said with a smile, revealing a dimple in each cheek.

Piper giggled. "I like yours too."

The knot of worry in Brock's chest dissipated. Piper didn't always warm to people easily, but Ms. Spencer had put her at ease right away with her sweet smile and easy manner.

"School dismisses at 3:30," Principal Ben said. "Do you have any questions for either myself or Ms. Spencer?"

"May we talk privately for a moment?" Brock asked.

Ms. Spencer smiled. "Come with me, Piper. Nice meeting you, Mr. Hennessey. Once you access the school's website, you'll find my page, and you can message me anytime. I'll call you at the end of the week to let you know how things are going."

Moments earlier, Brock had been a bit nervous at Ms. Spencer's youthful appearance, but she impressed him with her crisp, professional manner. "Sounds great, thank you." He looked at Piper. He wanted to hug her but didn't want to embarrass her.

True to her nature, she latched on to him first. "Bye, love you." With a grin, she gathered her things and followed Ms. Spencer out.

"May I close the door?" Brock asked.

"Of course," Garritsen replied.

They both sat. Brock drew out a paper from his leather portfolio. "I wanted to give you this for Piper's file. I have full custody."

The principal looked the document over and nodded. "Looks fine. We see these a lot. California?"

Brock nodded. "Piper must never leave with anyone but me."

Garritsen didn't say anything.

Brock continued. "If you need details, I can share some of them." He usually had a good first read on people, and this man had made a good impression.

Garritsen seemed to size Brock up too, then shook his head. "Not at this time. Is her mother in her life at all?"

"No. She's still in California. Our situation is a little more complicated."

The principal nodded. "If and when the time comes, we can talk. Until then, Piper will be flagged in a special category, and our school security officer will know to keep an extra eye out for her."

Brock exhaled a deep breath. Every muscle softened in relief. "I appreciate the extra effort, thanks."

"Anything else?"

Brock stood. "We arrived in town last night. I should have an apartment rented by the end of the day and have an address to put on the enrollment papers."

Garritsen stood and nodded. "If you need any other help settling into the community, my door is always open." He handed Brock a card. "You can also message me through the parent portal on the school's website."

Brock didn't want to explain his current offline status. He shook the man's hand. "Thanks again for everything."

He thanked Ms. Fleming on his way out, then quickly made his way to his truck. Once he started the engine, he glanced at the dashboard clock and winced. Mrs. Harper hadn't been happy with him setting the later arrival time, and being even a few minutes late wouldn't help. He wasn't at fault, but he wouldn't be able to explain why. Having

Piper settled and happy in school was his top priority, and his heart rested much easier now.

As he drove through town, he was struck again at how tranquil and simple life appeared in the sparkling morning light and crisp, gentle breeze. His breath caught as his gaze roamed around the town square, and he checked his mirror before braking sharply and turning a corner.

The house didn't have a coffeemaker, but here was his salvation, *Mountain Mist Café and Bakery*. Brock was already a little late, so what would a few more minutes matter? He wasn't sure how long he could stay awake and alert without a serious infusion of caffeine.

He parked and entered the shop, passing three tables on the sidewalk where people sat enjoying their morning repast. Inside, nearly every seat was taken, and Brock took a place in line. He glanced at the clock behind the counter and almost turned around and left, but the swirling aromas rooted him to the spot. Not even the prospect of Mrs. Harper's ire could move him.

"Welcome to Mountain Mist. What can I get started for you?" A fresh-faced girl who looked to be in her late teens smiled at him. Her nametag read *Lark*.

"Whatever your dark roast is, large."

While she fixed his order, he studied the mouthwatering breakfast treats and other desserts in the glass case. The artistry of the decorations was impressive. There were colorfully decorated cakes, bars, and cookies with a fall theme—pumpkins, autumn leaves, and cornucopias.

Brock handed over the cash for his coffee and promised himself this would be a one-time treat. Their prices sure beat California's, but until his job situation was settled, he needed to watch his spending.

"You must be new in town," Lark said.

Brock chuckled. "You know everyone here?"

The brown-eyed blonde smiled and tilted her head. "No, but most. Born and raised here."

Something occurred to him. "Do you know—" he realized he didn't know her first name. "Mrs. Harper? The woman who owns the hair salon?"

"Gianna? Sure. She's a regular."

Gi-AH-na. The name rolled around in his head. "Has she been in yet today?" Lark shook her head.

He took out his wallet again. "Give me a large of whatever her favorite is." He would swallow the extra expense. Lark filled the order, and within a couple of minutes, he held a cup in each hand.

"Come back soon," Lark called out with a smile and a wave.

Brock climbed into the truck and took a tentative sip of his coffee. Perfect. He took a deeper swallow, and the liquid sparked through his veins all the way to his fingertips. *Oh, wow.* This might be the best coffee he'd ever tasted. His resolve to stick to the store-bought stuff would be tested.

In five minutes, he arrived at the salon, which sat between a store selling snowboarding equipment and a florist. He found a parking spot right in front. A painted sign hung above the salon door, *Ladies and Gents,* which Brock hadn't noticed yesterday. A silhouette of a woman faced one way, a man faced the other—with a red-and-white barber pole between them. *Ladies* was in a fancy font, *Gents,* a bold one. He grabbed both coffees and pushed through the door.

The bell tinkled, and Mrs. Harper turned from where she was stacking bottles on a shelf. She wore a lavender v-neck, long-sleeved knit shirt topped by a quilted vest in dark purple, black leggings, and white running shoes. Tall and slender, she moved with a dancer's grace. Her ebony hair was piled on her head and secured with a clip. A few pieces tumbled around her face.

And what a face, Brock realized. He hadn't noticed yesterday afternoon, but in the morning light, Gianna Harper was stunning. She had high, prominent cheekbones and a dusky complexion, but her eyes were her most arresting feature, a shimmering blue changing to lavender. But they were weighed with grief, trapped within dark circles. A pang of shame hit him. She was a new widow, and he had no business forming any opinion about her physical attributes.

She looked at him, her face void of expression. "Right on time, I see. I love punctuality in my employees. Especially on the first day."

"Sorry, boss." He couldn't resist. He tried not to smile too broadly and instead, offered the cup, making sure the logo faced her. "A peace offering."

Her features registered astonishment. "You discovered Mountain Mist already?"

He nodded and took a sip from his own cup. "Best coffee I've ever tasted."

She smiled wanly and came toward him, extending a slim hand. "What are you drinking?"

"The dark roast."

She took the other cup from him and bent her nose to sniff. "But this is—how did you know?"

He lifted his shoulder and sighed. "I have a gift."

A dry laugh spilled out, and Brock's heart did a backflip. An honest to goodness backflip.

"You do not." She took a hearty drink and her eyelids drifted shut.

Brock's heart did a double backflip. A reaction to Mrs. Harper? Not good.

"You must have met Lark."

He nodded.

"Thank you," she said. "This almost makes up for your tardiness."

Brock started to make a retort, but realized she was serious. "I—I had some important business to take care of this morning," he said, hoping he sounded contrite. "It won't happen again."

She walked toward the back room. "I have a nine-thirty appointment, so we'll need to be quick. We'll start you on a few things, you can come back later this afternoon, and we'll discuss the rest."

Brock didn't want to come back later this afternoon. He planned to collect Piper from school and keep her with him the rest of the day. He didn't want his boss to know about her yet, wasn't ready to explain the complication.

Mrs. Harper pulled a stool to the counter and motioned for him to take a seat on the other one. She pulled out a pad of paper and a pen. "Where are you from, Mr. Hennessey?"

Brock smiled. "I asked you to call me Brock."

She took another sip of her coffee. "I'd rather keep things professional," she said primly.

He would follow her lead. "I'm a west coaster."

One perfectly formed eyebrow lifted. "Good. That covers about a thousand miles. Where was your last job? Do you have a résumé?"

This wasn't going well. "No. I told you, I'm a general contractor. I've been working construction for over—"

"Do you have any references I can call?"

Brock looked away to try to formulate his next statement. "I was introduced to your husband by a mutual acquaintance. Or an acquaintance of someone he did business with, I think."

Her lovely eyes narrowed, and she crossed her arms. "Nothing suspicious there at all."

"I spoke with your husband on the phone, twice. We emailed back and forth. He sent me a contract, which I signed, and then he countersigned and sent me the completed copy."

"Do you have any of those emails?" Her chin lifted a notch, which Brock took as a sign she already knew the answer.

"No." He should have printed copies of them before he closed his account. Brock fought the urge to sigh out loud. He wasn't doing anything to alleviate her well-founded suspicions.

Because he had nothing except his good word.

Mrs. Harper huffed. "I searched through all of my husband's files last night and didn't find one thing about any plans to hire you, not one paper with your name on it. You show up here with some 'contract' and expect me to hand over ten grand and a job."

"You saw his signature on there," Brock countered.

She tossed her head. "For all I know, you could have found his signature somewhere and concocted the whole thing."

Brock shook his head in disbelief. "Where would I find his signature?"

"I don't know," came the sharp retort. "People forge documents all the time. You could be some shyster who stalks widows and tries to wrangle money out of their husband's estate. You could be—"

Brock interrupted her. "I could be an honest man who came here to accept a job offer and fulfill my end of a *legal contract*."

Her voice rose in volume. "I can't find one iota about you on social media. You might not even be who you say you are. It's not as if your name is *John Smith*. Something should come up under Brock Hennessey." Her beautiful eyes were stormy.

Brock ran a hand through his hair, at a loss to explain. "Being on social media isn't a requirement of the human race, you know." He hesitated, then reached into his back pocket. "I have a driver's license." He flipped open his wallet and held the document out, making sure his thumb covered the address, then returned the wallet to his pocket.

She threw up her hands. "What? A California license, your name, and a years-old picture."

"A legal form of identification is enough."

"You're hiding something. For all I know, the license is fake. Are you running from the law?"

The irony almost made him laugh. "I said I'm an honest man. You'll have to trust me."

She shot from her stool. "I have no reason to trust you." One hand sliced through the air. "We're done here, Mr. Hennessey. Wherever you're from and whatever you're doing, I won't partake."

He stood and stared her down. "You need me."

The beautiful blue-lavender eyes blinked. "I beg your pardon?"

"You said so yesterday. You have all these crumbling rental properties. You're grieving and overwhelmed, and you need help."

She bit her lip as though trying to keep her composure but didn't respond.

Brock lowered his voice. "I'll make you a deal. Let me stay in the rental house in exchange for doing all the work you need on your properties. I'll buy my own groceries, and you don't have to pay me." He still had a little in reserve. The most important thing was having a roof over his and

43

Piper's heads. "We can reassess in a week. You can keep looking in your husband's things, and maybe, you'll find something to support my claims." He paused. "Because I am telling the truth."

She drew her lips together in a straight line. "My gut is telling me not do to this."

Brock drew out his trump card. "We shook hands last night. We had a deal."

He should have felt triumph when her shoulders sagged, but instead, a stab of pity pricked him.

She exhaled loudly. "All right. Today's Tuesday." She handed him a single sheet of paper on which was a typed table listing the tasks needing to be done along with their locations. "Finish these by close of business on Friday."

Brock scanned the list and totaled nine addresses each with anywhere from one to three tasks—some minor, some leaning to major—all of which he was more than qualified to complete. His mind ticked them off one by one. Finishing on time would be a challenge—achievable if no other issues arose, which in Brock's experience was unlikely.

"This is a lot to accomplish in four days."

She shrugged. "Enjoy your trip back to California."

Brock folded the list of chores and stuck the paper in his pocket. "How often must I report in?"

"You can email me—"

"Nope. I want to meet face-to-face, so you know I'm still here and holding up my end of the deal."

"All right. Come here each weekday morning at seven-thirty."

Brock calculated his new morning schedule getting Piper to school without Carmen's help. "Seven forty-five."

Mrs. Harper put her hands on her hips, and her eyes narrowed to slits. "You are *really* pushing my buttons."

Brock grabbed his empty cup off the counter and aimed for the trash can. Slam dunk. He strode toward the door and tossed a smile over his shoulder. "I'll bring Mountain Mist."

CHAPTER 6

Gianna listened to the voicemail and resisted the overwhelming urge to throw her phone against the wall. Another delay in receiving the toxicology report from the accident. Could the police do *nothing* right?

She looked at the clock. Sally Abbott was under the dryer. Most of Gianna's customers preferred having their hair blow dried, but she kept two of the old-fashioned bonnet dryers for the older women.

Gianna rolled her aching shoulders, grateful for the week's end. Between Monday morning's teeming rain, Paisley's overdue school account, the missing money from hers and Greg's bank account, a full schedule at the salon, and dealing with Brock Hennessey, Gianna was exhausted.

She finished Leon Porter's trim, and Van was completing haircuts on a young brother and sister before taking off for a weekend trip with her boyfriend. Gianna would be done with Sally by the time Brock came by to give her his final report. He'd been punctual every morning since Tuesday with neatly handwritten notes next to each item on her list. When they met this morning, he assured her everything would be finished by Friday afternoon, which she hadn't expected. When she smiled at him and said, "great job," he looked shocked, and Gianna felt a flush of guilt. She had probably set him up for failure by piling on so many tasks.

She applied gentle pressure to the back of Leon's head to trim his neck. Why was she uneasy about Brock Hennessey? First, he was hiding something, and still had an unsubstantiated claim about Greg offering him a job. But he seemed responsible and was different from most of the men who came through town looking for temporary work. Gianna was certain he wasn't doing the bar circuit at night. He was always clean, alert, and clear-eyed.

And he brought her Mountain Mist.

She was also beginning to wonder if his story about Greg offering him a job was true. She had found some cryptic notations on Greg's task list. Gianna wasn't ready to share any of this with Brock, however. She still didn't trust him.

She finished with Leon, dusted off his neck, removed the drape, and checked him out. Van's young customers left with their mother.

"You OK to finish Sally?" Vanessa asked.

"Absolutely. Go on." She smiled. "You've been counting the minutes till you and Reid leave."

Van bounced on her toes and grinned. "This is the first time he's taking me to one of his dad's rallies. I think I'm being tested."

"Is Senator Hendrickson exploring a run for the presidency?" Gianna asked.

"Yes, according to Reid." Van stepped in front of the mirror and finger-combed her hair. "I wish I had time for you to work some of your magic on this mop."

Gianna waved her hand. "Your hair always looks gorgeous. Are you wearing one of your dresses?"

"Yes, an electric ice-blue silk, and the finished product is even better than I envisioned."

Gianna shook her head. "You have the most amazing flair for fashion and are such a talented seamstress. I can barely sew on a button."

Van laughed. She clasped her hands in front of her and grinned. "I feel like Cinderella, moving in the Hendrickson family circles." She blew her wispy bangs off her forehead. "Is hunky Brock coming by?"

Gianna rolled her eyes. "Stop. He's not hunky. We agreed this morning he would have a final check-in with me today at five."

"What will you do with him?"

Gianna frowned. "Do with him? What do you mean?"

"You said he's done a great job, better than you expected. Are you keeping him on?"

Gianna twisted her wedding ring around. "I don't know. I still don't trust him. I can't pay him a full salary, and I'm not any closer to getting any of the insurance money." She was about out of funds otherwise. She rubbed her temple, which had begun a painful drumbeat. "I don't know what to do."

Vanessa patted her arm. "Take one step at a time. Do you still need someone to manage the maintenance on the properties?"

Gianna nodded. "Definitely. Even though Mr. Hennessey has made a huge difference this week, at least a dozen new issues have cropped up."

"And he's happy staying in your A-frame rental house, right?"

Gianna nodded.

"There's your answer. Ask him to stay on another week or two. One less headache for you to manage."

"You're right." Gianna managed a tired smile. "Thanks, you're the best." She wrapped her arms around Van and squeezed. "Go. Have a wonderful weekend and I'll see you Monday. Send me pictures."

Van scurried toward the back room and blew Gianna a kiss on her way out. "I will. Bye, sweets."

The buzzer on Sally's dryer sounded, and Gianna helped her into the chair. She listened with one ear as Sally chattered about her new great-grandbaby while Gianna combed her out.

Thirty seconds after Sally left, right at five, Gianna was sweeping the floor to ready the salon for the morning when the door opened, and the bell tinkled.

There he was, filling the doorway. Brock gave her a lopsided smile. He wore a charcoal gray T-shirt and faded but clean jeans over new work boots. He had a two-day beard growth, neatly trimmed.

Why should she care about his appearance? Gianna could resist everything attractive about him, except the tool belt hanging from his slim hips. She mentally shook herself.

Better to keep things professional and skip any small talk. "Did you finish?"

He lifted his clipboard on which the list rested. "Almost."

She walked over to him and leaned against the lobby desk. "Either yes or no."

He lifted an eyebrow. "The leak in the basement bathroom in the house on Route 56 has seeped into the drywall. There's mold back there, and someone should have caught the problem sooner. In fact, at least half the things I worked on this week have been sitting for a long time. Anyway, I discovered the mold problem at 3:30 today, and I'm not sure of the extent." He held the clipboard out. "Everything else is one hundred percent complete."

The throbbing drumbeat returned in Gianna's temple. Mold issues could quickly become costly.

Brock sighed. "I hate to add to your list of woes, but the paint on the west side of the house on Bison Trail is flaking pretty badly. I did a walk around when I went by to work on the garbage disposal. If you repaint and seal now, you'll save money later."

Gianna winced. "The house is only two years old."

"But most of the storms move through from the west, so the side facing west should have had at least an extra coat of sealer for protection." He shrugged. "A lot of builders skimp where they can to save money."

Gianna didn't want to be impressed by his expertise and initiative, but she was.

"Am I hired?"

Something in Gianna snapped. "No, you are not hired, Mr. Hennessey. I appreciate your efforts this week, but I'm going in a different direction." She didn't know what she would do. Her financial situation was dire. She had little money to pay him or to fix mold issues or repair paint. She was reeling with grief. With each passing day, she grew more uncomfortable about her late husband's business dealings. But she was done with Brock Hennessey and his deep brown eyes, broad shoulders, and confident assurance. She didn't want to talk with him anymore, didn't want anything to do with him.

"Great," he muttered. He stood. "Give me a check for the ten thousand signing bonus your husband promised, and you and I will be square. You'll never see me again."

Gianna's jaw dropped. "I already told you, Mr. Hennessey, I cannot and will not—" The door swung open, and the bell shook. Gianna looked up. A skinny man of medium height entered.

"Evening, Miz Harper," he drawled, doffing his battered hat. Gianna thought she recognized him as one of Greg's employees. Mark? Another name beginning with M? He shut the door.

His clothes were stained and dirty, his boots cracked and dusty. He had a scraggly beard, and an aura of stale tobacco surrounded him.

"How can I help you, Mr.—"

"Riggs. Mort Riggs. I manage your husband's—your late husband's—properties."

She crossed her arms. "Where have you been for the last four weeks?"

Riggs sniffed and ran his sleeve under his nose. His gaze didn't quite meet hers. "I—ah, I was so upset when your husband—I had to tend to some things. I'm real sorry, ma'am. But I'm back now."

The smell of alcohol radiated off him, and his story didn't ring true. "Did you tell anyone you were leaving?"

Riggs gave her a blank stare and shook his head.

"Did you make arrangements for anyone to cover your duties while you were gone?"

Another shake.

Gianna now understood Brock's observations about all the issues gone unfixed. She drew in a breath. "Unfortunately, Mr. Riggs, your services are no longer needed." She tipped her head at Brock. "I've already employed a new property manager."

If Brock was surprised at her pronouncement, he hid his emotions well.

Riggs blinked. He looked at Brock, and a hard edge crept into his bloodshot eyes. "I'm not sure a new property manager is a good idea, ma'am."

Gianna opened her mouth, but Brock stepped forward, towering over Riggs. "You heard the lady, Mr. Riggs. Your services are no longer needed. You'd best be on your way."

Riggs's gaze flashed, but he didn't move. Silent seconds ticked by. Then he hooked his thumbs in his belt and stepped toward the door, never breaking eye contact. His eyes appeared almost black, and Gianna suppressed a shiver.

"Be seeing you."

As soon as the door shut, Gianna exhaled. To her surprise, Brock turned and took hold of her arms, gently rubbing them. "Are you OK?" he murmured, his voice laced with concern. His tenderness caught her off guard, and she stepped behind the desk. She needed to put some distance between them.

Gianna cleared her throat and picked up the clipboard. "Mr. Hennessey, if you are still available, you have a job." Crispness coated each syllable. She reached into the desk drawer and pulled out another sheet of paper. "More things have gone wrong this week. They need to be addressed, along with solving the drywall issue and fixing the paint and sealing."

He leaned against the counter and reached for the list. Gianna fought to keep her gaze off the corded muscles on his tanned forearms. "These tasks won't take the whole week."

"I'm sure you'll discover even more things the *former* property manager let go," she snapped.

Brock straightened to his full height. "Wait a minute," he said with a frown. "I hope you aren't insinuating I'd fabricate things to create work for myself."

Gianna closed her eyes briefly. "No, I didn't mean—" Even though she still didn't trust Brock, the differences between him and Riggs were blatantly apparent. She swallowed. "I—I apologize. Now I remember Riggs. He's worked for Greg for about a year, and Greg wasn't happy with his work on the properties, but I asked him once why he didn't let him go, and he said the man was 'useful,' which made me uncomfortable."

Brock glanced at his watch. "Listen, um, I'm so sorry, but I must go. Can we finish this Monday morning?"

Gianna wondered what kind of plans he could have, being new in town and not knowing anyone. Her gaze roamed over his muscled chest and strong jaw. He probably had a date.

"Sure. This weekend, I'll figure out what Greg was paying Riggs, and transfer his salary to you." She would find a solution, somehow. She owed Brock something. "And you can remain in the house."

"Thank you, I appreciate it. I really do. Thank you." Impatience fell off him in waves. He opened the door. "See you Monday morning."

Gianna locked the deadbolt behind him, flipped the sign to *Closed,* and walked to the back room. Paisley met her at the door.

"Ready to go, Momma?"

Gianna smiled. "Sure am." She slung her arm around her daughter's shoulders and pressed a kiss on her hair. "I'm looking forward to spending the weekend with you. I'm sorry I have to work tomorrow morning."

Paisley's arms squeezed her around the waist, and she rested her head on her mother's shoulder. "I understand, Momma. Some of your customers can only come on the weekend. Can we go hiking at Sapphire Falls? We haven't been there in a long time."

"Sure," Gianna said. "All the summer tourists will be gone, and the fresh air and sunshine will do us both good." Gianna switched off the lights and gathered her things while Paisley zipped her backpack.

"I made a new friend at school this week."

"I'm glad."

"She just moved here and doesn't have any friends. I wanted to invite her along to hike, but she doesn't have a phone."

Gianna loved her daughter's generous heart. "Maybe another time." She opened the back door and ushered Paisley through. For the first time in almost a month, Gianna felt something other than utter worry and despair.

CHAPTER 7

Brock burst into a full run once he exited Gianna's salon. He'd been so concerned about her after Riggs left, he had nearly forgotten about Piper. He'd left his daughter alone on a bench halfway down the block in front of an art store. His sense of security about the bucolic small town was unrealistic. Crime occurred everywhere, and men like Riggs were capable of anything ... for the right price. He recalled the dark hatred in the man's eyes and hoped Riggs never discovered Brock's connection to Piper. *God, please protect my little girl.*

His heart resumed its normal rhythm once he saw her copper-colored hair gleaming in the sun. He slid onto the bench and drew her close in a crushing hug.

"Oomph—you're squeezing me."

He exhaled and drew back. "Sorry." He didn't mean to scare her. He closed his eyes and kissed her hair.

She pointed to the window behind them. "Look, they have art lessons for kids. Can I sign up?"

Brock took in the bright yellow bench they were sitting on and the other bright, whimsical tables and chairs lining the walk. His gaze landed on the display windows on either side of the door filled with colorful arts and crafts, things he couldn't afford right now. And art lessons wouldn't be free.

But he didn't want to crush Piper's hopes. He ruffled her beautiful hair and smiled. "I'll see what I can do."

Her grin was all the thanks he needed. "Are you done now?" she asked, her amber eyes magnified through her glasses.

"Sure am. Let's start this weekend."

Her eyes lit up. "I heard some kids from school talking about a fall festival."

Brock winced inwardly. Since he wasn't ready for Mrs. Harper to know about Piper, they should lie low. Anything in small-town Canadian Meadows was out, for now. "There's a national park about an hour from here with waterfalls and hiking trails. How about we explore tomorrow?" And best of all, since she was in fourth grade, their admission would be free.

"Can we take a picnic?"

Brock tweaked her cute little nose. "You bet. Hey, how about homemade pizza tonight?" And the hot tub for him after Piper went to bed. Brock's back muscles were crying out for a long soak.

"What about Happy's Pizza? Everyone says they're the best."

A twinge of guilt needled Brock. He was squeezing pennies to afford Mountain Mist. "*Everyone* hasn't had Hennessey pizzas. We could put Happy's out of business."

Piper giggled. "You're silly, but fine, we'll make our own."

What? No argument? No dramatic sighs?

She hopped up, and Brock followed her to the truck.

Once home, they made their pizzas and sat at the counter to eat. "Can I have a horse?' Piper asked matter-of-factly.

Brock nearly choked on his pizza. She had never shown the slightest interest in horses. She must have seen them as they drove through the valley around Canadian Meadows. "I'm afraid the answer is no. Do you have any idea how expensive they are to buy, let alone maintain? Feeding a horse isn't like feeding a cat."

"Can I have a cat?"

He weighed the possibilities. "We'll see." Of course, not so long as they were staying here. He was wary of Mrs. Harper's eventual reaction to Piper and wasn't about to add an animal to the mix.

Piper licked her fingers. "You see how that works? If I wanted a cat and asked, you would say no. Instead, I asked if I can have a horse, which is horrifying, and makes a cat seem reasonable."

Brock frowned. "You didn't bring up a cat. I did."

"Even better."

Brock couldn't suppress a grin. "You're incorrigible, Piper Lee."

"Do you mean smart?"

He laughed. "I sure do."

They finished up, and Piper changed into her PJs and joined him in the living room. The air was chilly, so he built a fire in the fireplace. He sat in the Adirondack chair, which was more comfortable than the smaller upholstered one, and Piper flopped on the floor in front of him. Having a couch would be nice, but he wasn't sure how long Gianna would let him stay in the house.

He asked Piper some questions about school and was relieved she liked her class and her red-haired teacher. Brock had checked in with Ms. Spencer when he'd collected Piper that afternoon, and she said Piper was on track with the class in all her subjects and ahead in her reading and spelling. The teacher had no worries whatsoever.

"Are you making friends?"

She shrugged. "I'm always the last one picked for teams. Nobody ever wants me."

He'd heard this before. "They want you for Red Rover."

"Yeah, the *other* team does, because I'm the slowest runner and can't break through them. And then they send everyone toward me because my arms are the weakest, and they can break through."

Brock resisted the urge to sigh. Why did these things never change? He had been one of the tall, athletic ones growing up and had used these exact same tactics on little girls like Piper. He swallowed a wave of guilt. "I'm sure there are other kids who don't excel at sports."

"I met one girl on the playground. She isn't in my class. She's in fifth grade. And she doesn't like sports either and loves to read. She wears glasses too."

"Good. I'm glad you made a friend."

"Her name is Paisley. Paisley Laura. What a pretty name. We have the same initials, P.L."

"Hmm." Brock was drifting off.

"Can I have a phone?"

Brock instantly woke up. "You don't need a phone yet."

"But everybody—"

He tipped his head at her. "You know better." He sat up and pulled her onto his lap. Brock couldn't reveal why she couldn't be on social media or any device where she could be traced.

He stared into her eyes and made sure he had her full attention. "Piper, this is one of those times when you have to trust me. I promise, when it's the right time for you to have a phone, you'll have one."

She sighed. "OK. I'm going to read in my room, Daddy. Night." She leaned in for a hug.

"I love you."

"Love you more."

She skipped up the circular staircase, and Brock went into his room to change into swim trunks. He climbed into the hot tub and let out a sigh. Within seconds, his screaming muscles relaxed.

It was a perfect evening, clear with no moon. The stars formed a glittering, black-velvet backdrop above. The wind whistled through the trees, and other than the bubbling water and a few animal noises, silence reigned.

Brock had never lived anywhere but Southern California, never thought he would want to live anywhere else. But this corner of northwestern Montana was capturing his heart. He and Piper were here through an incredible turn of events.

Someone—he still didn't know who—had put Greg Harper in touch with him. Harper wanted him as the on-site project manager for some kind of huge land development deal. His timetable was flexible, and he was willing for Brock to come anytime within a specified three month period. But Brock had steady work in San Diego, and even with the enticement of Harper's generous signing bonus, Brock wasn't sure he was ready to make such a dramatic change in his and Piper's lives.

Until the call came.

Raw anger boiled through him, marring the idyllic surroundings. The prosecuting attorney had been as stunned as Brock when Cass made parole on her first chance—an unprecedented outcome, given the facts surrounding her case and sentencing. The addition of Brock's strong testimony at the hearing should have assured the outcome.

Even though Brock had divorced Cass, and her parental rights had been terminated, she had vowed to come for her daughter the minute she breathed free air. The only solution in Brock's mind was to leave. The unexpected opportunity to come to Montana had seemed an answer to prayer.

But was Montana far enough away?

Going on the run with Piper wasn't a healthy way to live. When the prosecuting attorney had suggested Brock take out a restraining order, he almost scoffed, but clamped his lips together and said he would think about it. The man couldn't understand a flimsy piece of paper would mean nothing to Cass and her dysfunctional family. Her two brothers had been in perpetual trouble and were more comfortable operating outside the law.

The answer was to stay one step ahead of them, exactly what Brock was doing.

He drew a deep breath and told himself to think of something else. Brock tried to soak in the peace of his surroundings, but his mind turned to the incident with Riggs. He was surprised at his fierce reaction and his concern for Gianna. He didn't believe she couldn't take care of herself. She was a successful business owner, and she held her own in her dealings with Brock. But she was vulnerable, and something beyond the normal grieving of a widow, which brought out a protective instinct in him.

He leaned his head back and sighed. At the least, he would keep a sharp eye out for Riggs. He didn't want the man anywhere near himself, Piper, or Gianna.

At her insistence, he still called his boss Mrs. Harper, but in his mind, she was becoming *Gianna*. The lovely name suited her. Brock needed to watch himself and keep things on a professional level. He had no intention of becoming involved with a woman, especially now. She was newly widowed. Even if she was single, they mixed as well as oil and water.

Brock was afraid the weekend would drag since he and Piper didn't have a lot to do, but they slept most of Saturday morning away. The long trip and getting settled into their new surroundings must have taken more out of them than he realized.

They took a picnic lunch to the park and hiked until almost dusk. Both he and Piper were enamored with the mountains, the valleys and wildflowers, the clear rushing streams, and the trees in more shades of yellow, gold, and green than he'd ever imagined. Brock asked a park ranger about the absence of red and orange leaves and received a long answer about tree species. Even without those colors, the landscape was unbelievably beautiful.

On Sunday, they slept in late again and went grocery shopping for the week. Brock found a mower in the shed and mowed the grass. Gianna hadn't said anything about maintaining the yard, but he wanted to make an effort. Piper helped with the weeds. He loved getting his hands into the soil and teaching her a little about the joys of gardening. Brock hadn't done yard work in years, and doing so now made him feel connected to the earth in a deeply fulfilling way.

Their idyllic weekend drew to a close, and Monday morning dawned. When Brock pulled into the school's circular drive to drop Piper off, she rolled down her window and waved to a girl with long, curly brown hair and glasses. "Paisley," she shouted.

"Piper, shh," Brock admonished.

"But I want her to hear me."

Brock rolled his eyes. "They can hear you in Texas."

The girl smiled at Piper and came over to the truck. "Daddy, this is Paisley Laura Rossi," Piper said. Brock recognized her as the girl who was in the back room at Gianna's shop the first day he went there, the one who Gianna's assistant led away. She must be the woman's daughter.

"Hello, Paisley Laura Rossi," Brock said. "Nice to meet you."

"I'm happy to meet you too."

"Daddy, can Paisley come over to play sometime?"

He nodded. "As long as her parents agree."

"I'll ask my mom." The girl had a sweet, gentle aura about her. Maybe she would be a calming influence on Piper.

Piper reached across and smacked a kiss on his cheek. "Bye, love you."

"Love you. See you at three-thirty." He smiled to himself as the two girls walked away. Paisley was about a foot taller than Piper.

His truck knew the way from the school straight to Mountain Mist, and Lark greeted him when he came through the door. "Hey, Brock."

"Morning, Lark."

"The usual?"

"Yes, ma'am." A warm feeling spread through his chest. At least three years going to the same chain coffee shop in San Diego nearly every day, and no one knew his name or even acknowledged his regular business.

"Morning, Brock," called one of the other baristas, JT. Brock greeted him back.

A slender woman with bright blue eyes and faded strawberry-blonde hair caught up in a bandanna and wearing an apron, bustled up. She balanced a tray of cinnamon rolls on one hand and stuck out the other. "I'm Barb, Lark's mom. I hear you've become a regular. Welcome to town."

The scent from the cinnamon rolls tickled Brock's nose. Could he afford one today? He nodded and shook her hand. "Yes, I am. Brock Hennessey. I've become addicted to your coffee. Best I've ever had."

Barb laughed. "Good to hear. How about a cinnamon roll to go with your coffee this morning? On the house."

"Sounds good, thanks."

"See Lark for your roll. Good meeting you, Brock."

"You too."

After he was in the truck, Brock recalled a recent sermon about how God cares about the little things in our lives. He had every intention of saving the cinnamon roll to split with Gianna but couldn't resist and gobbled the warm, gooey treat on his short drive to the salon. Barb sure knew what she was doing, comping him a roll. At this rate, he would have to take on a second job to support his growing Mountain Mist habit.

When he arrived at *Ladies and Gents*, Gianna and her assistant were getting their workstations ready for the day. Gianna wore jeans and a long-sleeved cobalt-blue tee slanting off one shoulder. The color brought out the blue in her eyes but also accentuated the dark circles under them. She didn't greet him.

The other woman shot him a friendly smile. She was similar in height and build to Gianna, with streaked brown/blonde hair and bright green eyes. "Good morning," she said in a cheery voice.

"Hi, I don't think we've met," Brock said. He set the cups down and extended his hand. "Brock Hennessey."

"I'm Vanessa Kingston." She had a firm grip.

"I think I might have met your daughter this morning," Brock said, then mentally kicked himself. What was he thinking? He didn't want Gianna to know about Piper yet. How could Brock explain why he was at the school and how he could have met Paisley?

Vanessa frowned. "I don't have a daughter."

"Oh," he said. His mind raced for an explanation.

Gianna stopped sweeping and leaned against the broom. "Why would you think Vanessa has a daughter?"

Couldn't he have kept his mouth shut? "The girl who was in your back room the first day I was here. I ... Lark from the coffee shop asked me to drop something off at the school and the girl was there." Brock's heart hammered, and he doubted he was convincing anyone. He was a terrible liar.

Gianna frowned. She opened her mouth, but Vanessa interrupted her. "Oh, sure. Since Lark's brother is the principal." A wave of unease passed over Vanessa's face.

Brock laid a hand on the counter to steady himself. "Yes, her—um, yeah, the principal." The man's name was Garritsen, but Brock didn't know Lark or her parents' last name, so hadn't made the connection. His lie could be completely serendipitous.

He handed Gianna a cup. "Here's your coffee." He looked at Vanessa apologetically. "I'm sorry I didn't bring anything for you."

She laughed and flapped her hand at him. "Oh, I don't drink the fancy stuff." She rolled her eyes at Gianna. "I'll go in the back and wring out the dishrag to start my morning pot. Nice meeting you, Brock." She sashayed away.

Brock took out the clipboard. "I have a lot of work to do. Let's start." He took a gulp of his coffee. He wanted to steer the conversation away from the issue with—he almost said *Vanessa's daughter*. Who was Paisley Rossi to Gianna? A niece, maybe? Vanessa didn't acknowledge her in any way. Something was off. Piper said Paisley was a year older. Gianna would have to have been a young mother. And he didn't see any resemblance between them whatsoever. Paisley's hair and eyes were brown. He couldn't sort this out now. His head pounded.

Gianna stepped to the desk and took a sip from her cup. She looked exhausted, and appeared to be assessing him. He motored ahead. "I've made a list of how much is needed to repaint and seal the west wall on the Bison Trail house and the estimated cost for materials. You want me to purchase the supplies at the Ranch and Farm Center, right?"

"Yes, they'll charge my account." Gianna looked at the clipboard and gasped. "What are you using—gold flake?"

"Look at the calculations. The entire side of the house, all two stories, has no windows. I know how much is needed for proper coverage."

Gianna rubbed her forehead but didn't check his work. "Is there any way to cut the cost?"

Brock sighed. "I'll go over there and see what kinds of sealers they have. I think their prices are a little high. Maybe we could order something online—"

She took another gulp of her coffee and shook her head. "No. Buy whatever you need locally." Tension sliced through her words.

"I want to check the mold problem. I'll list out what I need and purchase everything when I pick up the paint and sealer."

"Run the totals by me first."

Brock huffed. "Why? You don't want to mess around with mold. If you cut corners, you'll pay the price later. Literally."

She blinked as if she were trying not to cry. "Just do as I ask."

"Do you want to go to the house and investigate the mold problem?"

"Do you want to stay here to cut and color hair?"

Brock shook his head. "This is my area of expertise. You're micromanaging."

She fisted her hands on her hips. "You don't have the right to make *any* unilateral decisions about my business."

Gaining even a sliver of trust from this woman was like trying to climb a greased rope. She was obviously having a terrible day, and he wished he could do something to help. He sighed. "Gianna—"

Her gaze flashed. "Mrs. Harper."

Great, another slip. Brock was full of them today. He gathered his papers and turned to go. "Mrs. Harper," he said formally. "I will investigate the mold problem and submit a written proposal to you for your approval." He strode through the door. The slam echoed behind him.

CHAPTER 8

Gianna spun on her heel and marched back to her workstation to finish setting up for the day.

Vanessa followed, wiping her hands on a towel. "I'm surprised the glass didn't shatter out of the door."

"Mark my words. Brock Hennessey is hiding something. He's a liar and will shaft me for money, materials—"

Van stepped to her and laid her hands on Gianna's shoulders. "Whoa, whoa. Where is all this coming from?"

"What was his story about meeting Paisley at the school?" Gianna shouted. Her entire body shook. "What business could he have there? He's brand new to town. We—we don't know anything about him. What if he's lying about Greg offering him a job? Why did he come here? What if he has designs on Paisley—to kidnap her or something?" Panic clawed at her, and her heart beat thundered erratically.

Van led her into the back room and guided her to a stool. "Sit, sweets." She set a small bottle of water from the fridge on the counter in front of Gianna. Then she scooted another stool over and sat, keeping her hand on Gianna's arm.

Gianna put her head in both hands. "I can't do this, Van." Her whole world was crumbling. The police refused to accept the possibility of Greg's accident being anything other than a suicide, and until the cause of death was determined, the insurance company refused to pay out on his policy. Gianna's name wasn't anywhere on Greg's business accounts, so she had no access to those and couldn't sell off any of the properties. Worst of all, he hadn't left a will. He always said he had plenty of time to make those arrangements. Gianna didn't know if she and Paisley would even be able to stay in the house.

And the accountant had called last night and admitted he was stymied about where the money from the joint account had gone. They could tell a lump sum was transferred out, but there was no trail. He promised to escalate the search but said the investigation would take time.

Gianna was running out of time. She was alternatively furious at Greg for leaving her with such a mess and drenched with guilt for her anger at him. Paisley was the only thing holding her together right now, the reason she could face each morning, Sometimes, she wanted to run to the school, grab her daughter, jump in the car, drive away, and never look back.

Van scooted closer and looped her arms over Gianna's shoulders, rubbing circles on her back. "We'll work everything out together."

Guilt washed over Gianna. She wanted to confide in her best friend but didn't want to include details Van might innocently share with her attorney boyfriend. Gianna also wanted Van to have plausible deniability in case she was ever asked about Greg's accident.

Gianna took a sip of water, the icy liquid soothing her parched throat. Time to change the subject. "The pictures you sent me from the senator's fundraiser were amazing. Your dress was gorgeous. What a color."

"I was the only woman there wearing ice blue." Van clapped her hands. "Both his sisters-in-law asked who the designer was. They were impressed when I said, 'me.'"

"You and Reid looked like a total power couple."

Van fanned her face. "My man sure knows how to fill out a tux."

They both laughed.

Gianna studied her friend. "Are you two getting serious?"

Van twisted her hands in her lap. "I think so, but I don't know." She looked away. "Marriage is a big decision."

Gianna knew there'd been a lost love in her friend's past, something deep and painful she had never shared. She squeezed Van's hands. "Do you realize you could be the daughter-in-law of the president of the United States someday?" she squealed. The words sounded surreal.

Van threw back her head and laughed. "I can't imagine."

A voice called from the front. Oh, no. Selma Miller's standing appointment. Gianna couldn't face her now.

"I'll deal with Selma." Van could always read her mind. She turned her head and called, "be right there, Selma," and squeezed Gianna's hands. "You stay here. Don't move."

Gianna nodded.

Van jumped up and scooted Gianna's bottle of water closer. "Drink this, take deep cleansing breaths." She gently shook Gianna's shoulders. "Look at me, sweets."

Gianna lifted her eyes to Van's.

"If you need to take today off, I'll handle things here."

Gianna twisted a tissue in her hands and shook her head. "I can't. There's so much to do."

"But you're in no shape to do anything. Be kind to yourself. Let me start on Selma. Then we'll make a plan."

"You're the best, Van. What would I do without you?"

Van pursed her lips. "Good thing you'll never find out."

She blew out of the room, and Gianna was left with her own swirling thoughts. She uncapped the water and took a cleansing drink. Then she closed her eyes and took several deep breaths through her nose and released them through her mouth.

I am with you always.

Gianna's eyes flew open, and she looked around. Seeing nothing, she closed them again. The words whispered through her soul. She had no idea how long she sat there, not moving, and then Van sailed into the room. She eyed Gianna warily. "You doing better?"

Gianna nodded and stood. Van pushed her back down. "No, you're not going out there today. I have everything covered. I made some calls, postponed a couple of folks, and I can handle the rest of today's appointments."

"Van," Gianna protested.

"Van nothin'. I'm chasing you out of here in a few minutes. But I need you to tell me something first. The total truth."

Gianna's stomach bubbled, but she nodded.

"If you could change one thing today, to make life bearable and give you the confidence to go on, what would you change?"

Gianna clamped her lips together. *For the accountant to find the missing money.* But she couldn't tell Van. "I need a pretty serious infusion of cash right now." Her heartbeat skittered with panic.

Van reached out, touched her hand, and her gaze bore into Gianna's. "Now, don't you freak out on me." She paused. "But what about your portion of your mama's life insurance money?"

Gianna shook her head, causing her hair to flop against the back of her head. "No. I won't touch Paisley's college fund."

"But Paisley's not going to college now, honey."

"There's not much in there, but I don't—"

Vanessa squeezed her hands. "Consider this. You can dip into your mama's insurance money to see you through and replace the funds when Greg's mess is straightened out. You don't have to lose anything."

Maybe. A sliver of hope dripped into Gianna's soul. But as quickly, the darkness swallowed the light. "I can't."

Van's eyes glistened. "You can't go on like this. I can't stand to see you so … terrified and lost. Go see Harv at the bank. Maybe he can think of something. Promise me you will."

Gianna's and Greg's accounts were at a big bank in Kalispell, but the account with Gianna's mother's insurance money was at Canadian Meadows' small bank. Gianna stood and reached for her purse. She owed her sweet friend a concession. "It may not do anything, but I'll talk with him."

Van all but pushed her out the back door. "Then you go home and sleep or take a bubble bath."

Gianna gave her a weak smile. "I might." She gave Van a quick hug and left before she lost her resolve.

Two hours later, Gianna left the bank with a spring in her step and a lightness in her heart. Never had she imagined she could take out a modest loan against the money in Paisley's fund without losing a penny of the principal.

She intended to drive straight home, but instead found herself outside Mountain Mist. She hadn't been there since before Greg's death, and suddenly had a hankering for their chicken salad. She hadn't eaten all day and decided she would treat herself this one time. Her stomach growled in agreement as soon as she stepped through the door.

"Hey, Gianna," Lark greeted her. The junior college student was one of Gianna's favorite people. Lark came out from behind the counter and gave her a hug. "I've missed you. I've been praying for you."

"Thank you. Your prayers make me feel less alone."

Lark resumed her spot behind the counter. "Chicken salad and raspberry iced tea?" she said with a grin.

"You know me." Gianna felt at home here.

"You want to sit outside? I'll bring your lunch to you."

Outside sounded good. "Yes, I think I will."

She passed Barb coming in, laden with shopping bags. The woman set them down and enveloped Gianna in a warm hug. "How are you?" Barb was old enough to be Gianna's mother but was more like a big sister. She'd been a steady friend for years, especially during the weeks after Greg's death.

Gianna put on a brave smile. "Better."

"We need to meet to pray and chat. Call me and I'll come out to the house."

"I will, Barb, thanks."

Gianna took a seat at an outdoor table and stared out over the town square until her food arrived.

"Here you go," Lark said. "On the house, Mom's orders."

Bless sweet Barb. "Tell her thanks." The sight of the buttery croissant made Gianna's mouth water. She picked up the sandwich and took a bite.

"I'm glad you're still getting your morning lifeblood," Lark said with a wink. "Brock is the sweetest thing, bringing coffee to you each morning."

The croissant crumbled into sawdust in Gianna's mouth. "He's not sweet," she mumbled, reaching for her iced tea.

The girl gave her a dreamy look. "I look forward to seeing him every day."

At least someone did.

Lark patted her shoulder. "I'll let you enjoy your lunch. Don't be a stranger."

"I won't."

Gianna ate leisurely and didn't even feel the urge to jump up and leave when she was finished. She continued to look out over the beautiful scenery when she saw a tall, dark man climb into a truck halfway down the block. He had the same broad shoulders and long, muscular arms as Brock, but he was wearing sunglasses and she couldn't be sure. Had Brock come into Mountain Mist, and she didn't see him? He would have walked right past her.

A few moments later, Lark appeared at her side and handed her some folded papers. "Brock was here. Said to give this to you and have you write your answer, give everything back to me, and he'll retrieve the stack in the morning."

Irritation flashed through Gianna. What was this, third grade? "Of all the—" She opened the papers and read his neat printing. He'd given her three options for the mold issue, and two for the paint and sealer. She scribbled a reply and handed the papers back to Lark.

"Are you guys having a fight or something?" Lark giggled.

Gianna rolled her eyes. "Or something." She forced a smile for Lark. "Thanks." She shrugged. "Guess I won't be having my coffee tomorrow."

Gianna spent the rest of the day puttering around the house. She washed clothes and made a new budget based on her improved situation. She texted Paisley and told her to take the bus home instead of coming to the shop, then prepared a treat to have waiting for her daughter. Their freezer was still full of food from kind friends and neighbors who visited after Greg's death. Gianna found some decadent chocolate-chunk cookies and put them in the microwave to thaw.

She sat on the porch to enjoy the lovely day and wait for Paisley to arrive home from school. Fall was Gianna's favorite time of year. The towering birch and aspen trees blazed yellow gold in the sunlight, blanketing the hills and distant mountains along with the pine trees.

Soon, the school bus came up the hill and stopped at the end of the drive. Gianna basked in the sight of her daughter running up the sidewalk, her beautiful curly hair sailing out behind her.

"Hi, Momma. Why are you home?"

"I came home a little early. How was your day?"

Paisley slid her backpack off and sat on the glider next to her mother. She pushed her glasses on her nose. "It was good. Our class and the fourth-grade class are doing projects together. Everyone works with a partner. Remember I told you about my new friend who just moved here?"

Gianna had a vague recollection and nodded.

"She's my partner. We're doing a report about Switzerland."

"Sounds like a fun project."

"We have to make some authentic food from our country. Can you help us?"

Gianna let out a dry laugh. "Better to let your friend's mom do the cooking."

Paisley nodded. "I'll ask her. Can I meet her at the library after school tomorrow? We have to turn in our outline next week. We want to start right away and do a good job on our project."

Gianna smoothed her hand over Paisley's silken curls. "Yes, you can meet her at the library."

"Cool. Can I have a snack?"

"Yes, you *may* have a snack. There might be cookies waiting for you."

Paisley's brown gaze sparkled. "Cookies, yum." She gave Gianna a smack on her cheek. "Thanks. You're the best."

Oh God, thank you so much for my precious daughter. Gianna rested her chin on her hand as the glider swung back and forth. She loved their home. When she married Greg and moved to Canadian Meadows, he gave her carte blanche to do whatever she wanted. Coming from a one-bedroom apartment shared with a toddler into life as Mrs. Greg Harper was like stepping into a shimmering fairytale. He was handsome and wealthy and adored Gianna. Their intense, whirlwind courtship had swept her into a world she hadn't even begun to dream about.

A tear slipped down her cheek. She had loved Greg. Their marriage had been good, but their family life had some cracks. Paisley had deserved better, and Gianna held deep regret for not choosing the right father for her. Not when she conceived Paisley, and not when she married Greg.

Gianna would never marry again, wouldn't trust herself to choose a father for Paisley. She still had insurmountable problems to solve. Today's loan was a temporary fix. She had no idea how she would survive. But she would. She and Paisley would be OK.

The mountains drew Gianna's gaze. *I am with you always.* A long-ago forgotten Psalm swam before her: "I will lift up mine eyes unto the hills, from whence cometh my help. My help cometh from the LORD, which made heaven and earth."

A peace settled over her. She was not alone.

For the first time in over a month, Gianna slept through the night. She still didn't feel like her normal self, but a good night's sleep made an amazing difference.

She put Paisley on the bus with instructions to text when she arrived at the library after school. "Go straight to the library, and I'll pick you up at 5:30."

A burst of energy surged through Gianna when she was getting ready, and instead of waiting until she arrived at the shop, she dried and styled her hair at home, taking a little extra care. She even put on a little mascara. She flew through the back door at 7:45. She couldn't be late for her and Brock's morning meeting.

"Hey, sweets, look at you." Van smiled as she finished putting her things in the fridge. "What a difference a day makes." Gianna had called Van last night to tell her about her success at the bank.

Gianna dumped her things on the counter and headed for the front. "I can't be late for Brock."

Van nibbled her lower lip. "He's already been here and gone."

Gianna's feet ground to a halt. "He has?" A spear of disappointment flashed through her, which she tried to ignore.

Van pointed to papers lying on the counter. "He said he picked these up from Lark." She frowned. "Although I don't understand how Lark is involved. And he wrote some questions for you. Said to text your answer to the number at the bottom."

Gianna collected the papers, annoyance raining on her. "He's such a child," she groused. She ignored the slight upturn of Van's lips.

"Did you guys have a fight or something?"

"No," Gianna snapped. "He's so annoying."

"He sure is more handsome every time he shows up here," Vanessa drawled.

"You're almost engaged," Gianna said.

Van laughed. "Maybe so, but I'm not blind."

Gianna rolled her eyes. She donned her apron and stuffed the papers in the pocket. "I have a full morning."

As she arranged her things for the day, Gianna grew more and more irritated. She would let Brock Hennessey know in no uncertain terms he couldn't avoid her because he was mad or didn't agree with her decisions. She needed to meet with him each morning, face to face, boss to employee. Using Lark and Vanessa as go-betweens was immature and not acceptable.

Gianna didn't have a free moment until after she'd gobbled a fruit salad for lunch, and then she called him. She had her speech all prepared and was even more annoyed when the call went straight to voicemail.

"Mr. Hennessey, this is Mrs. Harper," she said crisply. "I don't recall canceling our morning touch base meetings. I expect to see you at 7:45 sharp tomorrow." There. Her message should be crystal clear.

They had nine walk-ins in the afternoon, and Gianna couldn't believe when the clock read 5:20. She finished her last customer, and Van was almost done with hers. "I need to pick up Paisley at the library."

"I'll lock up," Van replied. "You have a good evening."

Gianna arrived at the library and stepped out of the car. She hadn't been outside all day, and drew deeply of the fresh, crisp fall air. She leaned against the hood of the car to wait for Paisley. She should be coming any moment.

About a minute later, the library doors opened, and Paisley came down the steps with a short, red-haired girl with glasses and a pixie haircut. The little girl was so cute.

Her hands moved around animatedly as she talked, and Gianna could tell Paisley was enjoying herself.

Gianna was about to call out when a man walked out the door behind them. What was Brock doing here? Why was he following Paisley?

Gianna's heart leapt into her throat. She jumped up and ran. "Paisley!" she screamed.

Paisley frowned. "Hi, Momma."

"Paisley, get in the car. Now." Gianna's voice shook.

Paisley's brow furrowed. "This is my friend, Piper."

Gianna ignored the girl. She grabbed Paisley's arm and pushed her toward the vehicle. "Paisley, *now*." Her daughter shuffled off, her features drooping.

Brock noticed Gianna. His mouth hung open. Gianna pointed a finger at him. "You—you stay away from my daughter," she hissed.

His jaw dropped. "Your daughter?"

Gianna glanced at the little red-haired girl. She should ensure the child's safety as well. She rested her hands on the girl's shoulders. "Go to the car with Paisley, honey." She'd sort everything out after they were both safe and away from Brock, and then she would call the sheriff.

"You want to take your hands off *my* daughter?" Brock's icy words shattered the air around them.

"Your daughter?"

His gaze bore into her. "Piper, get in the truck." He pointed his key fob toward the vehicle and clicked it.

"But Daddy, Paisley and I wanted to ask if we could go to Happy's for dinner."

"Now, Piper."

The little girl pushed her glasses on her nose and skittered away.

Brock's gaze remained on her until she reached the truck and closed the door. Then he turned back to Gianna. "You are one crazy lady," he barked, pointing at her.

Gianna parked her hands on her hips. "You have a daughter? What other secrets are you keeping from me?"

"You don't deserve to know every detail about my personal life."

"Every detail?" she shouted. "I don't know any details. I know nothing about you. You're a stranger to town. You talk about meeting Paisley at her school, but as far as I know, you have no reason to be there, and then you follow her out of the library today. What am I supposed to think?"

He palmed the back of his neck. "I—OK." He exhaled loudly.

The danger was past, and Gianna shook. "Paisley is my world. I have nothing else right now." Her throat closed.

Brock took a tentative step toward her. "Piper is all I have too. She means everything to me." His Adam's apple bobbed, and a rare, raw vulnerability shone in his gaze.

They stood there for a moment staring at one another, and then everything shifted in slow motion. Brock cleared his throat. "Somehow, you and I had a terrible start, and I'd like to try to make amends." His attention drifted over her shoulder to where Paisley was sitting in the car, and his lips turned up in a ghost of a smile. "What's Piper doing right now?"

Gianna looked past him to his truck, where Piper was hanging out the window, making wild gesticulations with her hands. Gianna tried to suppress the laughter bubbling inside her. "I think she and Paisley are up to something."

Brock gave her a full-on grin now, almost robbing Gianna of breath. "Piper is *always* up to something." He whirled around and gazed at his daughter, who ceased her movements.

Gianna spun and looked at Paisley. She sat in the front seat staring out the window with a wide-eyed innocent expression.

"Can we all go to Happy's?" Piper yelled.

"Puh-leeeeze?" Paisley called out.

Brock turned back to Gianna. "Please, will you come? Our treat."

Gianna shook her head. "I can pay."

"No—"

"My circumstances—things are looking up a bit. It'll be a business dinner, and I'll expense the bill," Gianna said.

"We'll decide later." He gave her another full-on, devastating grin.

Gianna gulped. She still needed to put up walls against Brock Hennessey, but now for a completely different reason.

CHAPTER 9

Brock opened the door to Happy's and ushered Gianna and the girls through. He stepped to the check-in station. "Four," he said to the hostess.

"We'll have your table in a few minutes," she said.

Brock stood with his hands in his pockets. Gianna also stood, looking a little uncomfortable. Paisley and Piper sat on a bench with their heads together, whispering.

The hostess came back and beckoned them to follow. She looked at the girls. "Do you want crayons and something to color?"

Paisley and Piper frowned.

"No, they're fine, thanks," Brock said quickly. He didn't want the hostess subjected to Piper's *I'm not a baby* speech.

They followed the hostess to a booth. Brock stood back and waited for Piper to scoot in. Paisley and Gianna slid in across from them.

When their server appeared with menus, Piper spoke up. "Could my friend and I sit over there?" She pointed to a table for two about fifteen feet away and looked at Brock. "Paisley and I need to talk about our project. I'm sure you would be bored."

"Sure, if you'd like," the server answered.

Paisley looked at her mother. "Please?"

Brock raised an eyebrow at Gianna.

"It's OK with me," she said. She and Brock rose and let the girls out.

Brock sat, and Piper leaned over and pecked his cheek. "Thanks. Have fun on your date."

She did not say that. Heat bathed Brock's face. He glanced at Paisley, who wore a wide smile, and at Gianna, who looked at her lap, her face pink.

Brock stood and took Piper by the elbow. "Excuse us," he said stiffly. He marched his daughter out to a corner of the lobby area where they couldn't be overheard. He gestured for her to sit on the bench and stood, towering over her. "Piper Lee Hennessey, I cannot believe what you said." He didn't know where to start. His relationship with Gianna was so fragile, and he wanted to gain her trust and build a friendship one step at a time.

Piper blinked at him. "But she's soooooo pretty, and you need someone like her. You're lonely."

How was his daughter dreaming up these ideas? "Piper, I am not lonely. I have you. And Gi—Mrs. Harper's husband, Paisley's dad, died very recently. She doesn't want to date anyone right now." He injected more sternness into his voice. "Regardless, our relationship is not your business, young lady. Do you understand me?"

Piper sighed. "Yes."

"I will let you sit at the other table with Paisley, but if you say one more inappropriate thing, you and I will leave. Do you understand?"

Piper nodded. "Do I have to apologize to Mrs. Harper?"

Brock took her elbow. "You bet you do."

They returned to the booth where Gianna sat. Paisley was at the other table.

Piper blinked at Gianna. "I'm sorry, Mrs. Harper," she said politely. "Sometimes I say inappropriate things."

Gianna's lips twitched. "Thank you, Piper."

Piper tapped Brock on the arm. "What kind of pizza are we ordering?"

"Mrs. Harper and I will decide." He tipped his head toward Paisley. "Go." Piper turned and walked away. By the set of her shoulders, she might be a little contrite, but knowing his daughter, he doubted it. She was probably planning her next attack.

Brock sat and reached for his water glass. He wished he could douse himself and melt away like the wicked witch in the *Wizard of Oz*. His face was still on fire, but he forced himself to make eye contact with Gianna. "I'm sorry. She—" his voice cracked, and he took a gulp. "Sometimes I have no idea what will come out of her mouth."

To his shock, Gianna burst out laughing. "Oh, Brock, she is adorable."

He was so relieved, he couldn't resist laughing too. "Easy for you to say. Paisley seems much more ... controlled."

Gianna shook her head. "She has her moments too."

He opened the menu and peered over it. "I'm glad you've moved past Mr. Hennessey," he said lightly.

Her lovely face flushed again, but she didn't respond.

Brock so wanted to call her *Gianna* but didn't want to shatter their fragile truce. They busied themselves deciding what to order, agreeing on small personal pizzas for the girls and a medium pizza and salad for the two of them to share.

When the server left, Brock rested his forearms on the table and tented his fingers. "We've had enough awkwardness for the evening." He tipped his head toward Piper. "Way more than enough."

He was rewarded by a soft laugh from Gianna.

"What would you like to talk about?"

She opened her mouth to speak, and he had another idea. He held up a finger. "No business. Not tonight." He wanted to begin building a bridge.

Gianna pursed her lips. "For me to write this off as a business dinner, we need to talk a little business."

Brock grimaced.

"I promise, nothing bad."

He relaxed a bit, and she continued. "I appreciate your attention to detail, and I can tell you have a lot of good experience. For example, the information about the peeling paint and how a lot of builders skip on the sealer."

Brock was stunned. "Thank you."

"You're welcome. Now we're done talking business. What do you want to talk about?"

Brock considered her question and admonished himself to slow down. He measured his words carefully. "You said you don't know anything about me, and I don't know much about you. How about we play twenty questions, sort of. You ask me a question, and then I'll ask you one. And if either of us is uncomfortable, we can say 'I'm not ready to answer,' or something."

She mulled his proposal over. "No pressure," he added.

Gianna nodded. "OK."

"You go first."

After the server brought their salads, Gianna picked up her fork. "Where did you live before you came here?"

"San Diego." Brock stirred his salad. "How long have you lived in Canadian Meadows?"

"Eight years." She lifted a forkful of salad and held it. "Are you running away from something or someone?"

Not a trick question, but close. He took a hearty bite, buying time to measure his words. Her gaze met his, and something told him he could trust her. He swallowed and took a sip of water. "Yes. But I'm not breaking any laws." He waited for her to look at him. "Why is Paisley's last name Rossi?" He took another forkful of his salad.

Gianna bit her bottom lip. "I'm not ready—" She looked at her lap. "Rossi was my maiden name. She was born when I was eighteen."

Brock wanted to know more, but now wasn't the time. "Thank you for trusting me," he murmured.

"It's not a state secret." She wiped the corner of her mouth with her napkin. "Are you and Piper in any danger?"

Brock reviewed what he'd done over the past two weeks to cover their tracks. "No one will find us here."

The server came with their pizza and took the girls theirs, providing a perfect place to end their twenty-questions exercise. He asked Gianna some general questions about the town and the area while they ate. The girls finished their pizza and joined them.

Gianna picked up the bill from the server.

"May I leave the tip?" Brock asked.

She nodded, showed him the total, and he left some bills.

When they reached their cars, Paisley and Piper hugged as if one of them was leaving for an overseas voyage. "Won't you see each other at school in the morning?" Brock asked.

Piper rolled her eyes at Paisley. "He doesn't understand."

"Definitely," Paisley agreed. Brock opened Piper's door, and she hopped in. He closed the door behind her.

"Please go to the car," Gianna said to Paisley. "I need to ask Mr. Hennessey something."

When both doors were closed, she stepped away and turned her back to the vehicles, and Brock followed.

"One more question," she said.

"Shoot."

"Do you drink the same coffee every single morning?"

He nodded. "Yes. Do you?"

Her gaze, still tired but brighter than he'd seen them all week, perked up. "No. Are you planning to bring me coffee tomorrow morning?"

"Yes. Would you like something different?"

"Yes."

"And?"

She shrugged. "Surprise me."

He smiled. "I will. Thank you for dinner, Gianna."

"You're welcome. See you in the morning, Brock."

CHAPTER 10

The next morning when Van arrived, Gianna was checking her hair in the back room and moved away from the mirror. She'd made sure to arrive plenty early.

Van's eyes went wide. "Don't you look nice? Your blouse looks new."

"This? No." But maybe the garment had hung in Gianna's closet for months and she'd taken the tags off this morning.

Van still stared. "You look good, better than you have for a long time. Are you sleeping a little better?"

Gianna nodded. She'd slept straight through for the second night in a row. After she'd lain awake for almost two hours thinking about Brock, about Piper, about dinner, about twenty questions.

"Is Brock coming by this morning?" Van opened the fridge and put her things in.

"Um, yeah. For our regular touch base."

Van leaned against the counter and crossed her arms. "Something's changed between the two of you, hasn't it?"

"What? No." Sometimes Gianna wished her friend's intuition wasn't so sharp.

"Come clean, sweets."

"OK, yes, maybe a little." She exhaled. "He has a daughter."

Van's eyebrows flew to her hairline. "A *daughter*?"

"Yes. She's a year younger than Paisley. They met at school and now they're best friends. Her name is Piper, and she's adorable."

"Is he married? Is her mom in the picture?"

Of course, Gianna wondered too. "I don't think so." And she wondered why Brock fled San Diego. But she didn't want to share those details with Van right now. Gianna gave her the abridged version of how they met at the library—minus all the screaming and shouting. "The girls wanted to eat at Happy's, so we all went."

Van grinned. "Sounds like a date."

"You have an overactive imagination." Gianna's heart skittered. "The girls are working on a school project together ,and they've bonded, so we came to kind of an understanding, and I don't hate him anymore."

"No other reason you're wearing new clothes and you already fixed your hair before you arrived?"

The front doorbell tinkled. Gianna stuck her fingers in her ears. "La la la," she sang. "I can't hear you, Van." Her friend's laughter followed Gianna as she headed for the front.

Brock stood at the counter, dressed in his usual jeans, work boots, and a navy T-shirt under a plaid flannel shirt. He raised his cup in a salute and grinned. "Morning."

"Good morning. Are you wearing a new shirt?"

He lifted a shoulder. "New to me. I visited the consignment shop. I thought plaid might help me fit in better around here."

Gianna laughed. "You're right." She pointed to the cup sitting on the counter. "For me?"

He nodded.

She took a tentative sniff. "Mmm ... interesting." She took a sip. "Delicious."

"Whew, I'm relieved."

"Is Lark responsible for this?"

"Nope. I am."

"Good job. Thank you." She indicated the clipboard he held. "What do you have?"

"I wondered if you could give me a complete list of your properties. I'd like to visit each one and make sure Riggs didn't let any other issues go."

Gianna nodded. "Great idea. I can email you." Then she took in his expression. "I forgot you're not doing anything online right now. I'll print a copy."

"Thanks."

They spent a few more moments looking over Brock's list. "I still want you to run anything by me before you purchase materials," she said.

"No problem."

Gianna glanced toward the back room and lowered her voice. "I—I found something in Greg's things I'd like to share with you."

His eyebrows lifted, but he didn't say anything.

"I'd rather have the discussion later. Can you come back after I close at five tonight?"

"Piper will be with me."

"No worries. She and Paisley can hang out in back." Something occurred to her. "Where is Piper after school if you're working?" Gianna couldn't imagine Brock would let his daughter stay home alone.

He straightened. "She's with me. Reading and doing homework. She doesn't interfere with my work at all, I promise. I ... I pretty much can't let her out of my sight when she's not at school."

Gianna's curiosity was piqued, but she didn't want to push. "Some days, if you want Piper to come here with Paisley, she's welcome. Paisley would love the company."

His gaze softened a bit. "I appreciate your offer. I'll think about it."

"Now that I know you have a daughter, some of your earlier behaviors I was puzzled about make sense. Being late the first morning."

Brock nodded. "I had to register her for school."

"And running off after our first Friday afternoon meeting."

Brock let out a breath and winced. "Piper was waiting on a bench down the block. After Riggs left, I panicked."

"Why didn't you tell me?"

He cocked his head. "You weren't in the mood to make any concessions for me."

Gianna was ashamed and looked away. She sighed and turned her gaze back on him. "Point taken. I know how tough single parenting is. I'll do whatever I can to help keep Piper safe."

Brock swallowed. "Thank you." He turned toward the door. "I'd better go. See you at five."

"Have a good day."

At five o'clock, Paisley ushered Piper and Brock through the front door. She'd been waiting outside for at least ten minutes. She and Piper chattered like two magpies as they sailed past Gianna.

"Hello, Mrs. Harper," Piper said.

"Hi, Piper," Gianna replied, smiling at the little girl.

"May we have a snack?" Paisley asked.

"You already had a snack. Dinner will be soon."

"What are we having?"

Gianna scrambled. "Ah—I'll have to see what we have at home."

"We're having taco night," Piper announced. "We already had them once this week, but I love tacos. Daddy, can they come over for taco night?"

Gianna looked at Brock, and awkwardness danced between them.

"I looove tacos too." Paisley crooned. Gianna bit back a laugh. Her daughter acted as if tacos were the most exquisite delicacy in the universe.

"Maybe another night, Paisley." Then Gianna saw the devastated look on Piper's little face and wanted to call the words back.

"Please come."

Gianna was surprised to hear Brock's voice. Her gaze flew to him, and he looked sincere.

"It would be a great way to start the weekend," he said.

"If you're sure," Gianna said. The girls hugged each other and bounced up and down.

Brock nodded, his gaze loaded with an additional message. "We'll have a chance to talk business."

"OK. Should we go ahead and leave now? For your house?"

Brock smiled. "You own the house." Gianna's face must have registered surprise. "The A-frame?"

She laughed. "We'll follow you there. Paisley, gather your things." She turned back to Brock. "Do you need me to stop at the store for anything?"

Brook shook his head.

Piper nodded. "We need more taco shells."

"We'll bring those," Gianna said. She was amused Piper seemed to have a better handle on their food stocks than her dad did.

The girls had their heads together. "Can Paisley ride home with us?" Piper asked.

Gianna hesitated, but she wasn't sure why. "Paisley, come with me. Help me shop."

"For *taco shells*?" Her daughter rolled her eyes.

Brock winked at Gianna, and her heart did a little flip.

"Come on, Pipe, let's go. You'll see Paisley in a little while."

"Bye, Paisley," Piper said, her voice dripping with sadness.

"Bye, Piper." Paisley was equally dejected.

"What's the house number again?" Gianna asked.

"Fifty-eight-ten," Piper chirped. She sure was a sharp little thing.

Gianna locked the shop, and she and Paisley drove to the grocery store. They came out with taco shells and chips, lettuce, an eight-pack of sparkling water, and a package of refrigerated cookie dough.

When they drove up the long driveway to the A-frame, Piper was waiting on the porch and ran to the car. She and Paisley floated into the house on a bubble of happy laughter.

Brock met Gianna at the door. "Good, you're here. They had to be apart for fifteen whole minutes."

Gianna laughed, and he reached for the sparkling water.

"What's this?" he asked.

"One of my favorites."

"Looks good." He led her into the compact kitchen overlooking the living area. "Have you ever been here?"

"No, never have."

The girls came running down a quaint spiral staircase leading to a loft. "Momma, Piper has a reading nook in her room," Paisley cried.

Piper pointed to the hallway. "Daddy's boring room is down there. Let's go in the backyard." They disappeared like the wind.

Gianna looked at Brock, and they shook their heads and laughed. He held his arms out and turned around. "Here's ninety percent of the house. You already heard Piper's directions to the bathroom and my 'boring' bedroom, if you want to see."

A room where he slept and dressed. Gianna's face flushed. "Piper sleeps in the loft?"

"Yes. Thirty seconds after we arrived, she staked her claim."

"Is there a bed up there?"

He shook his head. "We brought an air mattress with us. She doesn't mind." He took out ingredients from the fridge and set them on the counter. "I was afraid she would feel disoriented and a little scared the first few nights and want to sleep with me, but she didn't."

"I don't think much scares Piper, am I right?"

Brock nodded. "Yeah, she's pretty fearless."

"Paisley is more cautious," Gianna mused. "I think Piper is good for her." She watched his long, capable fingers slicing tomatoes like a pro.

Brock smirked. "If she doesn't cause Paisley to commit a felony."

Gianna laughed. "Do you need help with anything?" She should have offered sooner. She held up the bag of lettuce. "OK if I make mine a taco salad?"

"Sure. I think everything's about ready." He pulled a bowl of savory meat from the microwave.

Gianna looked around. "I knew this house didn't have much furniture, but—wow. I'm sorry, Brock."

"Don't be. Piper and I aren't used to much." His face went a little pink. "I didn't mean to sound pathetic. We lived in a little furnished duplex in San Diego. The fireplace and yard here more than make up for the lack of furniture." He walked around the counter and called out the open patio door. "Girls, come on in. We're ready to eat." They ran in, and he pointed toward the hall. "Wash up."

When the girls returned, Brock handed a plate to Gianna and one to Paisley. "Let's eat."

"We need to pray," Piper admonished.

"Oh. Right." He looked at Gianna. "OK with you?"

"Of course."

They all bowed their heads, and he offered a quick prayer. Gianna was surprised. The ease with which he spoke made Gianna think he talked to God on a regular basis.

They helped the girls settle at the counter. Brock grabbed his plate and two glasses of ice and motioned to Gianna. "We can sit outside. Will you bring the soda?"

"Yes," she replied, and followed him. They sat at a small, round, scuffed table.

"We eat out here almost every night," he said. "I suppose we won't be able to for much longer."

Gianna nodded. "Not without your parkas and gloves."

Brock laughed. Then his expression softened as he looked around. "It's gorgeous here. Peaceful. I've never seen so many beautiful trees."

"Do you miss San Diego?"

He lifted an eyebrow at her. "Are we playing twenty questions now?"

"Sure," she said with a smile.

"Then my answer would have to be no." He polished off his first taco and took a drink of sparkling water. "This is good. Where did you live before you moved here?"

"Helena. Were you raised in San Diego?"

"No, LA. When did you begin cutting hair?"

Gianna took a sip of her drink and pursed her lips. "Right out of high school. How long have you been doing construction work?"

"Since I was fifteen." He paused. "How did you meet your husband?"

Gianna dabbed her mouth with her napkin. She took a moment to choose her words. "He was a customer. I gave him a haircut. Is Piper's mom in the picture?"

Gianna thought she caught a flash of fear in Brock's eyes, but he recovered quickly. Was he running from Piper's mother?

"No. Was Greg older than you?'

"Yes." She didn't offer any other information.

Brock nodded and swallowed. "I thought so."

They'd asked and answered enough questions for tonight. Gianna pushed her plate away and looked in the house. The girls were still at the counter, talking and laughing. Brock was finished eating too. He scooted his chair back and stretched out his long legs.

He didn't say anything, and Gianna sensed he was waiting for her to tell him about what she had hinted at this morning. He didn't push, which she appreciated.

The girls opened the screen door, and Piper tapped Brock on the arm. "We have to make some Switzerland food for our project. Can you help us, since Mrs. Harper can't cook?"

"Piper Lee." Brock looked at Gianna, wide-eyed. "I'm so sorry." He turned his attention to his daughter. "Would you please apologize to Mrs. Harper?"

"Paisley said so. You helping was her idea," Piper insisted.

Paisley nodded.

Gianna laughed uproariously. "They're right, Brock. Beyond a block of Swiss cheese, I couldn't contribute much."

"The internet has some good ideas," Paisley said.

Brock sighed. "I'm sure we can come up with a good plan."

"Can we bake the cookies now?" Piper asked.

"If you can put the cookie dough on a baking sheet and preheat the oven." Brock said.

"We can handle that," Paisley said confidently.

Brock smiled. "I'll put them in the oven in a few minutes. Would you take our plates in, please?"

"Sure." The girls gathered them and left.

"They make a good team," Gianna said with a smile.

Brock dragged a hand down his face. "I'm sorry for what Piper said. Someday, my girl's mouth will land her in a heap of trouble."

Gianna couldn't help an escaping giggle. "She's so cute."

He gave her a lopsided smile, making her heart trip. "Easy for you to say." He leaned back and linked his hands behind his head.

Gianna took this as a signal to move to the next topic of conversation. She was more relaxed now and released a slow breath. "One reason I didn't believe Greg hired you was because he always surrounded himself with local people, most of whom he'd worked with and trusted for years. To bring in an outsider, someone clear from California, was out of character for him."

Brock didn't say anything.

Here came the hard part. "A while back, I found entries in Greg's task list with the initials BH, but none of his contacts corresponded with those initials, and the whole thing slipped my mind until ... until you came."

His brown eyes took on a spark, and he lifted his chin a notch. "You don't say."

She took a sip of her drink. "When we first met, you said Greg had hired you to work on a land development project. His business was property management, not land development. What did you mean?"

Brock leaned forward and put his forearms on the table. "Have you ever heard of Carson Bellmont?"

Gianna searched her mind. "No, I don't think so."

"In one of my phone conversations with your husband, he mentioned 'Carson' would direct my work when I came on board. He never used a last name. I'm not certain this is the same man, but searching 'land development' and 'Carson' led me to Bellmont." He paused. "He's been on the edge of some shady things. And he's not from around here."

Something was on the cusp of Gianna's mind, just beyond her reach. "Wait a minute." She snapped her fingers. "Oh, my goodness ... after the first entry of BH, the initials CB were always there too. CB and BH."

A low whistle escaped Brock's firm, full lips. "Interesting. Anything else with those entries?"

Gianna shook her head. "I'd have to go back and look." She bit her lower lip. "Will you help me?"

The oven beeped from the kitchen, and Brock stood. "Yes. Do you trust me now?" He looked down at her.

She stood so she could look straight into his eyes. "Yes. Do you forgive me?"

He tilted his head. "There's nothing to forgive, Gianna."

Gianna swallowed. "One more thing ... the job Greg promised you no longer exists, but your contract stipulated you would receive the hiring bonus upon your arrival. I can't—I still can't pay you the full ten thousand, but as soon as I can—"

Brock wrapped his hand around hers, and Gianna was surprised at its smoothness, considering he did manual labor. His deep brown gaze bore into hers. "Don't worry about the money now. I want to help you solve this mystery. OK?"

Gianna couldn't speak around the knot in her throat, so she nodded.

CHAPTER 11

Brock grabbed the last of the papers off the printer at the library and beckoned Piper. "Let's go. We don't want to be late."

"What are those papers?" she asked.

"They're for Mrs. Harper." Brock had some answers and was anxious to share them with Gianna. She said she had some things to show him too.

Piper scurried out the door and down the steps in front of him. She clapped her hands. "I'm so excited. A picnic and hike with Paisley." They were picking Gianna and Paisley up at the salon and taking a picnic out to someplace called Sapphire Falls.

When they arrived, Paisley was waiting out front with a big basket. She waved and bounced on her toes. Brock had barely stopped the truck when Piper unhooked her seat belt and launched herself out. She and Paisley fell into each other's arms as if they hadn't seen each other only last night. Brock shook his head. He sure didn't understand little girls.

Gianna glided out the door, and Brock did a double take. She looked like a burst of sunshine in jeans, hiking boots, and a bright yellow long-sleeved knit shirt, topped off by a white quilted vest. A long scarf in yellows and bright pink secured her hair and flowed behind her.

Brock shook himself and exited the truck. "Hi." He wanted to add, *you look gorgeous,* but stopped himself. He reached for the picnic basket.

"Hi," she answered, a bit breathlessly. Her bright pink lipstick matched the scarf. She handed him a small cooler and hers and Paisley's jackets. "Let me run back for my papers."

When Gianna returned, Brock held the truck door open for her. They headed out according to her directions and passed the turnoff to the A-frame on the way. Sapphire Falls was about twenty minutes out of town.

After he parked the truck, they retrieved their picnic things out of the back and ascended a set of wide-spaced wooden stairs built into the sloping hill. When they reached the top, Brock stopped and stared. A large plateau overflowed with towering pines, golden aspen and birch trees, and scrubby brush ranging from deep reds to oranges. The mountains rose before them and at the end of the plateau, spanning its entire width, a series of tumbling waterfalls spilled into several shallow pools connected by a rock-rimmed stream. To their left, a half dozen picnic tables sat in a shaded clearing, about half of them filled with other picnickers.

"This is awesome," Piper cried. She and Paisley ran to claim one of the tables.

The scenery was so beautiful, Brock had no words.

Gianna grinned at him. "I should make a note. Brock Hennessey, speechless."

He shook his head in wonder. "I wasn't prepared for this," he sputtered, then returned her smile. "The more I see of Montana, the more I'm struck by its beauty." He followed her to the table. The four of them unpacked the picnic lunch and sat.

"Pray," Paisley and Piper said in unison.

Brock smiled and removed his baseball cap. He looked at Gianna. "You want to, or should I?"

"You go ahead," she replied.

After they said *Amen*, Gianna put her palms up. "Full disclosure, I didn't make any of this. Mountain Mist to the rescue."

Brock smiled. "No apology needed. You had to work this morning. And I've been wanting to try their food."

"Everything they make is so good." The girls reached for their sandwiches and chips, and Gianna offered Brock chicken salad or turkey.

"Which one do you want?" he asked.

"I like either, honestly. You choose."

He took the chicken salad, plus a helping of potato salad and coleslaw. "Does Lark's family own Mountain Mist? I met her mom."

"Yes. Her parents are Barb and Tack Garritsen. They've been there for about fifteen years. They're a wonderful family. Tack used to farm exclusively, but now he splits his time between their farm and the restaurant."

"Principal Garritsen is their son?"

Gianna nodded. "Yes, Ben."

"Now I see the resemblance between Ben and his mom. Do they have other children?"

Gianna shook her head. "There's a big span between Ben and Lark. I think they had some miscarriages."

Brock swallowed his first bite of chicken salad. "This is good."

"I agree. Their chicken salad is my favorite."

Brock held out the other half of the sandwich. "Here."

"No. I'm fine with this."

He wiggled his fingers. "Take this, and trade me for half the turkey." She rolled her eyes, and he smiled and shook his head. "Stubborn."

After the girls finished, they asked if they could play in the stream and pools. Brock looked at Gianna and spun his hand in a circle. "OK if they go anywhere where we can still see them?"

Gianna nodded. "Stay on the plateau, girls."

"Can we take our shoes off and wade in the stream?" Paisley asked.

"Sure. Just don't walk in the grass without shoes." Gianna looked at Brock. "There's all kinds of stuff they can step on." She addressed the girls. "I have cookies from Miss Barb for later."

Paisley released a dramatic sigh and looked at Piper. "Miss Barb's cookies are the best." She turned to her mother. "Did you bring chewy chocolate chunk *and* peanut butter dreams?"

"Of course." Gianna laughed and shook her head as the girls ran off. "Barb is the baker in the family. The sandwich bread is homemade."

"Everything was delicious. I had one of their cinnamon rolls last week."

Gianna's eyes widened, and she opened her mouth. "Mmm," they said in unison. Then they laughed and grinned at one another, and Brock's heart fluttered.

"Their entire menu is family recipes," Gianna said. "They do so much for our community."

The two of them put everything back in the picnic basket, and Brock picked up the folder on the bench beside him containing the papers he'd printed off at the library. "I think I'm starting to find some answers about what Greg was doing. I have some papers to show you."

"Good. I have things to show you too." She held up a plastic sleeve secured with a string. "Do you want to move on this side so one of us isn't reading upside down?"

"Sure."

He settled on the seat next to her and smiled. "This way we can both look at the falls. This place is amazing." He opened his folder. "Mind if I go first?"

"Not at all."

"Carson Bellmont is from Seattle. He's in his mid-fifties and has been a land developer for over twenty years." Brock spread some of the papers out. "I haven't found anything to directly implicate him, but he seems to be on the fringes of some questionable things—properties being owned by shell companies and the like. There's something—I don't know, something doesn't sit quite right."

"What does this have to do with Greg?"

"I'm not sure yet. Do you know, did he ever have dealings in Washington? Oregon? Or anywhere else?"

Gianna shook her head. "I always thought his business was around here, but he did start traveling a lot, especially in the last year."

"Where to?"

She pursed her lips. "Seattle. Portland. Boise. Denver."

"Hmm." Brock drummed his fingers on the table. "Just because he traveled to those cities doesn't prove a connection. Did he ever share any details of his business with you?"

She shook her head. "He said he was working on some new deals and not to 'worry my beautiful head' over any of the business stuff."

Beautiful head, indeed.

"He ran his business, and I ran mine."

"Are all your books separate from his?"

"Yes, but he put up the capital for my salon when we'd been married for a few years."

They sat for a while, laughter from the girls piercing the silence.

"Was your marriage happy?"

"Yes." She sighed. "And no." She turned to meet his gaze. "Was yours?"

Brock hadn't admitted to ever having been married. "No. Not even a little. Did Greg ever want to adopt Paisley?"

"No. He didn't want children." She shrugged. "He only wanted me. Our courtship was short and intense. By the time I told him I had a child, neither one of us could walk away, but he was emphatic. Paisley was mine, and there would be no more children."

Brock wanted to reach out but held himself back. They had slipped into twenty questions, and he wondered if she would want to continue.

She cleared her throat. "How long has Piper's mom been out of the picture?"

"Seven years. Did Paisley consider Greg her dad?"

"No. She called him Greg. He provided for us, very comfortably, but they didn't have a strong emotional connection." Her chin trembled. "I had a wonderful marriage and a wonderful daughter, but the two didn't intersect. Not the kind of family life I'd always dreamed of."

Brock couldn't resist this time. He covered her hand with his. "I'm sorry, Gianna. Paisley deserved better." He immediately wished he could hit *delete* on the last three words. Talk about Piper's mouth getting her in trouble. "I apologize, Gianna. I overstepped." He tried to withdraw his hand, but she held tight. Brock enjoyed seeing her long, elegant fingers wrapped around his.

"No, you didn't. You're right, Brock. My daughter deserved better—on so many levels. She's had every creature comfort a child could want for most of her life, except a father's love. And now I look at you and Piper, with little but each other, and I—" She swallowed. "I think Paisley would have been better off the last eight years if I'd stayed single, even if we lived in the little one-bedroom apartment. I was so young and naïve when I married him, and I was certain once he'd spent time with my sweet, beautiful little daughter, he would turn into a loving father. But he didn't, and who knows what kind of long-term harm Greg's emotional rejection of her has caused." She removed her hand and covered her mouth, her eyes wide with regret and pain.

Brock rubbed her shoulder. "Kids are resilient. She's had enough love from you to fill in the cracks. I can see how close you are."

Gianna sighed. "Thank you. Paisley and I will be a team of two going forward."

The comment stung, which filled Brock with confusion. He wasn't looking for a love match, so why did Gianna's declaration bother him?

The girls ran to them, saving him from having to respond. "Cookies, cookies," they cried. Brock put the papers away and scooped up Gianna's folder, which they hadn't yet opened. They each had two cookies, and Brock sneaked a third peanut butter one.

"Daddy, can I grow my hair out?" Piper asked.

He tossed an amused glance at Gianna. "I like your hair short."

Gianna threw back her head and laughed. "So you don't have to deal with long hair."

"Shh." Brock smiled. He dusted cookie crumbs off his hands. "Those were fantastic, by the way."

"I can help, Piper," Gianna offered. "There are all kinds of ways to manage long hair."

"And I have a gazillion hair ties and ribbons and barrettes I can give you," Paisley said.

Piper rested her head on Paisley's shoulder. "Your hair is so pretty."

"Your hair won't be curly, Pipe, you know," Brock said.

Piper pouted.

"He's right, Piper," Gianna offered. She reached over and ran her fingers over the thick copper strands. "But your dad has the last word. Really, Brock, this is such a beautiful color, there should be more of it."

Brock threw up his hands. "I surrender. I'm outnumbered. You see this, don't you?" The girls giggled. He smiled at Piper. "You're old enough to take care of your own hair, so you can choose the style and length. You have my blessing."

The girls cheered and hugged, and Piper gave Gianna a high five. Then she and Paisley jumped up. "Can we go hiking now?"

"In a few minutes," Brock said. "Go on back over to the stream." He wanted to see the papers Gianna had brought. After the girls ran off, she opened her plastic folder.

"I printed out Greg's calendar and task list for the past year," she said. "I told you the places where I know he traveled, but for about the last four months, he wouldn't tell me where he was going, which was different. He used to always say, 'I'm going to Seattle, I'll be at the Hilton,' or whatever. At the beginning of summer, he stopped."

Brock thumbed through the sheets she laid out. He saw the BH and CB notations, but nothing else. "Did you press him for details?"

She shrugged. "A couple of times. I stopped asking because he wasn't willing to share."

"Do you have his credit card statements?"

She shook her head. "No. He would have used his business card for travel."

"Any chance you can find the statements? Would they be in his office?"

Gianna pursed her full, pink lips. "I'm pretty sure his accountant took care of those details. I can ask him."

Brock nodded, then scratched his chin and considered his next question. "Feel free to tell me if I'm stepping over the line."

She nodded.

"Could he have been having an affair?"

Gianna looked at her hands and picked at one of her nails. "No, I'm certain he wasn't. Everything was fine between us." She sighed. "We were very much in love. But I'm convinced he was hiding something concerning his business from me."

"Mind if I take these?" Brock asked, indicating the papers.

"Not at all," Gianna said. She inserted them into the folder and handed it to him.

"I think we owe some girls a hike," he said, and stood.

Gianna smiled. "I agree."

Brock picked up the picnic basket. "I'll put all this stuff in the truck."

"Can you grab our jackets?" Gianna said. The fall day was pleasant, but the temperature was falling.

When he came back to the plateau, they joined the girls at the stream while they put on their shoes and socks. Brock gazed at the water spilling over the rocks, most of the surface of which was covered with a blue-green moss. "What's the story I hear about the falls glowing like sapphires?"

"I've never seen the phenomenon," Gianna said, "but I know people who insist they have."

"Hmm," Brock said. "I wonder if the moss on the rocks has anything to do with it. Or the temperature. What kind of rock is this?"

Gianna laughed. "You're asking me? I'm a hair stylist, not a geologist."

Brock smiled. "Does the display occur often?"

She shook her head, her dark ponytail swinging behind her. "No. The claim might not even be real. Maybe just folklore." It happens only at sunset. I guess the light has to shine at the right angle."

Piper sighed. "I wish sapphire was my birthstone. Mine is a dumb light green one."

"Mine is an opal," Paisley said brightly. "They're pretty."

They hiked for two hours, and Brock fell in love with the landscape. He also learned from Gianna about the pine-ish looking trees with brighter green needles called *larch*. The girls ended up with pockets full of stones, twigs, pretty leaves, and other random things. The skies clouded over before sunset, eliminating any chance to see the falls turn blue. When they dropped Gianna and Paisley back at their car, darkness had descended.

Paisley climbed into the front seat, and Brock jumped out and met Gianna at her car trunk with the basket.

"I—we had a great time today," Brock said. "Thanks for lunch and being our hiking guide. I I can't wait to come back here to explore."

"You're welcome. I—we had a great time too. And thank you for looking through those papers. I don't know what else to do."

Brock reached out and squeezed her hand. If he bent forward a couple of inches, he could plant a kiss on her hair, or even her forehead. He was tempted but stepped back. Her words echoed in his head. *"We were very much in love."*

Even though Brock had been alone for many years, he had no plans for another relationship. And even if he did, he thought Gianna was still in love with her husband.

"See you Monday, Gianna."
"See you, Brock."

CHAPTER 12

Gianna peeked out the front window of the shop again, over the café curtains covering the lower half. *Whew.* He was gone.

When Gianna greeted her first customer of the morning after Brock left, she saw Mort Riggs across the street leaning against a light post, arms crossed, staring at her salon. Gianna couldn't imagine what he was doing there, and hoped he was waiting to meet someone.

Van had taken the day off, and Gianna didn't have a full schedule so found herself looking out the front window more than she normally would have. Riggs didn't move for over two hours. Sometimes he smoked a cigarette, but the rest of the time he simply stood there. His battered hat was pulled low over his eyes, but his gaze bored through the front window.

Gianna wished he would leave, but standing on a public sidewalk wasn't illegal. Hopefully this was an isolated incident, and he would be gone for good.

Her phone rang, and when she saw Brock was calling, she smiled. His cheerful voice greeted her, and she opened her mouth to tell him about Riggs, but then clamped her lips shut. No. She couldn't. "Glad you called. Things are a little slow. Van and I are splitting today. She's coming in late and I'm leaving early."

"OK if I come by? I need to show you something."

"Sure."

"What are you doing for lunch?"

"I brought leftovers from home. Do you have a better offer?"

"I'll bring Mountain Mist." His voice carried a lilt.

She laughed. "That's a *much* better offer."

He chuckled. "See you in a few."

Gianna disconnected. They had fallen into a too-comfortable pattern, but she couldn't tear herself away from their comraderie. They continued with their morning meetings, and Brock brought her coffee every day, sometimes surprising her with something different. About once a week, he brought along a couple of Barb's delectable pastries to share.

Piper came to the shop with Paisley almost every day after school. On the other days, Brock took both girls with him. Gianna was more and more assured of what a terrific dad he was, and she entrusted him with Paisley's safety. They all had dinner at least once a week and went hiking or did some other outdoor activity together on the weekends. Greg had never loved the outdoors like Gianna did and worked most weekends, although his concession was to work from home.

Gianna was sitting in the back thumbing through a new hairstyle magazine when she heard the bells on the front door. "Hey," Brock called.

"Hey," she responded.

He came into the room and hefted a sack. "Trying the roast beef today."

"I hope there's horseradish," she said. "Otherwise, your experience will be incomplete."

"Tack made sure." He took things out, and Gianna unwrapped her chicken salad.

Brock swallowed the first bite of his sandwich and groaned. "Yum. What's in the horseradish?"

"Trade secret, Tack's recipe." The familiar tastes and textures of Gianna's sandwich soothed her. "I'm such a creature of habit."

"You don't like to try new things?"

She lifted a shoulder. "Sometimes, but if my expectations aren't met, I feel cheated because I missed out on whatever my favorite thing was." She studied him. "I think you like taking chances and trying new things whenever you can."

Brock grinned broadly, and Gianna couldn't keep her gaze off the deep smile lines around his mouth. "Yeah ... I guess. Picking up and moving fifteen hundred miles away was pretty bold, even for me."

Gianna washed down her next bite with a drink of water. "I think both you and Piper have a spirit of adventure."

Brock shuddered. "I'm not ready to think about some of the adventures my daughter might seek." He tackled the second half of his sandwich.

"What did you and Piper think about the church service last week?" When Brock had asked her for a local recommendation, she invited them to attend the community church with her and Paisley.

Brock patted his mouth with his napkin and nodded. "I liked it a lot. The music was a good mix of hymns and praise songs, same as our church in San Diego. And Piper is fine with anything if it involves Paisley."

"I really like our pastor. He's only been here about a year."

Brock nodded. "He spoke right out of the Bible."

"His sermons are always doctrinally sound," Gianna said.

"We'll be back. I'm glad to be attending again."

Gianna tamped down a flush of pleasure. When the four of them sat together, she imagined tongues were wagging, but they'd done nothing wrong, and she held her head high and concentrated on the service.

"What are the two of you are doing for Thanksgiving?" she asked.

He gulped his iced tea. "We'll stay home. I'll cook a little turkey breast or something. What about you?"

She had overheard the girls talking about Thanksgiving the other day, and Piper seemed a little down. She talked about someone called Miss Carmen, who didn't sound as if she was a girlfriend of Brock's. Was she a neighbor? Apparently, she cooked for them a lot, and Piper would miss her Thanksgiving dinner. Anyway, Gianna was sad at the thought of Brock and Piper spending the holiday alone in the little A-frame. Piper said Brock loved to watch football, but the house didn't have a TV.

"We're heading out to Barb and Tack's farm. It's beautiful. Will you join us? Piper would love coming. They'll do all the cooking. You won't find a better meal in all of Montana."

"You're sure they won't mind a couple of extras?"

Gianna shook her head. "The more, the merrier. There will be some other random people there. They're always on the lookout for strays who don't have anywhere else to go." She sucked in a breath. "Brock, I'm so sorry. I didn't mean to imply you and Piper—"

He gave her a sincere smile. "No offense taken. Do you always spend Thanksgiving with them?"

Gianna's heart squeezed painfully. "Once, two years ago, when Greg was stranded somewhere on business and couldn't make a connection home. Barb heard we were alone and insisted we come." She dipped a pita chip in the hummus. "We had a great time. When he was here, our tradition was to eat out." She took another bite of her sandwich and swallowed. "Barb invited us back last year, but Greg didn't want to go."

Brock shook his head. "I know a lot of people eat out on the holiday, so they don't have to deal with the mess, but cleaning up is half the fun." He took another bite of his sandwich.

"I agree."

They finished their lunch and cleaned up. Then Brock took out the folder Gianna recognized from the other day. "I think I'm starting to untangle some things. But you can't ask how I found any of this out."

She stared at him. "Is it—did you obtain information illegally?"

"No. Do you trust me?"

"Yes." Even a week ago, she would have hesitated, but not now.

He opened the folder. "I think Carson Bellmont is the key to all this. I may have uncovered a pattern. He's built several big resorts in beautiful but accessible spots around the Pacific Northwest. There's always a lake involved, because water is such a big draw. He doesn't go for the big lakes, though. I think he takes aim at the smaller ones and builds resorts similar to planned communities, but without schools and houses and things you'd expect. They're not meant for people to live in. He puts up a big hotel, rental condos and cottages, restaurants, high-end shopping, a water park, mini golf, and so forth."

Brock slid some papers out, and Gianna looked through them. Cascade Falls in Idaho. Pacific Pines and Brookstone Hills in Oregon. Two more in Washington state. "Nothing in Montana," she murmured.

"Right. What if Bellmont was scouting out locations in Montana to build a resort? He'd most likely hire someone local to do the legwork for him."

"But there's nothing illegal or wrong about scouting locations, is there?"

Brock drew out another set of papers and set them in front of Gianna. They looked like court documents. The copy wasn't the best quality, and all the identifying information was blacked out. She flipped through the pages. "Where—" She clamped her lips closed, remembering her promise not to question him.

Brock flipped back to the second page and pointed. "Read the first paragraph."

Gianna skimmed the page, and her eyebrows lifted. "Someone's home was vandalized, pretty much destroyed."

Brock spun his finger. "Go to page four."

Gianna kept reading. "They arrested a guy named Dan Smith."

Brock nodded.

"Is he connected to Carson Bellmont?" Gianna scanned the page.

Brock tilted his head. "Not according to these documents. But about a month after this happened, the owners sold to a property management company, and Bellmont began construction on a mega-resort. The rest of the land already belonged to him, purchased piece by piece over the last six years. Everything was in place waiting for this one property to become free and clear."

"I think I understand," Gianna said. "What happened to Dan Smith?"

"Doesn't matter. He probably spent a little time in jail. I'm guessing Bellmont never met him—used a middleman to pay him in cash. There would have been no paper trail, nothing to link him to Bellmont. Guys like Smith—probably not his real name—are a dime a dozen. They take their chances and know they're on their own if they're caught."

Gianna mulled everything over.

Brock returned the papers to the folder. "There's more. I went back and looked at all the other properties around this lake. A couple of years prior, a house on one of them burned to the ground. Fortunately, no one was there at the time. The cause was ruled as accidental, an electrical issue. The owners settled, and the title transferred to—guess who?"

"The same property management company," Gianna said.

Brock nodded. "Bingo. It's the usual shell game, and I'm pretty sure all these properties eventually ended up with Bellmont."

"Do you think Bellmont may have been using Greg's property management business to buy up lakeside land somewhere in Montana?" she asked.

"I think it's a possibility."

"What's next?"

He tilted his head. "I want to think and do a little more research." Brock gathered the papers into the folder. "I have to do everything from a public computer, which means the library, so my time and access are limited."

She walked him to the front door, and out of habit, her gaze went across the street.

"Everything OK?"

"Um, yes. I have a client coming at one, and then I'm closing early. Paisley has a dentist's appointment."

He snapped his fingers. "That reminds me, can you tell me who your dentist is? Piper's overdue for a check-up."

"Sure. I'll write down his name. Can you pick up the girls after their art class tomorrow? I have a couple of late perms to do."

Brock nodded. "Sure. I'm glad they can walk to the community center after school. Hey, we can grab supper after. What about the Tex-Mex place over on 5th Street? I've had a hankering for some Mexican food."

Gianna grimaced. "Not for you and Piper."

"Why not?"

"Commercial Mexican food here isn't what you're used to. I don't think you'd survive the first couple of bites." She smiled. "I have a plan for you to sample some good, authentic Mexican food, but you'll have to be patient for a few weeks."

Brock grinned back at her, and her heart skipped a beat. She was struck again by his attractiveness, and felt sixteen again. "I can be patient," he said softly. The air around them shimmered, and Gianna wondered if the words held another, deeper meaning.

She tucked a piece of hair behind her ears. "There's something else I wanted to ask you. Paisley is dying to have Piper for a sleepover. She and I and Vanessa and some of her nieces get together every other month or so for a girls' night. We do their hair and nails and a little makeup, and watch chick flicks. G or PG rated," she assured him. "They don't stay over, but Piper could. I told Paisley I needed to talk with you first." She hesitated. "I know you're very protective of her, as I am with Paisley. But I promise, she'll be safe."

Brock looked out the front windows, his thumbs hooked into his belt loops. He exhaled and looked at Gianna. "Of course, I know she'll be safe with you. She's growing up so fast, and I need to start giving her some rope." He lifted a shoulder. "It's hard."

"Believe me, I understand. We're planning the sleepover for this Saturday night, kind of a party for Paisley. Her birthday is next week. We could pick Piper up in the afternoon and then bring her to church the next morning." Gianna was willing to have Piper come to the house, but for some reason, she didn't want Brock there, even to drop off or pick up. To her, the house was still hers and Greg's.

"Sounds good." He hesitated at the door. "Oh—I need to—there can't be any pictures of Piper on social media or any tagging. Nothing." His expression was solemn. "Will you promise me?"

Gianna nodded. "Absolutely."

One of her favorite clients, a cheery woman in her mid-fifties, approached. "Come on in, Carolyn." Brock held the door, and Gianna greeted Carolyn and made the introductions.

"Are you new to Canadian Meadows?" Carolyn asked Brock.

"Yes, my daughter and I moved here a couple of months ago."

"From where?" Carolyn asked. Gianna hid a smile. Carolyn loved everyone and always wanted to know everything about them.

"San Diego," Brock replied.

"Such a beautiful place. We vacationed there years ago." Her gaze bounced back and forth between Gianna and Brock, and Gianna could see the wheels turning in the lady's head.

Gianna hastened to explain. "Paisley and Brock's daughter, Piper, have become best friends." She looked at Brock. "Thanks for stopping by."

"Ah—yeah," he said, his lips twitching. "We'll see you and Paisley tomorrow." He bestowed a sincere smile on Carolyn. "Nice to meet you, Carolyn."

"Pleased to meet you, Brock." She beamed.

Once he was out the door and out of sight, Carolyn fanned her face. "Goodness, he's totally hot."

Gianna laughed, and her face heated up. Carolyn had been happily married to her high school sweetheart for almost forty years. Gianna strolled toward her station.

"Is he married? I didn't see a ring." Carolyn asked hopefully, following behind.

Gianna shook her head and tried to sound casual. "Ah, no."

The older lady lifted an eyebrow and smiled. "Interesting."

CHAPTER 13

Since the sleepover two weeks ago, Piper hadn't stopped talking about Paisley's house and Paisley's room and Paisley's dolls and toys and clubhouse in the backyard. She made Paisley's house sound like a palace. She'd had such a great time with Gianna, Paisley, and Vanessa and her nieces. Brock was thankful God had put women in their lives who would give Piper experiences a mother would, like sleepovers, doing hair and nails, and watching movies made for girls to enjoy.

He was preparing dinner for the two of them plus Gianna and Paisley, when Piper came into the kitchen, waving her fingers. "My nail polish is wearing off." Brock had let her keep the sensible, pale pink glittery coating on.

"I'll buy you some, and maybe Paisley or her mom will paint your nails."

She grabbed him around the waist. "You're the best." She skipped back up the stairs.

Brock busied himself for the next few moments pouring the ganache over the cake. Suddenly, he sniffed a burning odor. He grabbed the pot of spaghetti sauce off the burner and tipped the pan to look at the bottom. Definitely scorched. Maybe he could salvage the top part. He bent close and sniffed, then swiped his finger along the top and took a taste. *Blech.* He dumped the pan into the sink and ran a hand through his hair, then looked at the clock. By the time he drove to the store for more ingredients and back home, there wouldn't be enough time to finish the dish. This was more than dumping a jar of sauce in a pan. Brock created the recipe. At least he hadn't added the meatballs and noodles yet.

He grabbed a menu for Tony's Little Italy out of the drawer and made a call. "Piper," he called. "Come on, we need to make a quick run into town."

She peered at him from the loft. "Can't I stay here while you go? I'm old enough."

His heart quickened at the thought. "Absolutely not." He beckoned to her. "Come on."

By the time Gianna and Paisley arrived, Brock had the main dish assembled and the take-out container stashed in the trash. At least the salad, bread, and dessert were his.

The girls ran upstairs, and Gianna joined him in the kitchen. Tonight, she was dressed in skinny jeans, boots, and a long teal sweater with a patterned scarf. Her hair was loose, floating past her shoulders.

Brock wondered if the shimmering ebony waves would feel as silky as they looked, then caught himself.

Gianna drew in a breath. "Smells wonderful." She held an oversized shopping bag. "Here's everything. Coat, hat, scarf, gloves, snow pants, and boots."

"I appreciate this," he replied. "I would have paid you."

She waved a hand at him. "This is stuff Paisley outgrew last year. I would have donated everything to the church. I'm happy for Piper to have new outerwear." She tilted her head at him. "And you didn't have to make us dinner in exchange."

Brock would take any excuse to spend time with her. With them. "Girls, come on," he called. They ran into the bathroom to wash their hands and then returned.

"Wait till you taste my dad's spaghetti and meatballs, Paisley. They're sooooo good. He made everything from scratch except he burned the sauce. We went to Little Italy for more."

Brock placed his hands on Piper's shoulders and pulled her back. He tried to ignore his flaming face. Would his girl ever develop a filter? His gaze traveled to Gianna's, and one hand was clapped over her mouth. Her eyes were wide with hilarity as she tried to hold in her laughter.

Her reaction made him feel better, and they shared a smile. Brock shook his head. They prayed, dished up the food, and the girls climbed onto the stools at the counter. He had brought the little table and chairs in from the deck and arranged them near the fireplace. A plain, round tablecloth from a discount bin at the store covered all the scuffs. He set his and Gianna's plates there and she joined him.

After she'd taken a couple of bites, Gianna smiled at him. "Everything is delicious, Brock. Is this bread homemade?"

"Yeah," he said, willing his face not to heat up at her praise.

"I've never tried to make bread. My skills in the kitchen are almost nonexistent."

"There's no mystery, really. I'll show you sometime."

"I'd like to learn." Her smile made his heart trip. "What's your favorite thing to make?"

He took a sip of water. "Anything Italian. I love the spices and flavors. You can do about anything with them."

"Tony's sauce is good," she said.

"Mine's better." Brock nodded with confidence. "Someday, I'll give you the chance to compare."

Her eyes sparkled, and she lifted her glass in a toast.

Later, after they'd cleaned everything up, Paisley opened the bag and showed Piper all her new winter things. Of course, Piper was excited and had to try the clothes on and model everything for them.

Most of the clothes were somewhat big, which meant she could wear them for another winter, for which Brock was grateful.

"I can't wait for snow. I've never seen snow," Piper said.

Paisley's brown eyes went wide. "Never?"

"No, never. What do you do in the snow?"

"We go sledding and ice skating, and ride on snowmobiles, and build snowmen and snow forts. And some people go skiing."

"The church sponsors a lot of social activities in winter," Gianna said. "And Tack and Barb have people out to their farm almost every weekend. They have so much to do out there."

Paisley clapped her hands together. "Sleigh rides are the best."

"Sounds fun," Brock said. Having been raised in southern California, his only experience with winter was an occasional weekend trip to the mountains, which in the old days was more about sitting around a fire drinking beer than participating in any winter sports.

Brock brought out the cake and sliced it. The girls took theirs to the loft, and he and Gianna went back and sat at the table. Brock put some more wood on the fire.

Gianna took her first bite, closed her eyes, and moaned. "Oh, my goodness. This is delicious. I love chocolate mint."

Brock smiled. He recalled her making a comment last week. "Thanks."

"You could give Barb a run for her money with this."

He laughed. "Not likely. I've never seen cakes like the ones she makes." He rose. "I think the coffee's done." He returned with two mugs.

Gianna accepted her mug and took a drink. "I can't believe you've persuaded me to like plain, dark roast. At least sometimes."

Brock grinned. "One more thing I'm right about. Hang with me, and you'll discover many more. A dozen a day, at least."

"You wish, Hennessey," Gianna teased. "I still like my flavored coffee but not with cake like this." She took another bite. "The flavors wouldn't pop as much if they had to compete with the coffee."

He took another sip. "Did the accountant have anything about Greg's business credit card?"

"I almost forgot." Gianna handed him a folder from her purse. "Statements for a year prior to his death. But there's no travel charges here. No flights, no hotels, no rental cars. Nothing. To me, every charge seems legitimately connected to his property management business."

Brock thumbed through the pages. "He must have had another card he kept from the accountant." He measured his next words carefully. "Or somebody else was paying for it."

Gianna laid her fork on the table. "I'm having a bad feeling about all of this."

"Yeah, I know." He set the pages on the table and took a breath. Brock wasn't looking forward to sharing this next part with her.

"I've been doing some research, and started thinking about where Bellmont might have been targeting a land grab to build a resort. I found two possibilities within a couple of hours of here, Aspen Lake and Diamond Valley

Lake. I think I ruled out Aspen Lake because there's no easy access from the interstate—Gianna, what's wrong?"

Her face went white, and her hands flew up to cover her mouth. "No," she ground out. Wild-eyed, she shot out of her chair and made a beeline for the sliding-glass door. She threw it open and ran out onto the deck.

Brock stood and glanced toward the loft, where the girls were watching a movie. He looked out to the deck, where Gianna leaned against the railing, shaking.

Maybe Diamond Valley Lake had a special meaning for her and Greg. Brock needed to give her some space. The air was chilly, though. He grabbed a blanket from the closet, went outside and settled it around her shoulders.

"Come on back in whenever you want," he whispered.

To his surprise, she grabbed his hand. "No," she rasped. "I need to tell you."

"OK," he said.

She didn't speak for a long time, and he reveled in the feel of holding her hand. "Do you know anything about Greg's accident?"

Brock shook his head. He had discovered the crash involved a single-vehicle. He hadn't wanted to press Gianna about the accident, and the newspaper articles he'd found at the library gave no real details.

She released his hand and drew in a deep breath. "The last morning I saw him, he told me he would be in Kalispell for the day, which wasn't unusual. He called me around six-thirty in the evening and said he had something else to do and would be late, not to wait up."

"Did he stay out late sometimes?"

Gianna nodded, but didn't speak.

Brock squeezed her shoulder. "It's OK, take your time."

She cleared her throat. "From there, it's pretty much like an episode of any police show. He didn't come home. I called the sheriff first thing the next morning. He said they couldn't file a missing person report for twenty-four hours, but they would keep an eye out." She was silent for several more seconds and stepped away from Brock. "They found his car the next day at the bottom of a canyon on the east side of—" Gianna clamped her lips together.

Brock held his breath. She still didn't say anything. "Diamond Valley Lake," he finished for her.

She stared out into the inky darkness. "Kalispell is northwest from here," she said. "Diamond Valley Lake is in the other direction, due south. I couldn't think of any reason he would be there. We don't have any properties out there."

She hugged the blanket around her and looked so lost, so forlorn, Brock wanted to reach out but instead, crossed his arms.

"I haven't told anybody this," she whispered. Her glistening eyes blinked at him.

"You can trust me."

"I know." She swallowed. "There were no skid marks, and nothing was wrong with the vehicle." Her voice hardened. "They found a bottle in the car and said they could smell whiskey on him." Her eyes flashed. "Greg had an occasional glass of something at home or at a restaurant, but never— and I mean *never*—did he drink and drive. In the entire time I was with him, he never had more than one drink. I don't drink alcohol at all, and if we were out, I always drove."

She looked as if she couldn't go on. Brock reached out and rubbed her arm.

"They found a note at his office and ruled the accident a suicide, which means the insurance won't pay out." Her voice broke, and she bit out the next words with a breathtaking intensity. "I know my husband did not take his own life. He did not."

Brock's mind reeled from the news. He rammed a hand through his hair. "But—how do you explain the suicide note? Was it handwritten, or typed?"

"Typed. Unsigned. For one thing, the word "guilt" was spelled wrong—g-i-u-l-t."

Brock winced. "Anyone could—you know—mistype something or mix letters up. Especially if they were upset."

Her eyes blazed. "Greg wouldn't have. He was educated and a good writer. And he wasn't upset. He was meticulous. Spell check would have caught the error, and he would have fixed it."

Brock still wasn't convinced.

"He did not write a suicide note, because he did not take his life," Gianna insisted. "Greg didn't always go to church with us. He worked a lot of weekends. But—" she swallowed. "He had a religious upbringing, and he believed in God. We talked about suicide. He thought the choice was morally wrong. He *never* would have taken his life," she stated emphatically. "There's something else I haven't told anyone. All the money in mine and Greg's joint personal account has disappeared. The accountant has no answers. That's why— why I'm so—"

Brock couldn't resist. He drew her into his arms and held her. "I'm sorry," he whispered, stroking her hair. *So soft.*

She drew back and wiped a hand across her cheeks. "Now, you know everything."

They stared at one another, and she pulled the blanket tighter. "I think he was mixed up in whatever was happening at Diamond Valley Lake. And I think he was murdered."

Brock gently grasped her arms. "So do I."

CHAPTER 14

Paisley skipped into Gianna's bedroom. "I'm so excited for the Harvest Festival," She frowned. "Why aren't you ready?"

Gianna let out a frustrated breath. Everything in her closet went well with boots and jeans, but looked too festive. Greg had been gone for six weeks. Widows should wear black, shouldn't they? "Widows weeds" wasn't a thing anymore, hadn't been for, what? A hundred years? She supposed she read too much historical fiction, where the term was common for those time periods.

Gianna would rather stay home, but her daughter looked forward to the festival each year, and Gianna couldn't bring herself to say no.

She smiled and gestured toward her closet. "Help me choose."

"I like this one," Paisley said, pulling out a black eyelet, off-the-shoulder blouse with three-quarter length sleeves. "With this scarf. I love the bright colors."

"You made the perfect choice. Maybe you'll be a fashion designer someday."

Paisley's eyes brightened. "Like Vanessa."

"Go wait downstairs, and I'll be there in a flash."

Paisley skipped away.

Gianna checked her hair, freshened her mascara, and marched downstairs before she lost her nerve.

Against her better judgment, she had agreed to meet Brock and Piper at the A-frame and drive over to the festival together. It was innocent, but Gianna was worried everyone in town would think they were on a date. And her, a brand new widow. What would they think?

When the four of them entered the community center, conversations seemed to stop and every eye in the room rested on them. This had been a terrible idea. Gianna's heart thumped.

"Here, let me have your coats." Brock helped the girls out of theirs and then reached for Gianna's.

More people crowded through the door, and Gianna guided the girls out of the way. Brock made his way back to them. "Let's go find some tickets," he said.

"I'll buy Paisley's," Gianna said. They joined the line, made their purchases, and gave the girls their tickets.

"Can we go now?" Paisley asked. "I know where all the best things are. I can show Piper."

Brock frowned. "I'm not sure—"

Piper crossed her arms. "I'm not a baby, and neither is Paisley, Daddy."

"Please, let us go on our own?" Paisley begged, fluttering her lashes. When her daughter did her cow-eye routine, she was hard to resist.

Gianna looked at Brock. "They'll be fine. There're only two ways in and out, and they have good security here."

"And we can protect ourselves if we need to." Piper struck a pose and gave the traditional yell.

Brock laughed. Where had she learned karate? "Go on, then."

The girls raced off.

He slipped his hands into his back pockets and rocked on his heels. "Now what?"

Gianna looked around. "Oh ... um, there's all kinds of things to look at, the booths and games, face painting for the kids. And there's a whole area selling crafts, and food and drinks, and a pumpkin patch outside, and um, a dance floor." She looked at her boots and then back to him. "If you wanted to look around or whatever, you don't—I mean, you don't need to stay with me."

Brock looked a little bewildered. "Why wouldn't I want to stay with you?" He gave her a crooked smile. "It's not as if I know a whole lot of people here." Then his gaze registered understanding. He leaned in and lowered his voice. "You're afraid people will think we're here on a date."

Gianna exhaled. "Part of the problem with small towns."

"I don't have a lot of experience with small towns. Seems to me people should mind their own business. But I see Tack and Barb over there, so I'll go talk with them. I haven't had a chance to meet Tack yet." He gave her shoulder a quick squeeze and strode away.

Gianna watched him and then realized she was staring. She shook herself and took off for the refreshment area.

She wished Van were here, but she and Reid had gone to Helena for a concert. Come to think of it, Van always seemed to have out-of-town plans for any of the community events, which didn't make sense for someone raised in Canadian Meadows who claimed to love the town.

Gianna bought some lemonade and trail mix and looked for a place to sit. The main room was crowded, and she was never comfortable in social settings, anyway.

"Gianna." Lark called to her from a big round table. "Come sit with us." Lark pulled up a chair for her. "This is my best friend, Molly," she said, indicating a young woman with dark auburn hair and a ready smile.

Gianna shook Molly's hand. "Nice to meet you." Gianna glanced across the table. Three women, older than Lark and Molly, were engrossed in their own conversation. Gianna knew one of them, Bethany Knowles, but not the others. Their attention was riveted on something to their left, and Bethany didn't acknowledge Gianna's presence.

"I heard he's from California," one of the women said. Of course. They were checking Brock out where he was standing with Tack and Barb, looking tall and masculine.

"Hmm, nice," the other woman said, appreciation coating her words. "Wonder what brought him here?"

Nipped-and-tucked, Bethany straightened and tugged on her form-fitting, hot pink top. "It's nice to have a fresh face in this town." Gianna resisted rolling her eyes. More like fresh meat. Bethany was newly divorced—again, and probably looking for her next conquest.

While Gianna gazed at Brock, Tack and Barb's son, Ben, joined them, accompanied by a young, red-headed woman. Brock and the woman were certainly friendly. How would he know her? Annoyance flashed through Gianna.

Gianna and Ben's paths rarely crossed except for a quick nod and wave, usually at the school. He was a much loved and respected principal, a very nice man, but he seemed to have a deep aura of sadness surrounding him. He and his wife had divorced a few years ago. No one seemed to know why, and the word was she'd moved back to the West Coast where she was from. The breakup of his marriage must have shattered him.

Lark's voice brought her back to the present. "His name is Brock Hennessey," she said to the women. "He works for Gianna."

"Gianna?" Bethany gave a brittle smile. Her smooth, Botox-infused forehead refused to cave to the frown reflected in her eyes. "He works for you? At the salon? Whatever does he do?"

Gianna swallowed her lemonade. "No, he's doing the maintenance work on our—my properties," she said quietly.

"Is he married?" Bethany asked.

"I don't know. We've never talked about it." Truth. Brock had only admitted his marriage wasn't happy.

"He's a regular at Mountain Mist," Lark said. "And he's so sweet. Every morning he stops in—"

No. Gianna didn't want these women learning about how Brock brought her coffee every morning. She stood and gathered her things. "I need to go check on Paisley. Nice seeing you." She fled without a backward glance.

Gianna kept walking until she was around the corner and out of their sight. Then she sagged against a wall and rubbed a hand across her forehead. Why had she come?

She stood there alone until a couple of her regular clients walked by and greeted her, then she decided to go to the crafts area. She splurged and bought a couple of beautiful handmade things—one a perfect Christmas gift for Van—and strolled leisurely. The music drew her in and soon, she found herself on the outer fringe of the dance area. Sweet memories of last year's festival assaulted her. When she and Greg came to community events such as this, Gianna spent most of the time on her own since he insisted he needed to circulate and "work the room." But he always agreed to dance with her, and they were good together. Gianna closed her eyes and could almost feel his arms around her.

Gianna stood awkwardly until she spied a chair at a table in the corner. She slid her way between people and deposited herself there. She sat for a while, lost in her thoughts, hoping they could leave soon to go home.

"Hey, Momma." Paisley came running up, Piper trailing behind her. "Look at our faces. They painted our initials, P.L., with some flowers."

Gianna blinked. "Those are cute. Are you having a good time, Piper?'

"Yes. I've never been to anything like this. It's so fun." Piper's eyes were bright and her cheeks flushed. "My teacher is here—on a date with Principal Ben."

The redhead must be Piper's teacher. Gianna was relieved the woman who had seemed so familiar with Brock appeared to be taken, then shook the thought off. Then she wondered if a principal was allowed to date one of his teachers. *Stop. Ben Garritsen's dating life is none of your business.*

The voice over the PA system boomed through the room. "All right, here's the one you've all been waiting for, Ladies' Choice. This is your chance. Grab your man, gals."

A chorus of female shouts filled the air, and Gianna watched as they all landed their catch. Barb grabbed Tack's hand. He made like he didn't want to go, but his grin said otherwise. Ben Garritsen followed Piper's teacher to the dance floor but didn't look too excited about it.

Brock stood alone, and Gianna was a little sorry for him. Piper should ask him to dance. "Say, Piper—"

Piper jabbed Paisley's side with her elbow. "Momma," Paisley interrupted. "Go ask Mr. Hennessey to dance."

"Oh, no," Gianna said firmly. "Piper, your dad would love to dance with you."

Piper looked at Paisley and blinked. "No, I can't."

"No, she can't," Paisley echoed. She paused. "She hurt her, um, her foot."

Piper winced and grabbed her foot. "Yes, I hurt it bad."

Gianna wanted to laugh. Their tactic was about as subtle as an eighteen-wheeler blowing its air horn. Suddenly, she saw a flash of hot pink, and her stomach sank. Bethany Knowles was headed for Brock. Before her brain registered what she was doing, Gianna took off and approached him from the other side. She landed there two seconds before Bethany and grabbed Brock's hand.

"Come on," she said, pulling him into the dance area. She ignored Bethany's indignant look.

"Why, Miz Harper, are you asking me to dance?" he drawled. He gave her a crooked smile.

What was she doing? Gianna nearly turned and ran, but they had already attracted a bit of attention. She swallowed. "Yes, I suppose I am."

"I'm flattered," he murmured.

Gianna's heart skipped a beat as his hand slid around her waist. *Don't be. I'm saving you from the town piranha,* Gianna wanted to retort. Instead, she murmured back, "I felt sorry for you standing there by yourself."

He shrugged. "I'm used to being alone. I don't mind so much."

"Me too."

"Then we can be alone together," he replied.

His breath fanned her cheek and Gianna braced herself against the shiver threatening to overtake her.

He patted her back. "Hey, relax. I didn't mean *alone together,* I meant you're alone, and I'm alone—"

Gianna sighed. "It's OK. Never mind. Can we just dance?" Her face was warm, and she was having trouble meeting his gaze but finally made contact.

"Yes, we can just dance. I need to concentrate on not stepping on your toes, because I haven't done this in like seventy years, and I was never any good anyway." His smile was self-deprecating, and very attractive.

"You're doing fine," she assured him.

He pulled her a little closer, and she breathed in his woodsy aftershave, causing her heart to trip. "Bet your husband was a good dancer," he murmured.

She nodded. "Yes, he was." Being held by Brock was a different experience, but Gianna wasn't prepared to analyze her feelings now.

When the dance ended, they left the floor, and the girls came running over to them. "Daddy, Mrs. Harper, look at me and Paisley's new dance," Piper exclaimed.

They twirled around in a square dance do-si-do, then sashayed back and forth with their arms out hula-style, ending with a bunch of claps and high fives. "It's our sister dance." Paisley said. Her eyes sparkled and her cheeks were pink. Gianna loved seeing her daughter so happy. She bit back a laugh. She was tempted to ask if a faith healer had come by and prayed over Piper's foot.

"Great job, girls," Brock said. He put his arm around Piper and kissed the top of her head. "You're a better dancer than I am." He looked at Gianna and winked, then looked as if something else occurred to him. "Have you seen enough, girls? Why don't we go?"

"I wanted a pumpkin," Piper said.

"I always take home a pumpkin," Paisley said. "We could take them to art class and paint them."

Piper clapped her hands. "Awesome."

Brock handed them a wad of tickets. "Go buy your pumpkins and meet us at the front entrance." The girls nodded and ran off.

Gianna looked at him. "How did you—how did you know I wanted to leave?"

He took her elbow and guided her toward the lobby area. "I had a hunch."

Gianna recalled the dozens of times during her marriage when Greg ignored her wishes to leave an event or party after they'd been there for hours, claiming he needed to talk with one more person. One always turned into two, three, or more.

They drove to the A-frame. When they exited the truck, Brock drew Gianna away from the girls. "Do you and Paisley want to come in for a while?"

Gianna wasn't ready for the night to end. "Sure."

The girls disappeared into the loft once they were inside. Brock made a fire and offered Gianna the upholstered chair. "I'll brew the coffee."

She stared into the flames, and the tension of the night dissolved. Soon, Brock appeared at her elbow with a mug and a plate with a half dozen of Barb's cookies.

"You do know how to spoil a gal," Gianna smiled.

He lowered himself into the Adirondack chair. "Piper and I are hooked on Barb's cookies," he said, popping a whole peanut butter dream into his mouth.

Gianna took a delicate bite of a chocolate chip cookie. "Oh, these are dark chocolate mint. They're fantastic." She broke the treat in two and handed him the uneaten half. "Here, you have to try."

Brock washed the cookie down with some coffee. "I like the PB ones better."

Gianna reached for another chocolate chip one. "Good, more for me."

Brock laughed. "You know something? You're adorable."

A bubble of joy rose in her chest, and she tamped down the urge to giggle. "You realize this means more Peanut Butter Dreams for you."

His gorgeous eyes sparkled as he grabbed another cookie and raised his mug in a toast. "Works for me." They spent the next few moments polishing off the cookies.

Brock pointed to her mug. "Want a refill?"

"Sure, thanks."

He returned and handed her the fresh mug. "I need to ask you something."

"OK."

"I've been looking into all the land around Diamond Valley Lake, and I keep hitting walls. I believe most of the property is owned by the same person or corporation, but I can't find clear titles as I did with some of the other ones in Idaho and Oregon. In my opinion, someone has gone to a lot of trouble to make certain the information stays hidden."

Gianna pondered his line of thinking. "I wonder if Montana's laws are different from the other states."

"You may be right." He took a sip of his coffee. "Have you ever heard of Stanley Dole?"

She frowned. "I don't think so."

"He was eighty-one years old and had a cabin on the southeast side of Diamond Valley Lake. He lived there for forty-five years. His wife died about ten years ago, and they had no children." Brock set his mug down and tented his hands in front of him. "He was a bit of a hermit, and no one missed him. But then the mail piled up, and the mailman ordered a welfare check, and they found him. The house had been ransacked, and Dole was dead. He'd hit his head on the fireplace."

Gianna's heart squeezed at the thought of the elderly man dying alone. "How sad."

Brock nodded. "Very sad. But listen to this. The homicide investigation team found two hundred-dollar bills folded together, tucked inside a tear on the underside of the mattress."

Gianna frowned. "How strange."

Brock nodded. "Dole didn't have any bank accounts and had a history of some anti-government views. A person like him is a pretty good candidate to have stashed a fortune right there in his cabin. The working theory is the old guy might have hidden a lot more money under the mattress, and whoever found the treasure missed the two bills. They burgled the house, roughed Dole up, and he fell. Maybe he tried to fight back. Or maybe something else happened, and then they found the money."

"Did they find any evidence of someone else being in the cabin?"

Brock took another swallow of coffee. "No, which is strange too. They only said whoever cleaned up knew what they were doing."

Gianna shook her head. "How in the world are you finding all this out?"

Brock looked at her intently. "Someone with access." His gaze softened. "Someday, when this is all over, I'll tell you, I promise."

"I understand," she said, and sighed. "Do you think Dole's death had something to do with Bellmont trying to buy up properties around Diamond Valley Lake?"

"I do." Brock looked at her apologetically. "And I really don't want to tell you this next part."

Gianna held her breath.

"Stanley Dole died the same night as Greg."

Gianna clapped a hand over her mouth. Her heart pounded. "Do you think their deaths are related?"

Brock's gaze searched hers. "I hope not. I sincerely hope not."

CHAPTER 15

Brock put a forkful of enchilada into his mouth and was greeted by an explosion of one of the most flavorful combinations he'd ever experienced—a symphony of chili, tomato, and cheese. He chewed, swallowed, and groaned. "Barb, will you marry me?"

Laughter erupted around the table. Traditional Thanksgiving food as well as authentic Mexican food filled every plate. Brock was sure Gianna had asked Barb to fix the Mexican food for him and Piper. Of course, she'd made enough for everyone.

"I think this is better than Miss Carmen's," Piper said.

"No one here knows Miss Carmen," Brock said to her. He looked around the table. "Carmen Gonzalez was our next-door neighbor in San Diego. Such a wonderful lady." He smiled at Gianna. "And yes, a fabulous cook, who spoiled us." He wondered how Gianna knew how much authentic Mexican food meant to them. He'd never mentioned Miss Carmen to her.

Gianna gave him an answering smile. "I overheard Piper talking about her."

Brock was touched by the sweet gesture. He toasted Barb with his water glass. "Barb, thank you from the bottom of our hearts. This is like a taste of home."

"Montana feels like home now." Piper said.

"You're right, Piper," he said, surprised at his sincerity.

When they finished the meal, everyone helped take the dishes and extra food into the kitchen, and Barb shooed them all out. Gianna and the other women protested, but Barb held firm. "Lark and I will finish in half the time. You'd be in the way." Her smile assured everyone she wasn't upset.

Tack rolled his eyes. "Mama's in charge of her kitchen." He looked around the group, which included four other children besides Piper and Paisley. "Who wants to go out to the barn?"

The children erupted in an excited chorus.

Piper looked at Brock. "I can go, can't I, Daddy? Please."

"Sure," he answered.

Gianna pulled her coat on. "I'll go with them." They bustled out the door, taking their noise with them. Most of the other adults followed.

Ben Garritsen had greeted Brock when they first arrived, and Brock looked forward to getting better acquainted. "You a football fan?" Ben asked.

Brock nodded. "Sure am."

Ben walked toward the family room and Brock followed. "Who's your team?"

Brock grinned. "Chargers."

Ben made a face. "You're in Seahawks country now." Both men laughed. They sat, and Ben put the game on. They found a lot to talk about. Brock thoroughly enjoyed their conversation.

Later, the front door opened, and Piper bounced up to him, her eyes bright and her cheeks pink from the cold wind. "You have to come see the horses. Tack said I could have a pony ride if you agree. Hi, Principal Ben."

"Are you having fun, Piper?"

"Yes. I wish I lived on a farm." She tugged on Brock's sleeve. "Can we buy a farm?"

Brock rolled his eyes "Probably not."

Ben laughed. "You can come visit anytime."

"Thank you. Do you live here?" she asked.

Brock stood. Time to go see the horses, before Piper said something embarrassing.

"No, I have my own house in town," Ben said.

"Is Ms. Spencer your girlfriend?"

Brock took Piper by the shoulders and led her away while shooting Ben an apologetic look. "We're going to see the horses."

Ben laughed. "Tell Dad the game's on. He'll be upset if he misses much more of it."

Brock pulled on his coat and walked to the paddock where the pony rides were underway. Tack had the same height and build as his son, with thick blond hair turning to gray. He was patient and gentle with all the kids and looked as if he was having as much fun as they were.

Brock leaned on the fence and chatted with Gianna. Her deep-plum-colored coat brought out the color of her eyes, and the cold wind blew her hair around and put apples in her cheeks. Since the night of the dance, he'd done somemore digging and wanted to update her.

"Walk with me?" She nodded, and they stepped away from the group. "I've been trying to discover who owns the land around Diamond Valley Lake," Brock said. "I'm hitting solid brick walls now." Her beautiful features grew dark, and he regretted adding to her burden. "Maybe it's time to talk with the detective about what we think."

Gianna shook her head forcefully. "No. So long as they think Greg's accident was a suicide attempt, they're not willing to listen to anything I have to say. They give me the runaround when I ask about the toxicology report. Detective Gibson insisted the timeline for those to come back can be months."

"What if I talk with him?"

Gianna grabbed his arm. "No, Brock, please don't. You said you would help me. I want us to solve this together and then give them all the evidence." Her gaze pleaded with him, and she moved her hand to squeeze his. He would have given her anything she asked. "Promise me you won't."

He sighed. "I won't, I promise."

"Look at me, I'm on a pony," Piper shouted.

Brock and Gianna moved back to the paddock and smiled and waved at Piper. "She's having fun," Gianna said.

"As long as she doesn't get any bright ideas about having a pony," Brock muttered.

Paisley was next, sitting tall and composed in the saddle. Brock and Gianna agreed they'd never seen her smile so much.

When both girls were finished, they ran to their parents.

Piper waved her hands around. "We have a plan. You can pool your money and buy us a pony."

Brock looked at Gianna and groaned.

"We'll share her and save you so much money." Paisley said.

"Which will mean only half the work and expense for each of you to take care of Sunshine." Piper insisted.

Gianna stifled a laugh, and a soft snort escaped.

Brock bit the inside of his cheek to maintain control. "Where will Sunshine live?"

The girls looked at one another. "Here, with Tack and Barb," Paisley said.

Brock and Gianna collapsed on one another in a fit of laughter. The sound of a gong split the air, and Lark shouted to everyone to come in for dessert.

"Saved by the bell," Brock whispered, and they both laughed.

Brock couldn't believe the desserts filling the dining room table. Pies, multi-layered cakes, cookies and bars— all Barb's specialties—and homemade ice cream. Brock took his plate and a bowl of ice cream to the family room to watch the game.

Lark came around with a tray of mugs filled with coffee. "Here's your usual, Brock," she said with a smile.

A commercial came on. Tack turned to Brock. "Do you hunt?"

"No, I've never been." Brock didn't want to admit he didn't even know what kind of hunting Tack was referring to. Deer or elk, probably.

"We'll take you out some time," Ben said. "We have a cabin less than an hour from here, close to the border."

"Sounds great," Brock replied.

"What about fishing?" Tack asked.

Brock swallowed a spoonful of ice cream and shook his head. "Uh, I like fish sticks."

Tack looked at Ben. "We have our work cut out for us with this one, don't we, son?"

Ben nodded, and they all laughed.

One by one, all the other guests left. Paisley and Piper helped Lark clean the dessert dishes and went to the dining room table to play a board game.

Gianna sat next to Brock on the couch with her feet tucked under her. She'd tossed her hair into a clip and looked effortlessly chic, and he had a hard time keeping his gaze off her. His growing friendship with her, Tack, Barb,

Lark and now Ben, filled his heart with contentment. He was growing roots in Canadian Meadows. Could this be the answer? Was this the place God meant for him and Piper to make their home?

When the game finished, the four of them bundled into their coats. Gianna and Paisley had driven out here with Brock and Piper from the A-frame. Barb pressed a couple of plastic containers into both his and Gianna's hands. "Everyone needs enough leftover turkey for a sandwich," she insisted. She handed Brock an additional paper bag. "And there's cake in there—peanut butter cup, cherry almond, and lemon chiffon."

Brock groaned. "Is there a gym in Canadian Meadows?"

Everyone laughed.

Barb reached out for a hug, and Brock gladly complied. This sweet lady was beginning to feel like a second mom to him. Brock's mother had been gone for so long, he barely remembered her. "Thanks so much for having us. We had a wonderful time. And the Mexican food was so amazing. You were kind to go to all the extra trouble."

Barb swatted his arm. "Making the food wasn't a speck of trouble, and meant a lot to Gianna." She hugged the younger woman, then Paisley and Piper.

Brock shook the men's hands.

"We'll take you to the cabin sometime after the first of the year," Ben promised.

"I'll look forward to it," Brock said. When they had trailed out the door and were on the porch, he took the opportunity to hang back for a moment with Ben. "I'm sorry about Piper asking if you had a girlfriend."

To his relief, Ben laughed. "Oh, I'm used to it, believe me. Of course, I would never date anyone on my staff. Her teacher and I saw each other at the Harvest Fest, walked around for about five minutes and stood there talking with you and my parents, and everyone heard wedding bells."

Brock shook his head. "I have a lot to learn about small-town life."

"Ah, this is a great place to live," Ben said.

Brock smiled. "I'm starting to believe it. Well, I'd better go."

The Garritsens stood on the porch and waved goodbye as they drove off. Brock and Gianna chatted on the trip back, and by the time they arrived at the A-frame, both girls were asleep.

Brock transferred Paisley from his car to Gianna's, who buckled her daughter in.

Bone-chilling cold assaulted Brock when he exited the vehicle. Brock needed to take Piper in the house and let Gianna start her vehicle and go home. But he had to say something. In a bold move, he took both her gloved hands in his. "Thank you for an incredible Thanksgiving, Gianna. I mean it."

She smiled at him and nearly took his breath away. "I didn't do anything."

"You asked Barb to make the Mexican food, which meant so much to us." Brock squeezed her hands and let go. He took a step back. "Drive safely. See you—when I see you."

She backed up and walked around to her door. "Knowing these two, we'll see you soon." Her smile lit her beautiful face.

Whenever *soon* was wouldn't come soon enough for Brock.

CHAPTER 16

Only four weeks stood between Thanksgiving and Christmas. In addition to all the usual extra appointments to prepare clients for holiday events, Gianna and Van were in charge of hair for two weddings, and those were always stressful. Paisley was spending the day with Brock and Piper.

After the second wedding appointment, she and Van treated themselves to a late lunch at Mountain Mist, even though Gianna had to practically force her friend to go.

When they came through the door, Barb took one look at them and laid down her towel and bottle of cleaning solution. "You gals look all done in."

"We are," Gianna said.

"I can hardly feel my feet," Van added.

"Grab a seat, take a load off." Barb smiled. "Sandwiches and vegetable beef barley soup coming up. And a special dessert."

After they finished the delicious meal, Van bit into a chocolate peppermint brownie and groaned. "I'm gonna have to climb a whole bunch of stairs to make up for this. I have to fit into my dress for New Year's Eve."

"You and Reid are going to Helena?"

Van nodded. "Yes, we're attending some glittery party with his family."

Gianna reached for another brownie. "Glad I don't have to fit into anything," she said with a wink. "Do you think he'll propose?"

Van's beautiful green eyes twinkled. "I have no idea. But I'm pretty sure I'm ready with my answer." Both women clapped their hands and let out little squeals.

"Maybe Brock will invite you somewhere romantic." Van wiggled her eyebrows.

"Ah, no," Gianna said firmly. "I'll be at home. With Paisley."

Van closed her eyes briefly, then nodded. "I'm sorry," she whispered, and reached across to squeeze Gianna's hand.

The door jingled, and Ben Garritsen blew in, closing the door against the cold wind. Gianna faced the door, and his eyes connected with hers. A few snowflakes dusted his hair. "I think we're in for a few more inches tonight," he said with a smile.

"Hi, Ben. Good to see you."

"Good to see you too, Gianna." Van looked at her lap and didn't say anything, and something registered on Ben's face. Not surprise, exactly. Gianna couldn't decipher his expression.

He hustled toward the kitchen. "I need to—ah, find my mom."

Van jumped up and grabbed her coat and scarf as if she were off to a fire. "I need to go before I eat myself right out of my dress. I'll see you Monday."

Gianna found herself alone. *Hmm ... what was that all about?*

Gianna managed to power through the next week and a half and finished her Christmas shopping with four days to spare. Due to her financial constraints, she devised more economical alternatives for most of her gifts and even made some of them herself. The hard work delivered a deep sense of satisfaction.

Paisley and Piper were exchanging gifts, but Gianna couldn't decide whether to give Brock a present. She had something special for him but didn't think she would have the nerve to follow through. Gianna decided on a board game for him and Piper and a framed photo of the two of them she had taken on one of their hikes.

She was trying to survive the holiday and make some new traditions for her and Paisley. She still dealt with unexpected bouts of grief over Greg's death. He had never been into traditional, at-home Christmases. Last year, he'd taken them skiing in Aspen, the previous year, to Hawaii.

Despite his faults, he was generous, especially at the holidays. Every year, he hired a professional to decorate the house inside and out, which was out of the question this year. Their traditional massive, live tree in the great room soared to the top of the cathedral ceiling, dripping with hundreds of tiny white lights and red and silver ornaments. Gianna was afraid the six-foot artificial tree from the big box store would be a sorry substitute, but Paisley loved picking out brightly colored lights and other decorations, and even added some from her creations at the art center. Gianna's heart warmed to see her daughter having so much fun this Christmas.

But Gianna had decided on a very special Christmas present for her daughter, a gift Paisley would love for years to come.

Gianna glanced at the clock on the dash and decided she had time to stop at Mountain Mist. She'd skipped lunch and decided to treat herself to some hot chocolate and a muffin. Paisley would be coming to the shop from school in about twenty minutes, and Gianna had a client coming in.

The town square was all decked out for Christmas, more enchanting than ever. Gianna parked and walked past the windows to the front door of Mountain Mist, then stopped in her tracks. Through the window, she saw Brock standing by the deli counter, holding a cup. And standing next to him was Bethany Knowles. Gianna's insides twisted. Well, the piranha had caught him. The woman's boots cost more than Gianna made in a week. Bethany wore painted-on black jeans and a tight aqua sweater unbuttoned enough to show off her cleavage. Gianna rolled her eyes. Bethany had never met a push-up bra she didn't like.

Her platinum-blonde hair floated in clouds around her shoulders, and Gianna had to admit, looked spectacular. Bethany paid enough for the result, and Gianna endured the woman's simpering and self-indulgence because she was a loyal customer. Gianna needed all of those she could get.

White-hot envy coursed through her as Brock laughed at something Bethany said. Then the woman stepped in, reached out and touched her lacquered fingernails to the back of his hand, trailed up his arm, and squeezed. She fluttered her false eyelashes and flashed a crafted come-hither smile at him.

Gianna wouldn't watch one more second. She whirled and fled to her car, her appetite gone. She slammed the door and sat, willing her racing heart to slow. A maelstrom of thoughts pinged around inside her head like pinballs.

Why did she care? Brock could talk with anyone he wanted, or even date anyone he wanted. He was nothing more than the father of her daughter's best friend. Wasn't he?

To Gianna's horror, she realized she was jealous. She raised a shaky hand to her mouth. This couldn't be happening. Only three months had passed. She was still in love with Greg. Cold seeped in, and she started the vehicle.

She didn't know if she was angrier at Brock for succumbing to Bethany's outrageous flirtations or at herself for what she was feeling. The idea was impossible. Gianna didn't want anything but friendship with Brock. She never wanted to marry again or be involved with a man. She laid her arms on the steering wheel, dropped her head on them, and told herself to take deep, cleansing breaths. *In ... out ... in ... out.*

Gianna had no idea how much time had passed, until a knock came at her window, startling her. *Oh no.*

"Are you OK?" Brock said.

Embarrassment swirled through her middle, and heat infused her cheeks. She nodded.

Brock didn't look convinced. He made a spinning motion with his finger, and she rolled the window down. She wanted to put the car in reverse and leave, but with her luck, she'd run over his foot or something.

Gianna cracked the window. "I'm fine. I need to go."

Brock looked a little bewildered but stepped back. "OK, I guess I'll see you later."

Thankfully, he didn't press for details. Gianna rolled up the window and pulled out of her parking place.

When she arrived back at the salon, Van was finishing with a customer. Gianna's appointment was coming at four.

"Hey, girlfriend," Van called to her. As soon as her customer left, she marched over to Gianna. "What's up, sweets? You OK?"

Sometimes Gianna almost resented Van's keen powers of intuition. "Van, I'm fine. Christmas is hard." Truth.

Van pulled her into a hug. "I know," she murmured. "You and Paisley are still coming for dinner, right?" She pulled back and looked at Gianna, her large green eyes pleading.

"Yes, of course." Gianna said with a nod, and her dear friend let out a relieved breath. Van had grown up on a sprawling ranch about twenty miles from town, and had a wild, crazy family. She had five older brothers and about a gazillion nieces and nephews. Paisley always had a blast when they went out there.

Later, after she'd tucked Paisley into bed, Gianna went into her empty bedroom. She still hadn't worked up the courage to clear out Greg's things. Van had offered several times to help, but Gianna wasn't ready. Would she ever be?

She walked over to the bed and lifted her pillow, drawing out a soft, worn sweatshirt, the one he always wore around the house. She buried her nose in the cloth and took a deep breath, which morphed into a sob. For the first time, she couldn't detect his scent. She sat on the edge of the bed holding the sweatshirt as tears threatened.

Loneliness engulfed her. Would this be her life for the next fifty years? Their wedding anniversary was coming up, her first without him.

I am with you always. I will never leave you nor forsake you. Gianna heard God's voice as if he were right there in the room. The bands around her chest loosened, and she repeated the verse, the beautiful promises soothing her soul.

After tossing and turning most of the night, Gianna overslept and skipped her shower, gathering her hair into a haphazard bun. She pulled on the first set of clothes she found and arrived at the shop almost ten minutes late. Brock and Van sat in the back room chatting.

Gianna's already-bad day turned worse. He was the last person she wanted to see.

Van lifted a foam cup. "Look what I'm drinking this morning." She pointed to a box. "And ... Barb's Sparkleberry Peppermint muffins. To die for." She rolled her eyes dramatically. Gianna almost asked what happened to Van's resolve to fit into her New Year's dress.

Brock laughed. "I took a chance you'd be here, Vanessa. I always feel bad when I show up without anything for you."

Van lifted an eyebrow. "I don't think you're making the kind of money to supply all of us with Mountain Mist every day." She grinned.

"Didn't you hear? My boss added a coffee line item to my wages." Brock winked at Gianna. He pointed to the other cup sitting on the counter. "Yours may need reheating."

The drumbeat of a headache pulsed in Gianna's temple. "Maybe later."

Van and Brock exchanged glances.

Gianna cleared her throat. "Can you give me the daily update? I have a busy day."

Van hopped off her stool and pointed to the curtained-off area off the back room. "I'll inventory all the product back there. Thanks again for the caffeine and sugar, Brock."

"You're welcome." Brock turned back to Gianna and took out his clipboard. "It's a short list today." He ticked off a few items, and she gave him the go-ahead to purchase whatever he needed.

"You're doing great with all this, Brock. We don't need to meet every day. Maybe once a week, on Monday. You can text me if anything comes up." She busied herself tidying their kitchenette so she wouldn't have to meet his eyes.

He didn't say anything for several seconds. When Gianna was brave enough to look at him, her heart dropped at the wounded look in his eyes. "Is everything OK, Gianna?"

"Sure, why wouldn't everything be OK?" She hoped her voice sounded normal.

He looked a little puzzled. "I mean, um, you're sure?"

She pasted on a bright smile. "Yes, of course. Paisley told me she and Piper wanted to meet at the library after school today. Can you collect them at closing time, or shall I?"

"I will. I'll bring Paisley here. Tonight is Kids Eat Free night at Rollicking Ranch Buffet. Should we take the girls?"

"Ah, no. Tonight's not good." An uncomfortable silence wove its way around them. "Was there something else?"

He took a breath. "Well ... Piper wondered, I mean, she and I wanted to know—are you and Paisley busy for Christmas dinner? I thought we might ..."

Gianna's heart sank. She couldn't stand to hear what he had planned. She twisted a towel in her hands. "Oh, sorry, we're busy." Gianna regretted he and Piper would be alone, but the thought of the four of them in the little A-frame on Christmas day was too much.

She laid the towel on the counter and took a couple of side steps toward the front of the shop. "I need to set things up."

Brock hesitated, then stood and reached for his jacket. "Oh, sure. OK. Well, have a good day, and I guess I'll see you later." His shoulders slumped.

Gianna felt worse.

He gave her a weak smile. "Bye, Gianna."

"Bye, Brock."

CHAPTER 17

"Open it, open it, Daddy." Piper bounced up and down.

They'd finished breakfast and read the Christmas story from the second chapter of Luke. Everything about this Christmas was different except the timeless words, which gave Brock a tremendous measure of comfort.

Piper had opened her presents and now was his turn. He hadn't expected anything and was touched.

They sat on their slightly worn, but comfortable, used couch. Brock had found the sofa for sale online when he was at the library and decided this would be his Christmas gift to them. He was moved at the sight of the clumsily wrapped gift he was sure his daughter spent quite a bit of time and love on.

"Paisley and Mrs. Harper helped me."

Brock's heart gave a pop ... but not a happy one. Something was off between him and Gianna, and he couldn't pinpoint what. He had racked his brain trying to remember if he'd said or done something to offend her. She was creating distance between them, and Brock couldn't imagine why.

He pulled the last of the paper away, and his heart filled with love and gratitude. Inside was a beautiful forest-green sweater and a pair of socks. They were black, emblazoned all over with the words "best dad" and hearts in red. "Come here, Pipe." Brock drew her into his arms and planted a kiss on her head. As they lay there, he stared at their little five-foot live tree Piper had chosen. She was so excited she could reach the top if she stretched her hands. They'd put the decorations on together, and Brock thought the little tree was the most beautiful one he'd ever seen. The couple at the tree farm had thrown in several scrap pieces of greenery, which were now laying along the mantel. The holly with the red berries was cheerful.

Contentment washed over him. This might be the best Christmas ever—if he could repair things with Gianna.

Piper was too excited to sit still and jumped up. "I have to dress for Christmas dinner. I can't wait." She skipped upstairs to the loft.

Brock had been surprised at the last-minute invitation from Vanessa, but he was grateful. Piper was such a social butterfly, and she would have a blast. Vanessa said she had nieces and nephews of every age. All Piper would need to do was pick the ones she wanted to hang with.

He'd been tempted to ask if Gianna and Paisley were coming, but in the end decided not to say anything. He hadn't talked with Gianna in several days, since she'd refused his invitation to come over on Christmas Day. Piper hadn't shared anything about Paisley's plans for Christmas, and Brock couldn't think of a way to ask. His precocious daughter would be suspicious if he mentioned it.

Maybe if Brock could summon the courage, he'd call Gianna tonight to wish her a Merry Christmas.

Piper came back a few minutes later wearing her new boots, jeans, and the cowboy hat Brock had given her. She twirled around joyfully. "What do you think?"

Brock laughed. "I think you look like a real Montana girl."

"Did you know Montana girls can shoot guns and protect themselves and everything? Mrs. Harper showed us."

Alarm slammed through Brock. "She shot a gun?"

Piper continued twirling. "No, silly. When I was at Paisley's sleepover, she showed us karate and some other stuff."

Brock's heart went back to beating normally. He was certain whatever Gianna did was innocent.

Piper bounced on her toes. "Why aren't you dressed? Let's go."

He gathered his gifts. "Please clean up the wrapping paper mess." In his room, he donned the new forest-green sweater, pulled on a pair of black jeans, and carried his boots and socks to the living room.

"Do you like your new socks?" Piper asked.

Brock grinned. "I love them."

They put all of Piper's winter gear into the truck, since they'd had a fresh snowfall, and Vanessa had said the kids would spend a lot of time outside. The whole way to the ranch, Piper chattered about how excited she was to play in the snow. The trip went quickly with such beautiful scenery to feast their eyes on.

He followed Vanessa's directions—she had promised they couldn't miss it. Signs on the main road directed them to Kingston Valley Ranch, and when they pulled in, the large number of vehicles surprised Brock, and his pulse tripped when he homed in on Gianna's. Of course, this was where her Christmas dinner plans were as he'd suspected all along. He wondered if she knew Vanessa had invited him and Piper and if she would be upset when she saw him.

Before he could even park, Paisley came running toward them, holding onto a small, black wriggling mass of fur. "Did you know Paisley would be here?" Brock asked his daughter.

"Sure."

As soon as Brock turned off the engine, a swarm of children, ranging in age from about three years to young teens, appeared behind Paisley, all bundled up, dragging sleds and discs behind them.

"Look at my Christmas present," Paisley shouted the minute Piper climbed out of the truck. She set a barking, wriggling mass on the ground. "This is Sammy. Her real name is Samantha, but she looks like a Sammy."

"Oh, you're soooooo cute," Piper crooned as she bent to pet the moving target.

The moppy little dog must have eyes in there somewhere, but Brock couldn't see them.

Piper struck a pose. "Look at my new hat and boots, Paisley. Have you ever seen anything so awesome?"

"Of course I have, silly." Paisley giggled. "Who do you think helped your dad pick them out?"

Piper threw her arms around her friend. "You're the best. I love them."

Brock opened the tailgate and helped Piper up. "Put your snow pants on and switch out those new boots for your snow boots. And leave your hat in the truck." Once Piper jumped to the ground, she, Paisley, and Sammy ran off without a backwards glance.

The children covered the hillside like brightly colored ants. The slope was a perfect spot for sledding. Brock leaned against the truck and breathed in the cold, clear air tinged with pine and wood smoke. Colorful lights sparkled in the trees against the pristine white backdrop.

This was Christmas in Montana, a magical place. One he could see him and Piper settling into for the long haul.

He supposed he should go inside but was a little uneasy about meeting a whole new crowd of people and was on edge about seeing Gianna. He wished he knew what had gone wrong with them.

A few minutes later, a crunch of gravel sounded behind him, then a soft voice. "Hi."

Gianna.

He ignored the trip of his heartbeat and straightened. "Merry Christmas."

"Merry Christmas."

Brock drank her in. She looked tired but was unbelievably beautiful. Her scarlet red coat and matching scarf set off her dark hair and rosy skin. She stood next to him, and for a while, they watched the children.

He crossed his arms and grinned. "Sammy, huh?"

Gianna laughed. "Paisley screamed when she opened the box. I'm surprised you didn't hear the shriek clear in town."

Brock laughed. "What breed of dog?"

"Peekapoo—cross between a Pekinese and Poodle."

"Ah," Brock said. "Does she have eyes?"

He was rewarded with another one of Gianna's sparkling laughs. "Yes, somewhere under all that hair I'm sure she does."

Brock raised an eyebrow at her. "Will you let her have puppies?"

Gianna shuddered. "One is more than enough for now."

Silence settled around them. Then Gianna cleared her throat. "Brock, I owe you an apology. I've shut you out recently."

The tightness in his chest dissipated, and he didn't say anything for a moment. Then he looked down at her. "Do you need a friend?"

She frowned. "What?"

"Do you need a friend?" he repeated.

She blew out a breath. "Yes." She locked gazes with him. "Do you need a friend?"

He nodded. "Yes." They stood there for a moment, and then he lifted his arm. She stepped in, looped her arms around his waist, and he wrapped his arm around her shoulder.

Now, this was the best Christmas ever.

Several of the other parents—four of Vanessa's brothers and their wives and some cousins—came out to join in the fun with the children, and when they heard Brock had never been sledding, they descended on him. Someone shoved a pair of men's snow boots into his hands and wouldn't accept his protests to stay on the sidelines and watch. He was reluctant to try, but after the first time whizzing down the hill, he couldn't wait to go again. He went several times with Piper, on sleds and inner tubes, and the last two runs with Gianna and both girls on a big toboggan. His pants were soaked, but he didn't care.

"I'm so thankful we have the hot tub at the A-frame." He and Gianna climbed the hill one last time behind Piper and Paisley. "If I can even move by tonight to lower myself into it."

Her laughter sounded like wind chimes, and her sparkling eyes and bright red cheeks made her even more beautiful. "I think you must be out of shape, Hennessey," she teased.

"I'm sure I am."

"We'll have to take you out on the ski slopes."

Brock groaned. "Maybe next year."

Gianna's gaze softened. "Yes, next year."

They all trooped into the house and changed out of their gear. Vanessa greeted Brock with a warm hug. "Merry Christmas. I'm so glad you came," she said.

He greeted her back. "I wanted to come meet your parents earlier, but Gianna said I'd just be in the way. I wish you would have let me bring something for the meal."

She rolled her eyes. "Wait until you see the spread. There's enough food here to feed the entire state."

"Is Rand coming?" Gianna asked.

Brock frowned at Vanessa. "I thought your boyfriend's name was Reid."

"Yes, Reid. I was with his family for Thanksgiving, and we're doing New Year's together."

"Who's Rand?" Brock asked.

The women burst out laughing. "He doesn't know?" Vanessa lifted an eyebrow at her best friend.

Gianna giggled. "I guess he hasn't made the connection."

Vanessa looked at Brock, eyebrows raised, but he drew a blank. "Rand Kingston, my brother," she said slowly.

Brock's jaw dropped open in amazement. "Wait—you're telling me—Rand Kingston, the actor, is your *brother*?" Brock was in disbelief. Kingston was a Hollywood A-lister.

Vanessa nodded and took his arm. "Yep, he sure is." She tossed her head and looked at Gianna. "No, he's not coming. He's shooting on location somewhere in Europe." She squeezed Brock's arm and pulled him along. "Come meet our parents.

Vanessa introduced Brock to her parents, Pete and Marcella. A few minutes later, she thrust a pair of worn jeans into his hands. "Go put these on, and I'll throw yours in the dryer. They're Dad's, so they'll be big on you, but they'll do."

Dinner was a loud, noisy affair. One of Vanessa's other brothers rang a big gong, and everyone quieted long enough for Pete to offer a blessing over the meal. A big table filled the dining room, with another one in the kitchen area and a couple of other six-footers along with a smaller table for the youngest children. Piper, Paisley, and most of the older children sat on furniture or the floor in the great room.

They served the food buffet-style, and Gianna came and stood in line with Brock. He followed her to a seat at the big dining room table.

She looked over at him. "Nice sweater. Dark green looks good on you."

He grinned. "Thanks. Piper chose well."

Gianna let out a soft snort. "Piper wanted the bright orange one with black triangles. It wasn't even a good Halloween sweater. I talked her into this one."

Brock chuckled. "Why am I not surprised? Thanks."

Her eyes sparkled. "You're welcome."

Brock enjoyed meeting and talking with Vanessa's brothers and sisters-in-law. He could barely keep them straight, let alone the assorted aunts, uncles, and cousins. All the brothers worked on the ranch, but Todd Kingston handled all the construction projects, and the two men found a lot to talk about right away.

After Brock had finished his second helping of food, Gianna offered to take his plate to the kitchen. A few minutes later, she came up behind him and swatted his arm. "Time to work off your meal, Hennessey," she said, handing him a dish towel. She raised an eyebrow at Todd. "You too. Susy's saving a spot for you."

Todd stood. "The tradition is anyone who doesn't cook is on clean-up duty."

Brock rose and smiled. "I'm more than happy to help."

He and Todd continued their conversation in the kitchen. He enjoyed meeting Susy, a petite Filipino whom Todd had met at church camp back in high school. Brock also discovered Todd and Ben Garritsen had been best friends their whole lives.

After everything was cleaned up, Vanessa's dad called for everyone's attention. "Sleigh rides start in ten minutes."

The children clapped and squealed.

Pete looked around. "There's so many of us, we'll be outside a while, so bundle up. I think the sleigh will fit about six, a few more if the littles sit on laps. The sun will set soon, so we can take lanterns."

Brock and Gianna rode with the girls, Todd and Susy, and their two-year-old son, Marco. Brock sat on one bench with the girls, Gianna sat next to Susy on the other bench, and Todd held Marco.

The sun was setting as they glided along. Brock filled his lungs with the crisp, clean winter air and counted the blessings of the day. The sound of Piper's laughter filled him with joy, as did watching Gianna's animated conversation with Susy. He'd made a new friend in Todd.

Brock and Piper prepared to leave, and Vanessa and her parents escorted them to the front door.

"We had such a wonderful time. Thank you again for including us," Brock said.

"Thank you for the sleigh ride and the sledding and all the yummy food," Piper added. Brock was proud she expressed her appreciation without his prompting.

Pete Kingston accepted Brock's handshake with a strong grip. When Brock reached for Marcella's hand, she pulled him in a hug. "You're family now. Come back anytime."

"Thank you," Brock said, emotion swelling in his chest.

Piper hugged both the Kingstons and they left.

Brock settled Piper in the truck and walked over to Gianna's car. She climbed into the driver's seat, and he stood next to her, leaning on the open door. "Merry Christmas, again. I—we had a great time today," he said, for her ears only.

"I'm glad Van invited you," Gianna replied.

"Me too. I guess I'll see you—soon."

She poked a long, slender finger against his chest. "I'll see you at 7:45 tomorrow morning. Boss's orders." Her eyes twinkled.

Brock's heart swelled. "I'll bring coffee."

CHAPTER 18

After spending time together on Christmas day, Brock thought he and Gianna were back in their comfort zone. But when he suggested doing something with the girls on New Year's Eve, she declined with no explanation. He and Piper had a campout in the living room, and he tried to provide as much fun for her as possible.

He decided not to push and give Gianna some space. She was still a grieving widow experiencing all the first holidays and special occasions without her husband. When she contacted Brock a few days later, she was friendly and open, for which he was grateful.

Brock continued examining Carson Bellmont and Diamond Valley Lake and hoped to find a connection but kept running into walls. He was also convinced that Stanley Dole, the old man who died alone, was connected somehow, but had no leads there. He was determined to help Gianna solve the mystery and prayed daily for God to bring the truth to light.

The next several weeks flew by in a blur. The girls thrived in school, loved their art class, and participated in frequent service projects with a kids' club at the church, such as sorting and packing food for the needy. Brock and

Gianna continued to share the responsibility of getting them everywhere they needed to be.

Gianna and Paisley planned something different each weekend to introduce Brock and Piper to the joys of a Montana winter. They went both to Kingston Valley Ranch and Tack and Bev's farm several times to sled, hike, and take sleigh rides. Gianna planned a ski trip for all of them in about a month. Father and daughter were falling in love with their new state.

Saturday morning arrived, and Brock and Piper picked Paisley up at *Ladies and Gents*. Gianna and Vanessa were in charge of hair and makeup for a big wedding party. When Brock and Piper came through the door, music blared from a speaker, and excited chatter filled the air. Every seat was occupied by a woman or young girl in various stages of completion, some being worked on, others waiting their turn. Gianna and Vanessa ran from one to the other, smiles on their faces. They were clearly doing what they loved.

Brock sneezed several times in a row. So many different scents competed for air space, he couldn't tell what was setting him off. Hairspray? Some kind of bleachy concoction?

"Morning, Brock, Piper," Vanessa sang out. She was trimming the hair on a middle-aged woman, perhaps the mother of the bride.

"I hear congratulations are in order," Brock said.

Vanessa waved her left hand on which rested a large diamond. "Thank you. It was a New Year's Eve to remember."

Paisley ran up to them with her coat, hat, and backpack on, carrying Sammy, who was decked out in a little blue coat. Gianna followed, holding a big, round hairbrush in one hand and some kind of curling wand in the other.

She blew a wayward piece of hair off her forehead. "Thanks for taking her—well, them. This place is a zoo."

Her words tumbled out in a rush. "The wedding's at two, but I'm not staying. I'll call you when I'm free." She reached out and patted the little dog's head. "Are you sure this is OK? Sammy's pet carrier is by the door. There's a little container of food in there for her, her leash, and some plastic bags." She tapped Paisley on the shoulder. "Be sure to clean up after her, OK?"

"I will, Momma."

"No problem." Brock sneezed again and nodded, brushing his nose with his hand. "I'd better leave." He smiled, and he and the girls exited.

After they were in the truck, Brock turned to the girls. "Where do you want to go for breakfast?"

Piper and Paisley exchanged glances, and Piper rolled her eyes at him. "Really, do you have to ask?"

Brock smiled. "Next stop, Mountain Mist." They were busy, so when the girls were done with their waffles, they helped Lark clean some of the tables.

"It was so fun helping Lark," Piper said when they came back to him. "What's next? Are we going home?"

"Do you want to stop by the dog park?" Brock asked.

"Sammy loves the dog park," Paisley said.

They spent almost an hour there. Once off her leash, Sammy tore through the park, barking at everyone and everything. Brock and the girls walked along the paved paths winding throughout, and he was enchanted with the design featuring little bridges and shallow pools of water for the dogs to play in. They'd removed Sammy's coat so she could frolic to her heart's content.

Once they were back at the truck, Brock checked his phone. "Change of plans." He'd received a text informing him some materials he wasn't expecting until Monday had come in. Long-time renters in one of Gianna's houses had moved out, and she had agreed with Brock's recommendation to complete some significant work before acquiring a new renter.

Brock pulled on his jacket and motioned for the girls to move along. "I need to pick some things up and take them out to a house. Today isn't too cold, so you can play outside. There's a great yard."

Paisley and Piper's twin expressions brightened. "And we have our art stuff in our backpacks too," Paisley said.

"We can do a project inside if we're bored outside," Piper said.

An hour later, they arrived at the house on Autumn Hill Road. The home sat on about three beautifully landscaped acres. Brock went through the garage and led the girls inside. They removed their coats and looked around.

"Can we explore?" Piper asked.

"Sure," Brock said. He made multiple trips back and forth until the truck was unloaded.

The girls came running in. "This house is awesome," Piper said.

"Mine is bigger, but this is cool," Paisley added.

"There's four bedrooms, and two of them are kind of connected," Piper said. "We're playing in there. Come on, Pase."

"Be sure to watch Sammy, and don't wait too long to let her out," Brock said.

Brock organized his materials in the kitchen. About a half hour later, the girls came into the great room with Sammy and put their coats and hats on to go outside. Brock followed them out onto the back deck and looked around. The entire property was fenced, but there was a line of trees and he told them not to go beyond those.

It had warmed some, and Brock left the screen door open to the deck. He continued to work and thought about turning on the playlist in his phone, then decided he preferred the sounds of the girls' laughter and Sammy's barking as they ran and played.

After about an hour, he wandered over to the door.

The girls sat on the porch swing overlooking the yard, their backs to him and Sammy asleep between them. The excursion to the dog park and running in the yard had worn her out.

"Do you miss your dad a lot?" Piper asked Paisley.

She frowned and shook her head. "Not really. He was my stepdad. He married my mom when I was two."

"Where's your real dad?"

Paisley shrugged. "I don't know. He and my mom were never married. I don't think she even knows where he is. In a way it's OK. My friend Carlie's dad died last year, and they were close, and Carlie is still super sad all the time, like really bad." She pushed her glasses on her nose.

"You're lucky to have a mom. I never had a mom," Piper said.

A lump rose in Brock's throat.

"Did she die?" Paisley asked, her voice barely audible.

"I don't know. My dad told me once she was sick and did drugs and then did something against the law and went to jail."

Paisley's eyes grew wide. "I'm sorry, Piper."

Piper gave her a little smile. "It's OK. I don't remember her, so I don't miss her." Brock watched his daughter knead her hand through Sammy's soft fur. "Me and my dad are the perfect family. He's my best friend." Piper giggled. "Well, and now you."

Brock turned away from the door as his throat thickened and squeezed his eyes shut. The ringing of his phone pierced the silence, and he looked at the time. After two, already? He cleared his throat and answered.

"Are you OK?" Gianna asked. "How are the girls?"

"Ah, yeah. We're all fine. They've been playing outside. It's such a beautiful day. Are you finished?"

"Yes." He smiled at her relief coating the single syllable. "You survived OK?"

Gianna laughed. "Barely. Weddings aren't my favorite thing. Too much pressure and always some kind of drama. Anyway, are you at the A-frame? I can come by."

"No, we had a change of plans." He explained where they were and why.

"I haven't had lunch," Gianna said. "Have you?"

"We had a late breakfast," Brock said, "but the girls may be getting hungry."

"How about I grab pizza and come out there?"

"Sounds good."

"See you in about forty-five minutes."

They were all hungry by the time Gianna arrived, and since the house was empty of furniture, Brock lit the outside fireplace, and they sat on the built-in seating and polished off the pizza. After they were done, the girls insisted on taking their parents on a tour of the house.

"This is a beautiful home," Gianna commented when they returned to the great room and the girls had gone off to play. "The hardwood floors are gorgeous."

Brock's gaze was drawn to the stone fireplace and the shelves on either side. "These custom built-ins are my favorite. I'd fill them with books."

They stood at the back door, looking out over the deck and yard toward the snow-capped mountains. "I love the view to the backyard from this room," Gianna said. "The exposed beams and brick make it seem cozy even though it's a large space."

Brock tilted his head at her. "But this house isn't as big or as nice as yours, according to Paisley." He was curious about their home, but Gianna had still never invited him there.

She crossed her arms and shrugged. "It's an amazing house, but too big for the two of us, even the three of us. I'm not sure if I want to stay there."

"Where would you go?" he asked.

"No idea," she murmured.

Brock sneezed, and Gianna eyed him warily. "You've sure been sneezing a lot today. Are you allergic to something?" She grabbed his arm. "Are you allergic to Sammy?"

Brock smiled. "No, I'm sure I'm not. This was a regular sneeze. The ones this morning were itchy sneezes. Something in your shop."

"Hmm, *itchy* sneezes. I don't believe I'm familiar with that particular scientific term." She seemed so relaxed after the earlier whirlwind and tension of her day, and her smile was gorgeous.

Every time he was with her, Brock was drawn to her a little more.

The girls came running up. "We have an idea," Piper announced, all smiles. Paisley wound her arm through her mother's and laid her head on her shoulder.

Brock exchanged an amused look with Gianna.

"We want Paisley to come over to our house for a sleepover tonight." Piper tented her hands in front of her in a prayerful pose. "Please, please, please?"

Paisley bounced on her toes as she held onto Gianna's arm. "Please, Momma?" She lowered her voice. "I've never been to a sleepover."

Brock saw the hesitation in Gianna's eyes. "Let us talk for a moment, girls." He opened the sliding glass door and ushered Gianna onto the deck, then closed the door.

They walked over to the railing. "I understand if you don't want to let her come," he said.

Gianna twisted her hands in front of her on the railing. "I—there's no reason not to, but I—" She blew out a breath. "You probably think I'm an overprotective parent."

Brock touched her hand. "Not at all. I of all people know how you feel."

Gianna swallowed. "I need to start letting go. She's ten already. She'll be a teenager before I can blink." The disillusionment in her eyes made Brock ache for her. She was still newly widowed and overwhelmed at the prospect of being alone someday after Paisley flew the nest.

Brock moved his hand to rub her arm. "She'll be safe."

She nodded quickly. "I know, thank you."

He smiled. "You can call or text her as many times as you want."

Gianna waved her hand. "No, I'm not even sending her phone with her. It's only set up for her to text or call me or Van, anyway." She smiled beguilingly. "I'll call or text *you*."

He liked her idea and returned the smile. "You can do either, whenever you want."

They went back into the house and announced their decision, then covered their ears as the girls squealed and jumped around.

"I'll take Sammy home now and pack a bag for Paisley and drop it off at the A-frame," Gianna said. "I need to go back into town anyway to return some things from the wedding to the rental place."

"I'm at a good stopping point here," Brock said, "so we'll leave in a few minutes."

Brock offered to make the girls a light supper, but since they'd eaten lunch so late, they weren't hungry. He added wood to the fire, then lay on the couch. He crossed his arms and closed his eyes. Normally, he would have been watching TV or surfing the web, but he had to admit he didn't miss either one much. He much preferred listening to the backdrop of Piper and Paisley playing in the loft.

His thoughts turned to the house on Autumn Hill Road. The home wasn't new or fancy or even overly large, but it had a soul. Brock had been in hundreds of houses, if not more, during his construction career but had never connected with one, until now. If he could pull together the money, he would buy the house in a minute and move him and Piper in there.

The problem was, he had a greater chance of being struck by lightning than having a down payment to purchase the house. He must have dozed off because the next thing he knew, Piper was shaking him awake. "It's time for s'mores."

"What happened to not being hungry?" Brock yawned. "OK, you can take everything out." The girls skipped into the kitchen and rummaged around in the pantry. Brock went over to the basket by the fireplace and pulled out their coat hangers. Within minutes, they'd toasted the marshmallows and put the s'mores together. The girls sat at the counter, and he stood on the other side as they all ate.

"Those were awesome, Mr. Hennessey," Paisley said, licking the last of the sticky marshmallow from her fingers. "What's your favorite part of a s'more?"

Brock laughed. "Same as Piper's."

His daughter's eyes lit up. "The chocolate," they said in unison.

Paisley giggled. "Mine, too."

"Daddy, do you have the DVD player Mrs. Harper sent along for tonight?"

"Yes. I think Paisley has all the DVDs. Have you decided which one you want to watch?" Brock picked up the player from the other end of the counter.

Paisley held out her hand. "I know how to work this."

"We're watching a Disney movie," Piper said. "In the loft. You can go to bed if you want, Daddy. You look tired."

"OK," Brock shrugged. He looked at the clock. It was ridiculously early, but what else did he have to do? "In bed by nine, OK? Tomorrow's church."

"Nine-thirty?" Piper countered.

"Not a minute later," Brock said with mock sternness.

Piper gave him a hug. "Night, Daddy, love you."

"Night."

Paisley held the DVD player in front of her and looked a little uncertain. "Could—could I have a hug too?"

Brock's heart melted a little. "You bet." He wrapped one arm around her, snatched Piper with the other, lifted them up, and spun them around. "Here's double trouble," He shouted as the girls squealed.

"You're silly, Daddy," Piper said when he set them down. He'd never seen Paisley's smile so bright.

Their giggles chased them up the stairs. Brock extinguished the fire, turned all the lights off but one and headed for his bedroom. He thought he might be wide awake after his little catnap, but he soon fell asleep.

A knock came at his door. Piper's voice quavered. "Paisley is sick."

Brock came instantly awake. Probably the second s'more. He didn't want to have to explain to Gianna.

"Where is she?"

"In the bathroom. She started hurting a while ago. I helped her get down the stairs."

"Go back to her. I'll be right there." After Piper closed the door, Brock slid into his jeans and walked the short distance to the bathroom. Paisley was laying on the bath rug, curled into a ball.

Brock knelt beside her and instinctively felt her forehead, which was burning up. His stomach sank.

Paisley's arms were wrapped around her midsection. "It hurts." The fear in her voice worried him.

"Did you throw up?" he asked.

She nodded.

Brock was puzzled. Emptying the stomach usually helped.

"Will Paisley be OK?" Piper asked in a little voice.

Brock reached out and squeezed her hand. "Please bring me my phone, Pipe."

When his daughter returned, he checked the time. Nine forty-eight. Brock dialed Gianna, and after several rings, her voicemail picked up. He wondered if she was already asleep.

"Paisley, does your mom keep her phone in her bedroom when she sleeps?"

Paisley nodded.

Brock tried again, with the same result. Then he sent a text. *Everything is fine, but call me.*

Paisley let out a moan. "It hurts."

Brock knelt beside her. "Paisley, can you show me where the pain is greatest?" She nodded tearfully. She pointed to one area, and when Brock pressed lightly with his fingertips, Paisley bit her lip and moaned. They repeated this a few more times, and her reaction was the same. When he gently pressed on the lower right area just inside her hipbone, she sucked in a breath and crunched away from him.

Brock had a bad feeling about this. Piper had been sick before, but this was different. His mind raced. What should he do if he couldn't reach Gianna?

"Paisley, do you know your doctor's name?"

"I think maybe Dr. Johnson, in Kalispell."

Great. "Piper, can you bring me my wallet?" She scurried away and when she returned, Brock pulled out the business card from the medical clinic he'd taken Piper to for her school physical.

He dialed the after-hours number and spoke with the triage nurse. After relating Paisley's symptoms and answering some further questions, the nurse delivered news he didn't want to hear.

"It could be appendicitis," she said. "I would go ahead and take her to the hospital."

"Thanks so much," Brock said.

Piper stood in the doorway in her PJs. Brock led her out into the hallway. He spoke as calmly as he could. "Piper, go put your clothes on. We need to take Paisley to the hospital." Her eyes were wide with fright. Brock bent and grasped her arms. "Honey, she'll be fine. But she's scared right now, so I need you to be brave, so she won't be so scared, OK?"

Piper wiped her eyes and stood a little taller. "I can be brave."

"Go change, quick, and bring one of your blankets and a pillow." Piper ran off.

Brock stepped back in the bathroom and checked on Paisley. No change. He looked at his phone. Nothing from Gianna. He tried calling again and sent another text. He didn't give her any details because he didn't want to scare her.

Gianna's house was in the opposite direction from the hospital, and Brock had never been there. Even if Paisley gave him the address, Gianna might not be there. Was she with Vanessa? Maybe Tack and Barb? No matter, Brock didn't have any of their phone numbers. He needed to get Paisley to the hospital, now.

Brock knelt beside the little girl again, who was now shivering, partly due to her fever, and possibly due to being scared. He ran a gentle hand over her head. "Paisley, Piper and I are taking you to the hospital so you can see a doctor."

"I w-want my m-mom," she whispered.

"I know, sweetie. I'm trying to reach her. She's not picking up." Brock rammed a hand through his hair. "I'm sure she'll text me back soon."

Piper appeared in the doorway, dressed and holding a blanket and pillow. Brock stood. "Lay the blanket over her and stay with her while I dress."

Brock raced into his bedroom, changed into a clean t-shirt and a hoodie, and pulled on his socks and boots. He stopped in the bathroom doorway. "I'll start the car, Piper. I'll be right back."

He dashed out to the garage, grabbing a plastic bowl from the kitchen on the way in case Paisley threw up again. "Piper, go collect the pillows from my bed," he called out.

Then he ran back inside, wrapped Paisley in the blanket, and gently lifted and carried her out, He set her on the seat and put her seatbelt on, and she curled herself into a ball, holding her stomach.

Piper appeared with the pillows, and Brock set them between Paisley and the door. He told Piper to buckle in next to Paisley and hold the bowl for her.

As they rolled down the driveway, Brock tried to call Gianna again. *Pick up, pick up,* he prayed. Still nothing.

With no other option, he kept driving and praying.

CHAPTER 19

The road was clear and deserted, and they arrived at the hospital ER entrance seventeen minutes later. After instructing Piper to stay with Paisley, Brock threw the truck into park, jumped out, and ran inside. "I have a little girl who I think has appendicitis," he said to the young man at the registration desk.

"We'll bring a wheelchair out," the man said as he picked up the phone.

Brock ran back to the truck, and soon an ER tech showed up. Brock watched as the tech transferred Paisley into the wheelchair and rolled her inside. She was in so much pain and looked scared to death. The young man at the desk handed Brock a clipboard.

"Ah—I'm not her parent," Brock said. "I've been trying to reach her mom."

"Do the best you can," the man said. "We need some basic information before she can be seen."

Brock wrote Paisley's name on the form and asked for her address. She winced with pain, and tears rolled down her cheeks.

Piper stood next to him, her nose almost touching the clipboard. "It's 85 Rifle Mountain Road, Canadian Meadows," she said. "And her birthday is October 23. She's ten."

"Are you allergic to any medications?" Brock asked.

Paisley shook her head.

"Have you ever been sick or in the hospital?"

She shook her head again.

Brock handed the clipboard back to the young man at the desk. "I think we completed everything."

The man scanned the form and handed Brock another sheet. "This is a consent to treat form. Can you give me her mother's phone number? I'm required to try to contact her."

Brock handed his phone over and the man made the call. After a moment, he shook his head. "No answer. I'm not leaving a message."

"I've already left several," Brock said.

The young man made a notation on the form and held the paper out for Brock to sign.

They were directed to the waiting room and had only been there a few minutes when they heard Paisley's name announced. Brock wheeled her through the door and Piper trailed behind.

"I'm Gwyn, the triage nurse." The petite brunette had the biggest, brightest blue eyes Brock had ever seen. She laid a gentle hand on Paisley's shoulder. "We'll take a look at you, Paisley, and help you feel better real soon." She led them into a large, open area. "This is our triage area." She looked at Brock and Piper. "Is this dad and sister?"

"No, she's my daughter's friend," Brock said. "She was spending the night. I've been calling and texting her mother, but she's not picking up."

"Has she been vomiting?" the triage nurse asked. She swiped a thermometer across Paisley's forehead.

"Yes," Brock said. "I didn't take her temp, but she was hot when I felt her forehead."

"One-oh-two-point-four," Gwyn said, writing on the chart. "When did she eat last?"

Brock winced. "They had s'mores around seven. We had eaten a late lunch." He didn't want to admit he had fed them pizza. If the junk food police were patrolling the hospital tonight, Brock was in big trouble.

"I feel sick again," Paisley said. Gwyn grabbed a bowl and held it while she retched. When Paisley finished, Gwyn wiped her mouth. Gwyn looked at Brock. "We'll give her some pain and anti-nausea medicine soon." After washing the bowl out, she held it out to Brock. "You can be in charge of this."

Brock nodded.

"We'll take you to a room now where you'll see the doctor." Gwyn steered the wheelchair down the hall into another area. Piper walked next to the wheelchair and Brock followed.

Gwyn looked at Piper. "What's your name?"

"Piper Lee. My friend is Paisley Laura. We have the same initials."

"How fun. Those are pretty names," Gwyn said. "What's your favorite color?" she asked Paisley.

"Blue," Paisley replied.

"It's actually more aqua," Piper said.

"Well then, I think you'll like this room," Gwyn said. She wheeled them into a room with a wall mural depicting an underwater scene with brightly colored fish and other sea creatures.

"Oh, this is so pretty," Piper said.

Paisley smiled weakly.

Gwyn helped Paisley onto the bed, and Piper smoothed out the sheet and blanket.

A tall, slender man wearing a white coat entered the room. "I'm Dr. Jacobs," he said, extending a hand to Brock.

"Hello," Brock said.

"Let's see what's happening with Miss Paisley." He put his stethoscope in and listened to her lungs, asking her to take deep breaths, which Paisley did with various levels of discomfort.

"When did this start?" Dr. Jacobs asked.

Brock hesitated.

Piper jumped right in. "We were in the loft watching a movie, and Paisley started feeling sick, and later she said she felt even more sick, and the clock said 9:40 when we came down. And then she threw up. And whenever *I* throw up, I feel better right away. But she was worse, and laid on the floor holding her stomach, so I went to tell my dad."

The doctor smiled at Piper. "You gave a great answer, thanks. I'm not used to getting so much detailed information." He listened to Paisley's heart, then asked her where her pain was, and did a quick, gentle probe of her abdomen.

A younger man with a shaved head came in. "Hi, I'm Aidan, the primary nurse," he said to Brock.

Gwyn handed the nurse the chart. "I'll leave you in Aidan's capable hands," she said. "Bye, Paisley, I hope you feel better soon. Bye, Piper." She smiled at Brock and left.

Dr. Jacobs spoke. "I'm ordering an abdominal ultrasound, and someone will be in soon to take her down. I've already called for some basic blood tests and some pain and nausea medicine to help her feel better." He brushed past Brock.

Brock's mind was overloaded, trying to process all this. "OK, thank you."

Aidan pulled a cart over. "Hi, Paisley, I'm starting an IV so we can give you some meds so you'll feel better." He arranged his equipment and rubbed Paisley's arm with an alcohol swab. "I'll start the IV in your arm, and you'll feel a little pinch when I put the needle in, but you'll feel better soon. It's OK if you're scared or want to cry, but the most important thing you can do is to hold very still and not move your arm, so I can finish quickly and you won't hurt as much."

Paisley's eyes widened with fear. Brock stepped next to the bed, pulling Piper with him, and Paisley clung to his hand. "Piper and I are here, honey. Don't worry."

Brock's stomach bubbled as he watched Aidan start the IV, draw the blood, then inject the meds. The nurse patted Paisley on the shoulder. "You did great, Paisley. We're all done. And look, the needle doesn't stay in your arm, only this flexible plastic part, so if you move, there's nothing to poke you." He looked at Brock. "She should start feeling better in a little while." He held two vials of blood. "I'm taking these to the lab." Aidan left the room.

Brock transferred Paisley's hand to Piper's so he could sneak a look at his phone. Why wasn't Gianna picking up? Then Brock had another idea. He leaned close to Paisley, whose eyes were closed. "Honey, do you know Vanessa's phone number?"

Paisley shook her head, then her eyes fluttered open. "I think the first three numbers are 3-5-5. I don't know the rest. Momma programmed the whole number into my phone."

"Daddy, I think the last four numbers are 6-0-7-6," Piper said. "When I first saw Vanessa's phone number, I realized those are the same last four numbers as Miss Carmen's. But I don't know the area code. And I don't know for sure the part Paisley knows."

For the first time in over an hour, Brock felt a glimmer of hope. Montana had one area code. *Please, God, let this work*. He looked at his phone and winced. The device would run out of juice soon, and he had left his charger behind.

Holding his breath, he cobbled together the three parts of the phone number and dialed, uncertain of the outcome. *Please, God, please.*

Vanessa answered on the second ring. "Hello?" Her voice was hesitant.

Relief flooded his veins. "Vanessa, it's Brock Hennessey. Everything is OK," he rushed to reassure her, "but Paisley came to spend the night with Piper, and now, she's sick. I called the after-hours number for the medical clinic, and they thought I should take her to the hospital. I've been calling and texting Gianna for over an hour and she's not picking up. Do you know where she is?"

"Oh, Lord above," Vanessa said. "She's taking a bubble bath, I'm sure of it. I told her to light candles and play music on her iPad and not take her phone in—to shut the world out. The detective on Greg's case called earlier this evening with bad news, and she's upset."

Brock heard noises in the background.

"I'm on my way out the door," Vanessa said. I'll pick her up. She won't be in any condition to drive. You're at Valley Meadows Hospital, right?"

"Yes, in the ER. Thanks so much, Vanessa. Paisley is in good hands here, so there's no need to rush. Please drive carefully."

"I will."

Brock couldn't believe it. The instant Vanessa disconnected, his phone died. He leaned in and smoothed Paisley's hair. "Your mom is on her way," he murmured. The girl didn't open her eyes, but she nodded.

Aidan came back into the room with a young blonde woman. "Are you feeling a little better, Paisley?"

The girl nodded.

"We're taking you for an ultrasound. They'll rub a wand over your stomach to see what's happening inside. You shouldn't hurt since you have pain medicine now, OK?"

"OK," Paisley said.

"Can we go along?" Brock asked.

"Absolutely," Aidan said. He made sure the IV lines were free and clear, not dragging on the floor, and the young woman steered the bed out of the room. Brock held Piper's hand, and they followed her down a hallway into an elevator and to another room where a red-headed forty-something woman greeted them with a smile.

"Hi, I'm Ruthie, and I'll be doing your ultrasound." She adjusted the bed next to her machine and looked at Brock and Piper. "You want to come closer? Paisley, this won't hurt, but you might be a little uncomfortable because I'll have to press on your abdomen with this wand. The gel I have to use may feel cool and slimy."

Brock laid a hand on Paisley's shoulder, and Piper took hold of her hand.

Ruthie's part didn't take long. Brock watched the shadowy images on the screen and marveled at the ease of seeing inside the human body. Soon, Ruthie disconnected the machine and removed her gloves. She squeezed Paisley's shoulder. "You did great, Paisley. I'll be back."

"How are you feeling, Pase?" Piper asked.

"Better," Paisley said sleepily. "My tummy doesn't hurt very much anymore."

"Good," Piper said. She held onto Paisley with one hand and Brock with her other. He put his arm around Piper and planted a kiss on her head. She was scared but was trying to be brave for her friend. He was so proud of her.

Paisley dozed off, and Brock went back to the chair in the corner and sat, drawing Piper onto his lap. He needed to hold his girl.

In a little while, Dr. Jacobs, the ER doctor, came back into the room. "Her appendix needs to come out."

Brock's heart thundered erratically. "Is it—oh, wow, do you mean a full surgery?"

The doctor nodded. "It will be laparoscopic. She'll have three little holes across the lower part of her abdomen." He drew his index finger across the area on his own body. "The pediatric surgeon is here. She'll be in to talk with you soon, and then we'll take Paisley upstairs." He gave Brock's hand a quick shake and left.

Almost immediately, Aidan returned, preceded by a short, no-nonsense woman wearing a white coat over light blue scrubs, and a Peanuts surgical cap which hid some brownish-gray curls. "I'm Dr. Barker, the pediatric surgeon." She gave Brock's hand a firm shake. "Did you reach her mother?"

Brock shook his head. "But I reached her friend, and she's picking her up." He looked at his watch. "They should be here in about half an hour."

Dr. Barker shook her head. "We need to take her upstairs now and prep her," she said. "We don't want the appendix to burst."

Brock's heart sank. Gianna would be devastated if she couldn't see her daughter before she went into surgery. Brock would feel the same way. He stepped back as two transporters prepared to wheel Paisley's bed out.

"You can go upstairs to the third-floor surgical waiting room," Aidan said. "Dr. Barker will come find you there when she's out of surgery."

"How long will the operation take?" Brock asked.

The doctor shook her head. "I won't know till we're inside." She stepped past them. "I'll see you later."

Paisley had awakened and sensed something was happening. Her gaze flew to Brock and Piper. "Don't leave me. I'm scared."

Brock moved around the nurse to the side of the bed and took Paisley's hand. "Paisley," he said calmly, "the doctor is going to take your appendix out. That's what made you sick." He smoothed his hand over her hair. "You'll take a nap and when you wake up, your mom will be there, and you'll feel much better. OK?"

She nodded, and tears gathered in her eyes.

"We need to go," Aidan prodded. They wheeled the bed out the door. Brock and Piper held Paisley's hands as they moved through a maze of hallways, into the elevator, and then out into the hallway leading to the surgical wing. The large double steel doors yawned open in front of them.

Piper leaned in and touched Paisley's arm. "I love you, Paisley." Tears rolled down her cheeks. "S-s-sisters ever after."

"Love you, Piper. Sisters ever after."

Brock had no idea what they meant. He leaned in and kissed Paisley's forehead. "Your mom will be right there after you come out of surgery. We'll be praying for you." He squeezed her hand once more and let go. The bed rolled away, and he and Piper were left alone in the hallway. He put his arms around her, and she folded into his side, shaking.

Brock felt as if he'd been through the wringer. They walked into the waiting area, and he saw some vending machines. An infusion of carbs seemed like a good idea. "Do you want some juice or chips or something, Pipe?" They made their selections and sat.

Brock put his head in his hands. He wished he had his phone. How would Vanessa and Gianna find them?

Several other people were in the room. Brock spied a mousy middle-aged woman sitting next to an older man who was dozing. She tapped on her phone. "Be right back," he said to Piper.

He approached the woman. "Excuse me, my phone died, and I need to text my friend where to find me. Is there any way I could borrow yours to send her a text?"

"Sure thing." She handed the phone to Brock. He recalled Vanessa's phone number and typed, *It's Brock. My phone is dead. She's fine, but they need to remove her appendix. We're in the 3rd floor surg waiting room.*" He handed the phone back to the owner and thanked her.

Brock returned to Piper and pulled her into his arms, her head resting on his chest. He hoped she might drift off.

A few minutes later, Gianna flew through the door, followed by Vanessa. "Oh my gosh, Brock," she exclaimed. Her face was mottled and her eyes wild with fright.

She came right to him, and he jumped up, startling Piper. Without thinking, he opened his arms, and Gianna fell into them. She clung to him as if he was her last hope at life. "Oh God, I'm the worst mother in the world."

Brock rubbed circles on her back and held her close. "Shh, it's OK," he whispered. He didn't know what else to say.

"Her appendix? I didn't e-ven notice she was s-sick today." Gianna trembled. "What if—w-what if she—doesn't—" Gianna was escalating into hysteria. Brock had to take her away from Piper and the curious stares of others.

He caught Vanessa's eye, cocked his head toward the door. "Stay with Piper?" he mouthed.

Vanessa nodded and shooed her hands toward the door as if to speed his and Gianna's exit.

Brock led Gianna away, his arm firmly around her. He wanted to take her somewhere quiet and private. When they reached the nurse's station, he asked, "is there a chapel?"

"One floor down." The nurse pointed. "Take the stairs and turn right. Can't miss it."

"Thanks," he said.

Gianna still shook, although she had quieted some.

Brock opened the door and removed his arm from around her. Instead, he took her hand and led her down the stairs into the chapel.

The moment they entered, a cloak of serenity surrounded them. The room was windowless, ringed by false stained-glass windows in muted jewel colors with soft light illuminating them from the back. Four upholstered pews were on each side of the aisle. A simple altar sat front and center under a beautiful wooden cross adorned with a rustic crown of thorns draped with a deep purple cloth. Candles sat on various small stands and shelves placed across the front of the chapel, and after a quick appraisal, Brock realized they were battery-operated, not open flame.

They were alone. He led Gianna into one of the pews and sat. Without even thinking, Brock gathered her into his arms, and hers came around him. She sobbed into his shoulder, and he let her cry.

Vanessa said Gianna had been taking a bubble bath. A floral vanilla scent overtook Brock's senses. Her hair was like silk against his jaw, and she was unbelievably soft. Other than the one short embrace at his house a few months ago, Brock hadn't held a woman in a long, long time, and the walls he'd erected around himself came crashing down.

As he held her, he prayed for Paisley and her team of doctors.

They stayed there for a long time until Gianna's storm passed. She sat up and distanced herself a little from him, pulled a wad of tissues out of her bag, and swiped at her face. "I'm sorry," she whispered.

Brock stretched out his arm along the back of the pew behind her and stared into her wet, glittering eyes. "For what? You don't have anything to apologize for."

"I'm a terrible mother."

Brock's heart turned to stone. He knew *terrible mother*, and Gianna was not it.

"You're one of the most incredible mothers I've ever met. You work tirelessly to provide for your daughter, and it's obvious you love her with all your heart. I know you would do anything for her." Brock was surprised at the sternness in his voice and could tell Gianna was too.

He moved his hand a couple of inches to cup her shoulder and softened his tone. "Gianna, she wasn't sick earlier today, at all. Appendicitis comes on very quickly. She was fine, until she wasn't."

Her eyes filled with tears again. "But I *never* should have left my phone in the kitchen when I went to take a bath. It was all Van's idea and was so irresponsible of me." She shivered, and Brock realized she wore a light sweater. The hospital was cold.

He pulled his sweatshirt off. "Here, put this on."

Gianna stared at him for a moment, then shrugged into the garment and wrapped her arms around herself, her hands encased. Her leg bounced nervously. "I never should have let her out of my sight." Her voice rose in volume, and she shot to her feet. "I have to go back upstairs. I have to be there."

Brock gently grabbed hold of her hands. "Shh, calm down," he whispered. Her wild eyes darted around as if she wanted to escape. He didn't want her returning to the waiting room in this condition.

He stood and wrapped his arms around her as she quaked. Then he touched a gentle finger under her chin. "Hey, look at me." She took a deep shuddering breath and quieted. "You can't do anything to help Paisley by sitting in the waiting room. We can be there in thirty seconds. Text Van, let her know where we are, and tell her to text you back when there's any news. OK?"

Gianna nibbled on her bottom lip, then nodded. She dried her tears and handed her phone to Brock. "Will you text her, please?" She plopped on the pew, leaned her head back and closed her eyes.

Brock found Vanessa's number and texted, *It's Brock. Gianna is still very upset, we're in the chapel, and I'm trying to calm her. Text if you hear anything.*

The phone pinged seconds later, *Good plan. She needs to stay there with you. I'll text the minute I know something.*

Brock relayed the message to Gianna, then handed the phone back and she slid it into the pocket of his sweatshirt. She turned her luminous, swollen eyes on him. "What did the doctor say? Did he think the appendix would burst?"

Brock didn't want to discuss any specifics. He squeezed Gianna's arm. "They gave her something to control the nausea and pain right after we checked in. She was scared, but not in pain. The pediatric surgeon wanted to take the appendix out, but no one was acting alarmed."

"But I should have been with Paisley. Oh, Brock, I'm so glad you were there. Th-thank you so much." She hiccupped. "What if I lose her? I h-have n-n-nothing else."

Brock drew her into his arms again. "You won't lose her," he murmured. He stroked her hair.

"I can't imagine any greater pain," she murmured into his ear.

Brock's heart hammered.

Gianna shifted to look at him. "Since Greg died, I've told God he can take everything from me, but he can't have Paisley. I couldn't bear it. I couldn't lose my child."

Brock lost his breath and removed his arm. He shifted forward and rested his elbows on his knees, concentrating on breathing in and out.

Gianna peered at him. "Brock, what's wrong?"

He shook his head. He couldn't speak.

Her eyes widened. "Are you OK?"

Brock regretted scaring her. Darkness closed in on his field of vision. He shook his head to clear it.

"I—" a thousand-pound boulder crushed his chest, and another one filled his airway. He let out a weak cough. *Tell her.*

"Brock? What's the matter? Please talk to me." She shook his forearm.

He closed his eyes and looked at his feet. Four little words, and he could barely force them out.

"I—I lost a child."

What did he say? Gianna couldn't believe her ears. "You? You lost—?"

He nodded.

"Oh, Brock." His face was blanched white, and he had a look of devastation about him unlike anything Gianna had ever seen. She wrapped her arms around him and drew his head to her breast like she did when Paisley needed comforting. Did this have something to do with Piper's mother? Her heart thundered. She didn't know what to say, so she kept silent. Then she realized she was caressing his hair with one hand.

Silent sobs shook him, and they stayed there for several moments. When he sat up and composed himself, Gianna pulled more tissues out of her bag and handed them to him.

"Thanks." He swabbed his eyes and nose. "I—I think about him every day, but I haven't broken down so completely in a long time."

He'd lost a son. "I'm so sorry, Brock." Her words were inadequate, but Gianna had no other.

He nodded. "Would you like to see his picture?"

"Of course."

He pulled out his wallet and extracted a worn photo. Gianna imagined him looking at the picture every day. She held the photo between her thumb and forefinger and shifted a bit so she could see better in the dim light of the chapel.

Oh, dear Lord. He was a baby, maybe a year old, with dark hair, dancing brown eyes, and his father's chin. He was the spitting image of Brock.

Gianna didn't know how she had any tears left, but a new batch coursed down her cheeks. "What a b-beautiful child."

Brock nodded. "Yes, he was."

"What was his name?"

"Thomas James, but we called him TJ."

Gianna handed the photo back, and he slid it back in his wallet and returned the wallet to his pocket. Then he stretched his arm out on the back of the pew behind her. "He, um, was born right after Piper turned a year old. Their mother—" He swallowed. "Their mother had a hard pregnancy with him and didn't recover well. She was upset because she wanted another daughter. She had abused pills, and then she started drinking, which wasn't a new problem either, but she'd managed to curtail during both pregnancies." He exhaled and clamped his lips together in a tight line.

Gianna pushed the sleeves of the hoodie up and reached for his hand. "Brock, you don't need to tell me."

"No, no, I want to," he said, the words tumbling out. "One day, soon after his first birthday, she took the kids with her to a house where her brothers and some of his friends were drinking and doing drugs. The children never should have been there. I didn't know it then, but this wasn't the first time she'd taken them with her. She was a master at hiding everything from me. Anyway, when she arrived home with the kids in the afternoon, they had both fallen asleep in the car."

No. Dear God, no. Gianna's heart thrummed.

"She parked in the driveway under some partial shade and left the windows cracked. A male *friend* had followed her home." Brock went silent. Gianna looked at their clasped hands, at his thumb rubbing over the back of her hand.

He seemed to shake himself out of his reverie. His voice grew stronger and had a hard edge to it. "Ninety minutes later, a neighbor heard Piper crying. TJ was already gone." He swallowed. "Piper wouldn't have lasted much longer if the neighbor hadn't come along. She called the police, and they found Cass and the guy in our bed, passed out."

Gianna was so horrified, she thought she might be sick. She threw her arms around Brock and buried her face in his neck. His arms came around her. "I'm so sorry, I'm so sorry," Gianna whispered over and over. He shook with silent sobs.

They remained locked in the embrace for several moments. When they came apart, Gianna took out more tissues. Brock hesitated, then gently cupped her cheek.

"Gianna, you are a *wonderful* mother." His warm eyes and tender voice touched her deeply. "You didn't neglect Paisley. You didn't put your needs first. Even in your grief, you're *there*. You don't have anything to feel guilty for." He wrapped his hand around hers.

Gianna stared into his tortured eyes. "Thank you." She was lost in her tumbled thoughts for several moments. "Did your—did she go to jail?"

He nodded. "Yes, it was ruled negligence resulting in the death of a minor, a felony, with a typical sentence of twenty to twenty-five years. But she was released back in September."

Gianna's jaw dropped. "After only seven years? How?"

Brock snorted. "Our wonderful justice system. Prison overcrowding. By turning into a *model prisoner*, since she has no access to alcohol or pills." A tic worked in his jaw. "I testified at her hearing, and the prosecuting attorney was certain she wouldn't be released. She took a plea deal at the time of sentencing but should have been in for at least several more years."

"I'm so sorry," Gianna murmured.

His voice dripped with disgust. "I divorced her after she went to jail, and her parental rights were terminated. But the minute she was released, she contacted me and declared she expected to have a place in Piper's life."

Everything made sense now. Everything.

His eyes flashed and steel laced his voice. "I will take my daughter to the ends of the earth before she spends even one second in the presence of that monster."

Gianna squeezed his arm. Her phone vibrated, and she was transported back to the present. Her heart broke into a gallop. The text was from Van. *Nurse just came out. Everything fine. P in recovery. Dr will be out soon to talk to you.*

Gianna's heart burst with gratitude, and her voice shook. "Paisley is out of surgery." Grateful tears sprang to her eyes.

Brock wrapped his arms around her, and Gianna was cherished and comforted in a way she'd never experienced before. "I'm so glad God answered our prayers," he whispered.

"Me too."

When they arrived at the waiting room, Piper was asleep on a couch, and Vanessa jumped up. Her gaze took in Gianna swallowed in Brock's sweatshirt. The two friends threw their arms around one another.

Vanessa looked at Brock over Gianna's shoulder. "I don't know why I answered when you called. I never answer numbers I don't recognize."

"Thank God you did," he responded.

Vanessa nodded. "I'm sure he prompted me."

Dr. Barker approached. "This is Paisley's mom, Gianna Harper," Brock said. Gianna shook the doctor's hand.

"How's my daughter?"

"Everything went well. She'll be fine," Dr. Barker said. Brock was glad Vanessa was holding onto Gianna's elbow, or she might well have crumpled to the floor. Gianna swiped at her damp cheeks. "She's still back in recovery, and once the anesthesia team clears her, we'll take her to a room on the pediatric ward. One of the nurses will come for you soon."

"How long will she have to stay here?" Gianna asked.

"At least twenty-four hours." The doctor took a step back. "I'll be by in the morning to check on her." With a nod of her head, she turned to go.

"Thank you so much," Gianna said to the woman's retreating back.

Gianna and Vanessa sat, and Brock lowered himself onto the couch and put Piper's feet in his lap. He wasn't sure what he should do now. The crisis had passed. They could go home now, but something kept him there.

A few minutes later, a nurse approached. "Mrs. Harper?"

Gianna stood. "Yes?"

"They're taking Paisley to her room now. I'll be back in a few minutes." She nodded and left.

Vanessa stood and looked between Brock and Gianna for a moment, then touched her friend's hand. "I'll go by your house and take Sammy home with me."

Gianna dragged a hand down her face. "Oh, Sammy. I almost forgot."

"I'll take care of her, don't worry. I'll call you later tomorrow morning and come by when Paisley's ready for visitors."

Gianna reached out to hug her. "Thank you so much, Van. I love you."

"Love you too, sweets." She nodded to Brock. "Night."

"Good night, Vanessa. Thanks for keeping an eye on Piper."

Vanessa grinned. "Anytime. Piper's a hoot."

Brock smirked. "Yes, she is." He lifted himself off the couch then, trying not to disturb his daughter, but her eyes flew open, and she sat up.

"Is Paisley OK?"

"Yes, she's out of surgery."

Piper jumped up, ran over to Gianna, and threw her arms around her waist. "I'm so sorry, Mrs. Harper." Her eyes watered.

Gianna drew Piper close. "Oh honey, none of this was your fault." She sighed. "I'm so glad you and your dad were with her." She looked ready to cry again.

The nurse returned. "Are you ready?" she said to Gianna.

Piper looked at him. "Daddy, are we going home?"

Brock's eyes locked with Gianna's. She didn't say anything, but nothing could have dragged him away. "Not yet, Piper." He went to Gianna's side and the three of them followed the nurse to Paisley's room.

CHAPTER 20

Gianna's heart melted at the sight of her precious daughter in the hospital bed. She went to her side and leaned over to kiss her cheek. She stroked Paisley's beautiful hair. "I'm here, Curly Girlie," she whispered. "I love you. I'm not leaving you ever again."

Another nurse came in, early thirties with dark blond hair pulled back in a ponytail. She wore black scrub pants and a Minnie Mouse scrub shirt. "I'm Melanie, I'll be Paisley's nurse for the rest of this shift."

Brock nodded, and Gianna murmured a hello.

Melanie looked around. "We know our patient's families like to stay right in the room. There's a recliner, and the seat portion of this couch slides out a bit—it's not a full-sized bed, but mom and dad usually work things out." She bounced a smile between Brock and Gianna.

"Ah—" Brock sputtered.

"We'll be fine, thank you," Gianna said.

"Let me go grab some pillows and blankets," Melanie said.

"Piper, would you like to hold Paisley's hand?" Gianna asked. "I bet she'll know you're here."

Piper nodded and stepped to the bedside.

Erin S. Quint

Gianna approached Brock and swallowed. He opened his arms, and she leaned into his strength and closed her eyes. She wanted to ask him to stay but couldn't bring herself to utter the words.

"There's nowhere else on earth I'd rather be right now," he whispered. "We're not going anywhere."

How did he know? She swallowed past the lump in her throat. "Really?"

"Really."

"You and Piper can have the couch."

Melanie came in, her arms loaded with pillows and blankets. Brock pulled a small, cushioned chair next to Paisley's bed on the other side from where the couch sat and guided Gianna there. Melanie and Piper situated all the bedding.

"You're a great helper, Piper," Melanie said. She caught Gianna's attention and pointed. "Here's the call button. Do you need anything else?"

Gianna shook her head. "Thanks so much."

"I'll be in about every hour to check on her," Melanie said. "I'll do my best not to disturb you."

Piper sat on the couch/bed and yawned. "I'm sleepy, Daddy." She laid her head on the pillow.

Brock sat next to her and tucked a blanket around her.

"I'm so glad Paisley's gonna be OK," she murmured.

Brock leaned over and kissed her forehead. "You were awesome tonight, Pipe. You were brave and helpful, the best friend Paisley could ever have."

"She's my sister. Night, Daddy. Night, Mrs. Harper."

"Night, Piper." From her chair, Gianna held Paisley's hand, but her focus was on Brock, on how gentle and patient he was with his daughter. She didn't want to be caught staring, so she leaned her head back and closed her eyes.

204

Long-forgotten memories flooded Gianna's mind, when six-year-old Paisley had been hurt at soccer practice. The coach loaded her into the car, and Gianna headed to the ER at this very hospital.

Greg was in Kalispell for the day, and she called him on the way. After she explained what was happening, silence reigned.

"Honey, do you need something from me?" he finally asked.

"Well, I—could you come and meet me at the hospital? You could be here in less than an hour."

He sighed. "There's nothing for me to do there. Paisley doesn't need me. She'll receive great medical care. If they need a deposit or something, you have the credit card. OK?"

"Sure," she managed to choke out.

"There's my strong girl," he said. "I know you can handle this. I have another call coming in. I'll see you tonight."

Gianna felt so bereft at his response. Everything he'd said was true. Even though Paisley didn't need him, *she* did. Gianna wanted Greg to *want* to be there with her.

Paisley's leg wasn't broken but badly sprained. Gianna took her daughter home and texted Greg. He replied not to worry about dinner, he'd bring something for them so she wouldn't have to cook. An hour later, he arrived home with Chinese take-out, a dozen stunning red roses for Gianna, and a big teddy bear and balloons for Paisley.

And after Paisley fell asleep, he loved Gianna so thoroughly, she almost forgot how deeply he'd hurt her earlier in the day.

Soft footsteps interrupted Gianna's reverie, and Melanie mouthed "sorry" when Gianna lifted her head and saw her checking Paisley's IV. "Everything looks good," she added.

After Melanie left, Gianna's gaze returned to Brock. Piper was asleep on the couch, her feet in his lap.

Now she could stare at him without being noticed. His eyes were closed, his head tipped back. His hands were folded over his muscled chest and his long legs stretched out, crossed at the ankle. He'd removed his baseball cap, and his dark hair stuck out haphazardly. Unexplicably, she found it attractive. His strong, defined jawline was dusted with dark beard growth and—" Gianna shook herself. What was she doing? She still loved Greg and had no business thinking about another man.

Gianna pulled Brock's sweatshirt around her, and his words echoed in her head. *There's nowhere else on earth I'd rather be right now.*

Gianna awoke with a start, and for a moment, couldn't remember where she was. She sat up in the recliner and gazed at her daughter, who slept.

Ribbons of morning sunlight streamed in through the blinds. Piper's small, blanketed form curled on the couch. Brock sat next to her, wide awake and looking better than anyone should this early in the day. The clock read 6:50.

He smiled. "Morning," he drawled.

Gianna yawned. "Morning." She looked around. "How did I end up here?"

He stood. "You fell asleep by Paisley." He pointed to the chair sitting next to the bed. "And I helped you to the recliner."

Gianna recalled him carrying her, settling her in, and covering her with a blanket. A warm flush suffused her cheeks.

He picked up a white bag off the counter. "Be right back."

A few minutes later, he returned with a muffin and foam cup. He must have found a microwave.

Gianna's jaw dropped. "You've been to Mountain Mist already?"

He shook his head. "Remember, it's Sunday. They're closed. But the hospital cafeteria was open."

"At this hour?"

Brock smiled. "It's almost seven o'clock. For some of us, the workday is well underway by this time."

She reached for the cup and took a grateful sip. "Not for me," she murmured.

He laughed. "I know." He set the muffin on the table beside her.

"Thank you," she said. "You spoil me."

"I like spoiling you." The words washed over her like silk.

"Momma?"

Gianna almost sputtered her mouthful of coffee. She set the cup down and rushed to her daughter's bedside. Gianna looked into Paisley's tired but happy eyes. and smoothed back her hair with one hand. "How do you feel?"

Paisley smiled wanly. "I'm OK."

Piper and Brock appeared on her other side. "Hey, Piper," Paisley said.

"Hey, Pase, I'm so glad you're OK."

"Are you in any pain?" Gianna asked.

Paisley shook her head. "No, but I'm a little hungry."

Gianna pushed the call button. "We'll see what the nurse has to say."

A few minutes later, a tall brunette in a *Frozen* scrub shirt and bright blue scrub pants came in. "I'm Colleen, the day nurse." She stepped to the bed. "How are you feeling this morning, Paisley?"

"Pretty good."

"She's a little hungry," Gianna said.

Colleen nodded. "She can have some gelatin." She turned to Paisley. "What flavor would you like?"

"Strawberry?"

Colleen smiled. "And maybe some clear soda?" Paisley nodded.

Piper's gaze followed the nurse out of the room. "I think I want to be a nurse when I grow up. They wear fun clothes to work." She took up residence in the chair next to Paisley's bed. Brock sat on the couch, and Gianna made to go back to the recliner, but it was farther away from the bed and the couch, so she joined him there with her muffin, which had since gone cold.

She picked at the muffin, and Brock looked at her. "Do you want me to heat it up again?"

Gianna shook her head. "Wouldn't help." She laughed. Then regret filled her. "I didn't mean—it was so sweet of you to think of me."

He smiled. "But it's not one of Barb's. I understand."

Gianna finished the muffin and laid her head back. Soon, she heard a woman's voice.

"I'm Terri, one of the volunteers," a round-cheeked middle-aged lady greeted them. "How are you today, Paisley?"

"I'm OK."

Terri's gaze hopped from Piper to Brock to Gianna. "Oh, your whole family is here. How nice."

"Thank you," Piper said happily. Brock squirmed beside her, and Gianna wondered if she should correct the woman.

"We have books and puzzles you girls might like."

Piper and Paisley smiled and nodded. "I'll be back with those," Terri said. She turned on her heel and left the room.

Gianna rubbed her face. "Ugh, I feel like a swamp creature," she muttered. Her lovely bath from last night was a distant memory.

"Do you want to go home and grab a shower?" Brock asked. "We'll stay here."

Gianna shook her head. "I'm not leaving," she said firmly.

"Gianna," he said gently, lowering his voice. "She's surrounded by medical professionals. Nothing will happen."

"Van will bring me some things later and I can freshen up here." Gianna dozed off and when she woke up, she was surprised to find her head on Brock's shoulder, his arm resting along the back of the couch. Van stood in the doorway, staring at them.

"Good morning," she said cheerily. Gianna scooted away and sat up.

Van set her things down and placed a pot of colorful flowers on the table next to Paisley's bed. "How are you doing, sweetie?" She pressed a kiss on her head.

"I'm good, Aunt Van. Look what we're playing."

"Guess Who was always one of my favorite games."

Gianna stood and accepted the bag Van had brought. She'd never been so glad to see her own toothbrush in her life. "Thanks, Van." As she turned toward the bathroom, Colleen came in with Paisley's gelatin and a can of clear soda with a bendy straw.

"Would you like a soda too?" she asked Piper.

"Yes, please."

Colleen turned to Gianna. "Did you know we have a family bathroom down the hall?"

Gianna shook her head.

"There's a shower," the nurse said. She looked over at Brock. "You're welcome to shower too."

"I'm fine," Brock answered.

"Sounds like heaven." Gianna looked at Brock. "You'll be here?"

He nodded. "Right here."

"Promise you'll come for me if anything changes?" Brock quirked an eyebrow at her.

"OK, I'm leaving." Gianna followed the nurse out.

When she returned fifteen minutes later, she was much better. Van and Brock were sitting on the couch, deep in conversation. Gianna stepped to the bed to see what the girls were doing. They were drinking their soda and having a great time playing Uno.

Dr. Barker walked in, dressed as she was the previous night but wearing a Nemo surgical cap. "How's Paisley feeling this morning?"

"Good," Paisley answered. "Are you the doctor who did my surgery?"

She shook Paisley's hand and smiled. "I sure am."

"I think I want to be a surgeon when I grow up," Piper announced.

"But you can't stand being around blood," Paisley said.

"Oh, I forgot," Piper muttered.

"Piper, come over here," Brock whispered. Piper moved out of the way to make room for the doctor to conduct her examination, and Gianna stood on the other side of the bed.

When Dr. Barker had concluded, she made notations on an iPad. "We'll start her on some Jell-o and clear foods, then progress to simple foods. We could send her home today, but she's only a few hours post-op. I'll be back tomorrow morning and discharge her then. Any questions?"

Gianna shook her head, and the doctor nodded. "All right then, you folks have a good day."

Piper reclaimed her seat next to Paisley's bed. "Ok, back to our game."

Paisley yawned, and Brock stood and looked at Gianna. "Pipe, I think you and I should go home for a while. Paisley might need to take a nap."

"I want to stay," Piper whined.

Brock tapped her shoulder. "Put the game away and say goodbye to Paisley. I need to talk with Mrs. Harper in the hall for a minute."

Gianna followed him out, and they both leaned against the wall. "Vanessa and I talked," he said. "She'll stay with you now, and Piper and I will come back later. Then Vanessa will stay with Piper tonight and take her to school in the morning, and I'll stay here and take you and Paisley home when she's discharged."

Gianna couldn't believe it. "You—you don't have to go to the trouble."

"I know," he said with a shrug and a lift of his eyebrow.

Gianna found her arms wrapping around his waist, and he rested his chin on her head. "Oh, do you want your sweatshirt back?"

Brock smiled. "Nope." He stepped to Paisley's door and opened it. "Come on, Piper." He held the door open, and Piper came out.

She came to Gianna and gave her a hug. "Bye, Mrs. Harper, we'll be back later."

"See you later," she replied. She turned toward the door.

"Gianna," Brock's voice was so soft, she barely heard it. "Call me if you need me. OK?"

"I will, thanks." She watched them walk away, then stood for a few seconds collecting her thoughts. When she slipped through the door, her gaze landed on Paisley, already asleep. Gianna tiptoed over to the couch and sat next to Van, who stared at her expectantly.

They sat in silence for several seconds. "What?" Gianna finally said.

"You wanna tell me about you and Brock?" Van's smile stretched all the way across her face.

"What about us?"

Van grabbed her arm and shook it. "Sweets, that man is *totally* into you, and you know it."

Gianna adjusted a loose clip in her hair. "He hasn't done one thing to make me think he's *into me*." She made air quotes with her hands.

Van didn't blink an eye.

"The girls are best friends, so we hang out a lot. We've become friends. End of story."

Van emitted a dry laugh. "Right. When you were taking a shower, he thought of the plan to make sure one of us was here with you all the time. He stayed here all night. He's staying again tonight." She sighed. "It's so romantic."

Gianna huffed. "Van, stop. There's no 'being romantic.' He's been a perfect gentleman. He's—" She didn't want to reveal any of Brock's personal circumstances. "He's being kind." She pushed away the images of their intimate time in the chapel. She wasn't willing to share with her best friend now.

Van's brows knit together. "Did you ask him to stay?"

A warm feeling washed over Gianna, but she shook her head. "He offered." She sighed. "I didn't want to be alone and couldn't bring myself to ask, and ... he knew."

Van elbowed her. "See?" She had a cat-in-the-cream look on her face. "I'm tellin' you, the man has it *bad*."

Gianna giggled and covered her mouth. "Van, the man doesn't have *anything* bad." Heat rose in her cheeks.

Van kicked Gianna's foot playfully and pointed a finger at her. Her magnificent engagement ring glittered in the morning light. "See? You *have* noticed."

Gianna's insides twisted, and she let out a breath. *I sure have.* Immediately, shards of guilt stabbed her. "It's—Greg's only been gone a few months. Sometimes—sometimes I think I feel something for Brock, but then guilt pours over me. I loved Greg—I still love him. I still miss him. But—Brock is so different. I never feel put down by him. He respects me, and—" Gianna's heart tripped. "Oh, Van, when he goes all strong protector on me, I want to melt." She swallowed. "To have a man's support and a partnership." She paused. "You know I've never had either."

Van reached out and squeezed her hand but didn't say anything. For all her blustery, outgoing personality, her friend was a good listener, and Gianna adored her. "And the way he is with Paisley makes me think, makes me believe maybe—"

Then she shook herself back to reality. "Ah, I'm dreaming."

Van slid her a look. "Never say never, sweets. I *never* would have imagined I'd be marrying into a family who may be headed for the White House."

"I know, it's crazy. Any progress on setting a date?" Gianna asked.

Van rubbed her forehead. "You know I've always wanted a winter wedding, and I'm hoping for next January." She gave a little shrug. "It's all about the campaign, though, so the big day is penciled in for summer."

"*This* summer?"

"No. Next summer before the election. They want a big production at the ranch with fireworks." She shrugged. "For now, all my planning and ideas are on hold."

Gianna reached out and touched her friend's hand. "If you're marrying the man you love, everything will be OK."

Van nodded. "I never thought a bunch of political consultants would be planning my wedding, you know?"

Her eyes grew soft. "And I do love Reid." Her eyes grew bright, and she reached for Gianna's hand. "So long as my matron of honor is by my side, I can handle anything."

Gianna squeezed her hand. "You can count on me."

CHAPTER 21

Brock and Piper arrived home mid-morning. He made eggs and buttermilk biscuits and decided to lay down for a while. He hadn't slept much last night. "What will you do now?" he asked Piper.

"Go play in my room," she said. She'd slept some at the hospital and seemed to have boundless energy.

When Brock changed out of his jeans into comfy sleep clothes, drew his bedroom shades and lay down, he thought he would fall right asleep, but his brain whirred with all sorts of thoughts.

Thoughts filled with Gianna. The incredible feeling of holding her, comforting her, and being comforted by her. Brock couldn't remember the last time anyone had held him and been strong for him.

She was one of the strongest women he'd ever met, one who could bear her own burdens and take care of herself, but he wanted to share them with her. He wanted to see her beautiful eyes light up when he brought her favorite coffee and sandwich to her. He wanted to laugh with her and share private jokes with her.

He wanted to hold her, whenever he wanted.

He wanted to love her.

Love?

Brock let out a groan and buried his head in the pillow. Was this love? He'd never been in love, not before, during, or after his marriage. If Cass wasn't pregnant with Piper, they would have fizzled out. She was barely tolerable when she was clean, and terrible when she wasn't.

Was he in love now? Gianna was becoming his first and last waking thought of the day, not only because of her outer beauty—but Lord above—she was the most gorgeous woman he'd ever known. Her silky black hair looked incredible whether falling in soft waves around her shoulders, marching in a stock-straight curtain down her back, or gathered into a casual twist or ponytail. Her eyes— the window to her soul with a thousand nuances—drew him in every time, one-of-a-kind bright blue with hints of lavender. Her rosy, dusky complexion was flawless, with a look of smooth satin. He longed to run his lips over her cheek. Her slender, graceful form beckoned to him every time she moved. Brock had every line and curve memorized. They played in a loop over and over in his mind.

He sat up and put his head in his hands. *Hennessey, you're in a bad way.*

The timing was impossible, all the way around. First, because Brock's future was still uncertain. Piper loved Montana, and he felt as if he could grow roots. But he was still uneasy knowing Cass was out of prison. He'd gone off the grid as much as he could without changing their identities, but someday, one or both of them might be traceable online. Would Cass have the capacity to connect the dots, to find them, to come after Piper? The ramifications struck fear in his heart. Cass had no parental rights, but a little thing like the law wouldn't stop her.

Brock thrashed around and tried to find a comfortable position. He stared at the ceiling. The other reason the timing wasn't right was Gianna herself. She was a new widow, but the circumstances surrounding her husband's tragic death were shrouded in mystery. Her financial situation was a tangled, uncertain mess, and she was trying to come to terms with how she would provide for her daughter in the years ahead.

As strong as Brock's feelings were for her—whether or not they were love—anything beyond friendship was an unfair expectation right now. *Help me to trust your timing, God, and to do the right thing by her.*

Brock dozed off a couple of times but never slept. When Piper knocked on his door a few moments past three thirty, he was showered, changed, and ready to go. They met Vanessa on their way into the hospital. She'd gone home to pack a bag to stay with Piper tonight.

"Did you receive my text?" she said to Brock.

"Yep. You're in my caller list now."

"And you're in mine." She smiled and shook her head. "I'm still amazed at how everything went down last night."

When they arrived at the room, Paisley was awake, and Gianna dozed in the recliner. Piper and Paisley resumed their Uno game. Brock sat on the couch quietly chatting with Vanessa.

At one point when she answered a text, he put a hand over his eyes. "Gosh, you about blinded me," he teased.

"What? My ring?" she laughed.

"What's his name?"

"Reid Hendrickson."

"And his dad's a senator?"

Van nodded and put her phone back in her purse. "Yes, Montana's longtime senior senator, Sam Hendrickson.

Reid is the youngest of the three sons. His oldest brother is the governor of Colorado, and his middle brother is a congressman from Washington state."

Brock whistled softly. "Sounds like a political dynasty."

Van quirked an eyebrow at him. "Pretty much."

"What does Reid do?"

"He's an attorney and will probably manage the campaign if his dad gets the nomination."

About ten minutes later, Brock heard a rustle from the corner. Gianna stretched and yawned, then rose and padded over to them. She tugged at her topknot with slender fingers. "I must look like a monster."

Vanessa rubbed her arm. "You look nothing of the sort. Did you sleep?"

Gianna shrugged. "A little." She walked over to the bed. "How are you doing, Curly Girlie? Hello, Piper."

"Hi, Mrs. Harper."

"I'm doing good, Momma. Could we have some soda?"

Brock stood. "Coming right up." The nurse had shown them a fridge containing items for Paisley and themselves. He came back and handed the cans to the girls.

Gianna and Vanessa sat on the couch, talking in low tones.

Brock stood next to the window, looking out. He never tired of the beautiful Montana sky and the mountains.

A few minutes later, Vanessa stood and picked up her purse. "I think Todd and Susy wanted to come by later to say hi."

"We'd love to see them," Gianna said.

"I'll text them. Ready to go, Piper?" Vanessa shimmied her hips. "We're dining at the Burger Barn."

Piper clapped her hands.

"Aww, I love the Burger Barn," Paisley pouted.

Piper grabbed Van's hand. "I promise we'll go again when you can come with us. Right, Aunt Van?"

Brock's lips twitched with amusement. Vanessa was family now, and a warm feeling spread through his chest. He swept Piper up in a hug. "School night. Bed by eight-thirty."

Piper nodded.

Vanessa saluted. "Yes, sir."

"Thanks so much for doing this, Vanessa," Brock said. He handed over his house key.

"Hey, it's what family does. And I've been wanting to see the A-frame. Piper's told me all about it." She leaned over Gianna and hugged her. "Sleep well, sweets, love you."

"Love you, Van. Good night, Piper."

"Night, Mrs. Harper. Night, Daddy, love you. Night, Paisley. See you tomorrow."

Paisley lifted a hand. "Night, Aunt Van, love you. Night, Piper, love you."

"Love you, Pase." Piper flitted over to the bed for one more hug.

Brock shook his head at Gianna as the door closed after them. "I've witnessed the longest goodbye in history. Guys are like, 'see ya.'" He waved his hand.

Gianna burst out laughing. She looked at him. "I could use some real food soon. I've been eating out of the vending machines all day. Did you have something in mind for dinner?" She grimaced. "Hopefully *not* from the hospital cafeteria?"

Brock looked at his watch. "As a matter of fact, our dinner will be delivered soon."

Gianna raised an eyebrow at him. "I'm intrigued."

They sat for a little while talking about nothing, and right when Gianna rubbed her stomach and said she didn't think she could go one more minute without food, the door opened, and Barb and Lark came in with a large picnic basket. Gianna's face lit up and she looked at Brock. "You didn't."

His chest fluttered at her smile. "Yeah, I did."

The women hugged Gianna and greeted Paisley. After a few minutes, Barb and Lark said they needed to go. Gianna opened the basket. "Hold on, I want to see what's in here. She pulled out a large, sealed glass container. "This is still nice and hot—oh, please tell me it's mac and cheese."

Barb nodded and laughed. "Yes, Brock said comfort food. There's veggies and a little tomato vinaigrette salad and cupcakes."

"A new recipe I tried," Lark said. "I hope you like them."

Gianna hugged the young woman. "You learned from the best," she said, eyeing Barb. "I'm sure they're fantastic."

"And there's a thermos in there," Barb said with a wink.

Gianna moaned and hugged Barb. "Thank you so much."

"It was all Brock's idea," Barb replied, sending a smile his way over Gianna's shoulder. "Tack sends his love. Call us if you need anything."

"I will." The women said goodbye to Paisley and took their leave.

Gianna wasted no time grabbing plates, utensils, and serving the food. "Brock, you're amazing," she said. "How did you know how much I needed this?"

He smiled. "I had to admit, my motives were selfish. You think I wanted to eat hospital food?"

Gianna threw back her head and laughed. For the next ten minutes or so, they enjoyed their meal in the quiet. As they finished, a knock sounded at the door, and Todd and Susy came in. The men shook hands and the women hugged.

Susy stepped to the bed and squeezed Paisley's hand. "How are you feeling? We brought this for you." A teddy bear holding a cellophane bag with homemade treats peeked out of a basket.

"Thank you, Mrs. Kingston," Paisley said. "Those look good, but I don't think I can eat them right now." She petted the little teddy bear.

Susy looked at Gianna. "I'm sorry, I didn't even think."

Gianna squeezed the woman's arm. "No worries, Susy. She can have the cookies after she gets home. You were so sweet to make them."

The Kingstons stayed for a few more minutes and then left. "Call us if you need anything at all," they said.

Paisley had some soup for dinner and said she felt better, even though she was tired.

"Would you like me to read a chapter from *Little House on the Prairie?*" Gianna asked.

Paisley nodded.

After Gianna finished, Brock spoke a thought out loud. "Piper loves those books. Maybe I'll suggest we read together sometime."

"It's a great way to spend time together," Gianna said. "I'll bet she'll love to."

Melanie the night nurse was back and glad to see how much better Paisley was feeling. "Where's Piper tonight?"

"Oh, she's with our Aunt Van," Paisley said.

Melanie finished all her checks and readied Paisley for bed. The nurse looked at Brock and Gianna. "Ring if you need anything. Have a nice night." She switched off the overhead light on her way out, and the room was bathed in soft shadows and muted light from the area behind Paisley's bed, and the small lamp on the table over in the corner by the recliner.

"Goodnight, Melanie, and thank you," Gianna said. She smoothed her daughter's hair and leaned in to kiss her forehead. "I'll—we'll be right here, Paisley," she murmured. "Do you want me to pray for you?"

Brock stood and cleared his throat. "I'd like to pray, if you'll let me."

Gianna's eyes widened. "Of course."

He stepped to the other side of the bed, and he and Gianna each took hold of one of Paisley's hands, and Brock held his out for Gianna, closing the circle. He loved the feel of her hand in his. They bowed their heads and closed their eyes, and Brock waited for the peace of the moment to wash over them.

"Father in Heaven, we are so thankful for your protection over Paisley. From the moment her sickness started yesterday, your loving hand has been on her. Thank you for Gwyn and Aidan and Ruthie and Dr. Jacobs and Dr. Barker and Melanie, Colleen, and all the other medical professionals who have cared for her." He paused. "Jesus, we are so grateful for how much you care for every small detail of our lives. Please help Paisley to heal quickly, and help us to trust you for every moment, every day. In Jesus's name, amen."

"Amen," Paisley echoed. Brock saw Gianna's lips move, but no sound came out. Her eyes were shiny with tears.

"Goodnight, sweet girlie, I love you," she whispered, and pressed another kiss to Paisley's forehead.

"Love you, Momma." Her soulful brown eyes rested on Brock. "Thank you for taking care of me, Mr. Hennessey."

Brock squeezed her hand. "You're welcome, Paisley. Sleep well."

He sat on the couch and balanced his elbows on his knees, linking his fingers together. Gianna hovered near the bed, and he wondered what she was thinking.

She grabbed some tissues from the box on the bedside table, blotted her eyes. Then she walked over to Brock and sat next to him. She looked at him, and he wrapped her in his arms. He leaned back and took her with him and held her.

"I never would have survived this without you," she whispered several moments later.

"Yeah, you would have, Gianna." He lost himself in the feeling of holding her. "You're stronger than you think."

She sat up and looked at him. "Before Greg died, I never would have imagined I could handle everything I've gone through since then. I'm certain this is God's strength, not mine."

He nodded. "The Bible tells us his strength is made perfect in our weakness."

Gianna nodded.

"I'm glad I could be here to help." He recalled how he had confided in her last night, and about how she had held him and let him cry. "You've become a real friend."

Gianna blinked rapidly. "Your friendship has become important to me too."

They sat there, staring at one another. Then Paisley shifted and let out a little noise, and Gianna rose and went to her. She smoothed her hair and adjusted the bed clothes and stayed in the chair next to the bed for a little while. When Paisley was asleep once more, Gianna walked over to the little table.

"You ready to try Lark's cupcakes?" she asked.

Brock smiled. "You bet. Is the coffee in the thermos still hot?"

Gianna unscrewed the lid and watched the steam curl. "Yes, it's good." She looked around. "Are there any cups?"

Brock stood. "I'll go out to the family kitchen area and find some."

CHAPTER 22

Gianna watched Brock leave the room. He wore a long-sleeved gray Henley with the sleeves pushed up, black track pants, tennis shoes, and moved with a confident, but casual, gait. From the times she'd had her arms wrapped around him during the last twenty-four hours, she knew firsthand how trim and muscular he was.

She grabbed a tissue from the box on the table and lowered herself onto the couch. His prayer for Paisley tonight moved her deeply. Greg had been fond of Paisley, but in eight years had never shown the kind of concern and love Brock was demonstrating and had certainly never prayed over her.

Was Brock trying to gain her affection through her daughter? Gianna might be relenting. But if he was the kind of man who would stoop to such a scheme, he wouldn't be worthy of her, and she wouldn't want to be with him. And almost instantaneously, she realized Brock wasn't a schemer, and his concern and affection for Paisley was genuine.

And now she was more confused than ever because she'd made such a terrible choice on Paisley's behalf when she'd married Greg. Why were her thoughts heading down this road?

Brock's words played over in her mind. *You've become a real friend.* Gianna was shaken by this revelation. She and Greg hadn't been friends before their marriage. Friendship came later. Their romance had exploded from the start.

Her mind was swimming when Brock came back into the room and closed the door. Gianna poured coffee into the two cups, and they took their cupcakes to the couch.

Brock unwrapped his, leaned in and sniffed. "What is it?"

Gianna took a bite. "Hmm ... I think lemon with raspberry filling. Yum."

Brock sampled his and nodded. "Lark did a great job."

Soft light bathed the room. Muffled noises from the hallway and beyond surrounded them. She and Brock were encapsulated in a private cocoon, cut off from the real world. Gianna was tired but didn't want to sleep. All she wanted was to spend time with this man who was capturing her heart.

When she finished her cupcake, she wiped her hands on a napkin and took a sip of her coffee. "Are you cold?" Brock asked.

"A little."

He reached behind him and handed her a blanket.

"Thanks."

She tucked her legs under her and pulled the blanket around her shoulders. He pulled up a small ottoman and stretched out his legs.

"Want to play twenty questions?" he asked with an engaging smile.

She giggled. "Sure."

"How long did you know Greg before you married him?"

She tilted her head at him and smiled. "Aiming for the jugular, Hennessey?"

He drank from his cup and grinned back. "You can always say 'I'm not ready to answer.'"

"Three months." Gianna set her cup down, reached for a pillow and wrapped her arms around it.

"Wow, fast."

"What about you?"

"Six weeks."

Gianna slugged him with the pillow. They both laughed.

Brock sighed. "I was living in LA, had been dating a girl for a few months and thought things were great, and out of the blue, she broke up with me. I don't know if she met someone else or what. I never found out. The next day, a Thursday, I went to San Diego for a two-day job, and a bunch of guys went out after work on Friday. Cass was one of the cocktail waitresses. We closed the place down, and I left with her. She'd been flirting with me all night."

"Was she beautiful?" Gianna wasn't sure why she asked, but the words were already out of her mouth.

Brock exhaled. "She was ... no, not really."

Gianna lifted an eyebrow, and Brock shrugged. "She could have been, but her life was a mess, and she was into—well, she was pretty beaten down. But she didn't need to be beautiful. She just needed to be there, and willing, which doesn't say much about my character at the time, and I'm not proud, but—well, I was a different person then. Now, God has changed my heart in many ways, and I realize a woman's beauty comes from inside. What the world sees as outward beauty can mask a rotten core."

"True."

"The next morning, I went back to LA, didn't think I'd see her again, but we texted and talked, and I came down a couple more times." He shrugged. "She wound up pregnant and wanted to get married. She had a horrible home life—

her family was on the verge of being homeless—and wanted to escape. I was thrilled with the prospect of being a dad and thought the best way to be involved in my child's life was to be married to its mother. We weren't a great love match, but I wanted to make the relationship work, so I moved to San Diego, and we settled down."

Gianna didn't say anything, and they sat in companionable silence for a few moments. Then Brock spoke up. "Has Paisley's bio dad ever been in the picture?"

She released her breath. "No," she said, drawing the lone syllable out. She glanced at Paisley, who was sleeping, then lowered her voice. "Captain of the football team. I was from the wrong side of the tracks, but the issue was less about our family's economic status and more about us being Italian. His father paid mine $5,000 to release him from any further responsibility and to promise never to contact him. They had a lawyer draw up papers, neat and tidy. He left for college the next year, and his family moved away, back east, I think. I have no idea where."

"Have you ever tried to find him online?"

She shook her head. "No. He has a common name. And I don't care. He was a sperm donor, nothing more."

"Does your family still live in Montana?"

Gianna swallowed and shook her head. "My mother died about five years ago, and my dad moved back to Italy to take care of my grandmother and took my younger sisters with him. They all still live there."

"I'm sorry about your mom. Did you ever think about moving there too?"

She shook her head. "My life was here with my husband."

More seconds ticked by. "Was Piper's mom ever a good mother to her?" Gianna asked.

Brock grimaced. "Sometimes. She had an easy pregnancy with Piper and adored her. I realized later her better moments were due to the booze and pills. When she couldn't find them or whatever, she was impatient and out of sorts with Piper, which scared me sometimes. And when she was pregnant again, everything went downhill." He didn't say anything for a few seconds. "She hid so much from me. I had no idea how bad things were."

Gianna ached for him. She glanced at Paisley and lowered her voice to a whisper. "Does Piper know about her brother?"

Brock raised an eyebrow. "I'll answer your question with a question. Would you give Paisley a two-hundred-pound suitcase to carry?"

Gianna frowned. "Of course not, that much weight would be impossible for her to lift." Instantly, she saw his point. What a wise man he was.

He nodded. "Someday, when Piper can carry the weight of such a burden, I'll tell her." He shared the conversation he'd overheard between the girls the day before when they were at the Autumn Hill house. "They're both pretty resilient. Paisley seems to accept the relationship she had with Greg, flaws and all. I don't see any emotional scarring."

Gianna sighed. "Thanks, I appreciate your insight."

"Piper knows her mother did something bad and went to jail. When she was little and asked if she had a mom, I told her sometimes mommies and daddies don't live together, and her mommy had to go away. When Piper asked if her mommy loved her, I told her yes." He lifted a shoulder. "Despite Cass's deep defiencies, she loved her daughter in her own way."

Gianna's heart went out to sweet little Piper, of whom she had grown very fond.

Brock leaned his head back on the couch and spoke so quietly, Gianna could barely hear him. "From the first night with Cass, the whole thing was a disaster. But one terrible choice on my part gave me the two most precious, beautiful gifts in the world." He turned his head and his eyes shimmered. "I only had TJ for a year, and even for all the pain, I wouldn't take back a moment of it. He gave me so much joy. And I know I'll see him again someday."

Gianna's heart broke for Brock. She reached for his hand and sensed he was grabbing for a lifeline when he laced his fingers through hers and held on tight.

His eyes were like pools of dark chocolate, and Gianna found herself drowning in them. "We left San Diego in the middle of the night," he whispered. "Piper was asleep in the car. The last stop I made was at the cemetery. Saying goodbye was as hard as when I buried him." A heaviness settled on Gianna's chest as she imagined him kneeling at his little son's gravesite one last time.

The silence stretched between them while she scrambled for a reply. "I'm sorry, I can't think of anything to say," she whispered.

Brock squeezed her hand and gave her a sad smile. "You don't need to say anything. Being here is enough."

She nodded and looked at their hands. His thumb rubbed over her knuckles, and she couldn't tear her eyes away.

A wisp of a smile stole across Brock's face. "I'll bet Greg was swept away by your beauty."

Gianna's soft laugh sounded hollow in her ears. "Pretty much. I told you I gave him a haircut, and the next day he sent three dozen red roses to the salon with an invitation to dinner."

Brock let out a low whistle. Gianna pulled her hand away and tucked a loose strand of hair behind her ear. "It was a whirlwind. He was living in Helena but preparing to move here to start the property management business. He was deep into the social circuit there, one of the city's most eligible bachelors, and spent almost every night of the week at a party or reception. He filled my one-bedroom apartment with new dresses, gowns, shoes, purses—all designer labels—and jewelry." She shook her head. "Oh, my goodness, the jewelry."

"I'll bet you were the talk of Helena when you showed up on his arm. How old was he?"

"Thirty-six." Brock's eyes registered surprise. "Yes, we were quite the scandal. I had come from complete obscurity, a twenty-year-old hairdresser. No one knew what to think. He proposed three weeks later," she said. "By then, he'd hired a full-time nanny for Paisley. He brought me to Canadian Meadows and showed me the house he had bought, turned me loose with a decorator and told me to do whatever I wanted, spend whatever I wanted." Gianna picked up the pillow again and hugged it.

"A real-life Cinderella," he said.

She nodded. "Our wedding was a formal evening event with over four hundred guests, including the governor, and I knew about a dozen of them. My family couldn't come."

"Where did you honeymoon?"

"Paris. What about you?"

"El Cajón."

Gianna looked at him blankly.

He grinned. "One of the 'burbs outside San Diego."

She chuckled with him. "Greg loved to travel. I'd never been any further than Idaho, so when we did travel, every new place was total culture shock for me."

"Where was he raised?"

"Michigan."

Brock's eyes registered surprise. "Does he have any family there?"

She shook her head. "His parents and an older brother died before I met him."

"Until I came here, I'd never been out of California except Arizona once and Vegas a couple of times."

"California's beautiful," Gianna said. "But I've never been there."

Brock shrugged. "The ocean is amazing, and other parts of the state are too. But Montana is stunning."

Gianna nodded. "I agree. I've never wanted to live anywhere else. Greg didn't either, once we settled here."

"How did you end up with your salon?"

"When we returned from our two-week honeymoon, reality set in. Paisley wouldn't come to me." Gianna swallowed. "She had bonded with the nanny. I was devastated. Hysterical to the point where I almost considered taking her and leaving Greg. He sent the nanny away and let me be a stay-at-home mom. He was attentive and showered us with gifts and spent every night and weekend at home. But when Paisley started school, I grew bored, so he set me up in the salon."

"Do you enjoy it?"

She nodded. "I do. It's a creative outlet. For a while I thought I might want to go to college for a business degree, but you don't need an education to run a business, I guess." She shrugged. "Greg's accountant handled those details, anyway."

"How did Vanessa end up there?"

Gianna smiled. "What a story. You know she was raised here, but I didn't meet her when I moved to Canadian Meadows. I opened the salon about five years ago, and early last year, she came in for a haircut and *hated* it."

Brock whistled. "Did she threaten to sue?"

Gianna laughed. "No, she made me hire her. She'd been living in Wyoming or Utah for a couple of years and trained there before moving back. She promised to triple my business within six months. I liked her, so I hired her."

Brock chuckled. "You took a chance."

Gianna raised an eyebrow. "The business quadrupled in six months."

Brock nodded. "I'm not surprised. Van's a force of nature. Was the haircut you gave her a bad one or just not to her liking?"

Gianna swatted him with the pillow. "We agreed to disagree. She lets me cut her hair now." Gianna laughed. "But she gives me step-by-step orders. She's the best friend I've ever had. She's a few years younger than me, but that has never mattered. Don't know what I'd do without her." She wanted to know more about him. "Do you have a best friend?"

Brock exhaled. "Yeah." His eyes took on a wistful cast. "A kid I grew up with. I haven't seen Tim in years, but he's like a brother and the only person from my past who knows where I am right now." He looked at Gianna. "He lives in Sacramento, works for the state. Has access to all kinds of databases and information." He lifted an eyebrow.

"Oh, I understand."

"Everybody needs a Tim in their corner." He searched her eyes. "With everything happening with Paisley, we haven't been able to talk about ... Van told me you received some news from the detective working Greg's case."

A spear of dread descended upon her. "They lost the toxicology report. He said papers are routinely misfiled. They may never find the report."

"So now what?"

"The medical examiner's report will stand and state the cause of death as inconclusive." Gianna looked over at Paisley.

"What about the insurance payout?" Brock asked.

A wave of fatigue threatened to overtake her, and she stifled a yawn. "Don't know, don't care. So long as my girl is OK, nothing else matters."

Brock nodded. "I understand."

They sat in silence for a few moments, then Gianna spoke. "Can I make a confession?"

"Sure."

She took a breath. "The night at the Harvest Fest, I asked you to dance because I saw Bethany Knowles was about to ask you."

Brock looked confused. "Oh, the blonde?" He looked as if he had tasted anchovies. Or liver. Or anchovies *with* liver. Gianna's heart fluttered at his reaction.

She nodded. "I was saving you from her. And then, the Wednesday before Christmas, I was on my way into Mountain Mist and saw you through the window, standing with her. You looked ... very cozy."

Brock's eyebrows raised, and he took a drink of his coffee. "And you jumped to a conclusion."

Gianna couldn't meet his eyes. "I did." She picked at a thread on the pillow.

"I remember," Brock said. He stretched his arms out and emitted a noisy yawn. "Not that hordes of women have thrown themselves at me, but I know a piranha when I see one."

Gianna gasped. "The exact word came to my mind at the dance."

He grinned at her. "If you'd stayed around about two seconds longer, you would have seen me shut her down."

Gianna brightened. "Yeah? Give me details."

Brock laughed. "Well, first off, I removed her hand from my arm and stepped back. I told her she was in my personal space, and whatever she'd heard about me, I wasn't interested in dating her or anyone else."

Gianna ignored the *or anyone else* part for now. "What did she say?" She held her breath.

"I don't know. I left. I needed to pick something up at one of the shops on the square. And then I came back to my truck and saw you sitting in your car."

Gianna let out a breath. "I—I wish I could have seen you in action."

His lips turned up and he tilted his head. "Give me some credit, Gianna."

"I should have. I'm sorry."

He raised his hand. "Raise your right hand."

"Huh?"

"Raise your right hand and repeat after me."

She giggled and did as he asked.

"I, Gianna—what's your middle name?"

"Maria."

One dark eyebrow quirked up. *"Maria,"* he murmured in an Italian accent.

Gianna's heartbeat skittered.

Brock cleared his throat and spoke normally. "I, Gianna Maria Rossi Harper, promise to never again jump to a conclusion."

She echoed the words.

He continued, "About anything Brock ever says or does."

"What's your middle name?"

"David."

"About anything Brock David Hennessey ever says or does," she finished with a smile and lowered her hand.

"Amen," Brock said emphatically. His gorgeous eyes twinkled.

Mindful of her sleeping daughter, Gianna burst into soft laughter. "That doesn't warrant an *Amen*."

CHAPTER 23

By some unspoken agreement, both Brock and Gianna stayed on the couch, much like he and Piper had the previous night. She lay with her feet in his lap, and he stretched out his legs on the small ottoman.

She fell asleep first, and Brock took the opportunity to stare at her. He still hadn't resolved his thoughts from earlier in the day.

When Barb and Lark were there chatting with Gianna and Paisley, Brock was content to sit and watch and listen. He was becoming more and more enamored with the people in Canadian Meadows who were like extended family to Gianna—Vanessa, the big, noisy Kingston family, and the Garritsens. There were a few others, but these were the core of Gianna's support network. They truly loved one another. They had chosen to be family.

Brock smiled to himself thinking about the whole misunderstanding around Bethany. He recognized a woman on the prowl when he saw one, and he also knew jealousy. Gianna was jealous. The realization gave his heart hope, but knowing her as he did, he suspected she was upset and confused over those feelings, because she was still in love with Greg.

His smile dissipated when another thought hit him. If and when Gianna was ready to move on, would Brock be ready? He was still so conflicted over his thoughts about love. Maybe he was infatuated. He hadn't had as much as one date since his marriage dissolved. All his time and energy went into giving Piper a loving, secure life. After Cass, he'd sworn he'd never be involved with another woman, never marry again. Because Gianna was a wonderful, devoted mother to Paisley didn't mean she could love Piper as her own, as Brock did.

Most importantly, the timing was off, for both of them. *Keep trusting me for the timing*, God's voice whispered.

Brock finally slept and must have slept hard. The next thing he knew, Dr. Barker was concluding her examination of Paisley, talking with Gianna across the bed. Brock sat up and rubbed a hand over his face.

"She can go home today," the doctor said. "They'll give you discharge instructions about her diet. Keep her home for the week, lots of rest. She can do homework from there. Call my office for an appointment next Monday, and I'll clear her to go back to school. Any questions?"

"No, not right now," Gianna responded. "Thank you so much, Dr. Barker."

"Bye, Dr. Barker," Paisley said.

"See you next week." The woman nodded to them and left the room.

Brock stood. "I'll be right back." He walked down the hallway to the family bathroom, took care of business, and tried to make himself look presentable.

When he arrived back at the room, Paisley was there alone. "Where's your mom?"

"She went to do something."

"Oh. How are you feeling?"

"Good. I can't wait to go home."

Gianna bustled into the room, all smiles, carrying a box and coffee caddy. "Sit," she ordered Brock, pointing to the couch.

He flashed a smile and followed her orders. She opened the box and handed him a steaming cup, then set another down, followed by an assortment of four of Barb's muffins.

"Did you go there for this?"

She rolled her eyes. "Of course not. Lark delivered."

Brock took a hearty draw from the cup and waited for the coffee to work its magic. "Ahh," he murmured. "Perfect." He reached for a muffin and lowered his voice. "You spoil me." He hoped he sounded a little bit flirty.

Her beautiful face pinked. He'd hit his mark. "I like spoiling you," she said. Her eyes sparkled and—wait—did she almost wink at him?

It was the exact exchange they'd had yesterday morning in reverse, and Brock's pulse kicked up a notch.

She sat and cut one of the other muffins in half, then took a drink of her coffee.

"What are you drinking this morning?" he asked.

Her face flushed a little more. "The dark roast." She bit into her muffin.

He couldn't resist. "Ah, you've seen the light."

She bobbed her head back and forth. *Adorable.* "Maybe. Do you want the other half of this muffin?"

"Sure. I'm sorry, did you want half of this? I kind of dove in."

Gianna smiled. "I'm fine. There's another one." She reached into the box and cut the remaining muffins in half and as they finished, Melanie walked in.

"Are you ready to leave us, Miss Paisley?"

"Yes," Paisley said.

"I'll help you dress," Gianna said.

Brock stood and gathered their leftover items. "I'll wait outside." After he found a garbage can, he lingered in the hallway outside the door.

In a few minutes, Melanie came out. "You can go in now. I'll be right back with a wheelchair."

Brock and Gianna carried Paisley's things out, and Melanie pushed the wheelchair. Brock drove the truck to the hospital entrance and settled Paisley in the back seat, Gianna in the front. With a wave to the nurse, they were off.

When Brock first glimpsed the Harper home, he forced himself not to react. It could have been a magazine spread. The long driveway swept up a hill and curved around to one side. The house sat perched at the top, a shining jewel, two stories with dormer windows, all dark wood. The distant forested mountains formed a backdrop, and an inviting porch stretched all the way across the front. A large octagonal deck with a gazebo sat off to one side.

The house sat on at least five acres. The lawn, trees, and flowers were immaculate. Brock estimated the square footage to be at least thirty-five hundred, probably closer to four thousand. The materials, quality, and workmanship were top-notch.

"Go ahead and pull up to the garage," Gianna said. "I'll hop out and open the door." She entered a code, and one of the two double-doors of the four-car garage glided up.

Brock exited and went around to Paisley's side. He scooped her up and followed Gianna into the house. They entered a mudroom larger than his bedroom at the A-frame, and Sammy yipped from a pet cage in the corner.

"Sammy, I'm home," Paisley said. "Momma, let her come up to my bedroom, please, please, please?" She could barely be heard over Sammy's barking.

"Van took her home while we were at the hospital and brought her here this morning. I need to take her outside for a minute first. Are you OK if Mr. Hennessey takes you upstairs?

Paisley nodded. "I'll give you directions," she said to Brock.

"Yes, ma'am," he said in mock seriousness. He followed Paisley's instructions as they walked through an executive kitchen, then a sprawling family/living area with floor-to-ceiling windows and a massive stone fireplace. They headed up the stairs and along a hallway looking over the space below. Paisley told him to turn right and go through the second door on the left.

The room was beautifully decorated, as Piper had described. Brock set Paisley on the bed. The barking became louder and louder, and Sammy burst into the room, Gianna on her heels.

The little dog leaped onto the bed and licked Paisley's face. She hugged Sammy and dissolved into giggles. "Oh, Sammy, I missed you so much."

Gianna tossed throw pillows aside and pulled the teal comforter back.

"I'll collect the rest of your things from the truck," Brock said. They'd made a quick stop at the store on the way for Gianna to grab some clear and simple foods and drinks for Paisley.

"Are you sure you don't mind?" She pulled a set of PJs out of a drawer.

"I don't mind at all," he assured her.

Brock took his time going back downstairs. The vaulted ceilings and wood beams were spectacular. He stopped in the living room and peered out the windows overlooking the backyard. A wide deck ran the entire length of the house, and Brock spied an outdoor fireplace and kitchen. Beyond the deck was a rustic wooden staircase sloping to a stone-rimmed blue-green pond overlooking the valley. A rock-bottom clear stream ran across the back of the property. Evergreen, aspen, and birch trees dotted the yard, and Brock recognized the clubhouse Piper had described to him, tucked in a shady spot.

An oversized wedding portrait of Greg and Gianna hung on one wall, and Brock stared at it. Harper was handsome and looked as if he thought he was king. The tilt of his head gave the impression he was looking down his nose, and a flash of haughtiness shone in his gaze. Gianna was a spectacular bride but looked brittle enough to break at any moment. Brock recognized the lost, fearful look in her eyes. A frame with cut-outs for school pictures showing Paisley through the years, with several empty spots waiting to be filled, hung on another wall. He glanced around, looking for any family pictures, but didn't see any.

He put the grocery items away in the kitchen and took the rest of the bags upstairs. "Thanks. I'll go put these in my room," Gianna said.

Paisley was curled in bed, her arms wrapped around Sammy. Brock slid his hands into his pockets. "I bet you're glad to be home."

She smiled and stifled a yawn. "The hospital was so noisy."

Gianna swept back into the room. Her posture was relaxed, her movements fluid, so different from when they were at the hospital. "It's so good to be home. Paisley, we'll go back downstairs. Do you want to read for a little while and then take a nap?"

Paisley nodded. "May I have some juice?"

"Sure thing." Gianna turned to leave, and Brock followed her to the massive kitchen, where Gianna poured juice into a glass.

"Would you and Piper like to come over tonight?"

He studied her beautiful face, reached out and rubbed her arm. "You're exhausted. Let's wait until tomorrow night. You need to sleep and relax."

She suppressed a yawn and smiled. "You may be right."

Brock straightened. "Sweetest words a man ever hopes to hear." They both laughed.

"Can I text you if I change my mind and want you here?"

Was she kidding? He nodded. "And text me if you need anything between now and then."

"I will."

"I mean it. I can leave work anytime. I have a real understanding boss."

She laughed. "Thanks again." Then her face grew serious. "For everything. I wouldn't have survived without you."

He resisted the urge to hug her. "Happy to help," he murmured. He turned to leave.

"Um, Brock?"

"Yeah?"

"Hold on a sec." Gianna exited the room and came back in a moment with a large box, which she set on the counter. "This—well, I intended for this to be a Christmas gift, and I lost my nerve. I ... well, this isn't new, but I hope you won't—never mind." She blew out a breath. "Please, open the box."

She had certainly piqued Brock's curiosity. He lifted the lid and was surprised to see a high-quality, black Stetson, worn but still in good condition. "This is beautiful."

Gianna blinked rapidly. "It belonged to my father. When he left and moved back to Italy, he said he wouldn't wear something like this there and asked me to keep the hat for—well, someone special someday."

Brock couldn't have been more surprised. He wondered why she hadn't given the hat to Greg. Maybe she had, but he didn't want it. "Gianna, are you sure?"

She nodded vigorously. "Absolutely. You've—you've become a good friend to Paisley and me. I can't ever thank you—" She covered her mouth with one hand.

Brock set the hat on the counter and took her in his arms. Nothing could have kept him away. "Hey, everything is fine. Paisley's on the mend."

She held on for a moment, then drew back and sniffed. "I need some sleep." She held out the hat with a smile.

Brock settled the Stetson on his head. He grinned. "Feels like a perfect fit. What do you think?"

Gianna's smile warmed his heart. "You look like a real Montana cowboy now."

"Thanks, ma'am," he drawled, and was rewarded with one of her sparkling laughs. "We'll see you tomorrow night."

Driving back to town, Brock couldn't stop glancing in the mirror. The Stetson looked so natural on him. What a generous gift. With all they'd been through over the last three days, something had changed in his and Gianna's relationship. Until now she hadn't wanted him at the house. She always insisted on picking Piper up in town and bringing her back. Maybe she was uncomfortable at the affluence of her home for Brock's sake, or because Greg's memory filled the space. Brock suspected the latter.

Now, suddenly and for whatever reason, her reticence had vanished, and he was grateful. He had been trying to formulate a way to ask Gianna if he could search Greg's home office. The man probably had at least one hiding spot there, and Brock hoped he might find something to unlock the mystery of Harper's business dealings.

Brock planned to go over the next night and bring dinner, but the school texted him mid-afternoon saying Piper had an upset stomach, so a couple of days went by before they returned. He didn't want to chance Piper passing some bug on to Paisley.

Brock looked forward to preparing a meal in Gianna's massive kitchen. He'd never cooked in such a grand space. He'd thought about making his special spaghetti sauce, but settled on creamy chicken noodle soup instead.

Piper breezed into the house ahead of him as if she owned the place, greeted Gianna, and took off for Paisley's room. Brock set his bags on the counter. His gaze moved over Gianna like a man seeing an oasis after wandering in the desert. He hadn't seen her in over forty-eight hours, but it felt more like weeks.

She wore jeans and a teal-blue top and looked beautiful. "I'm glad you're here," she said a little shyly. "The hat looks great."

"Thanks. Piper thinks it's cool. You look a lot more rested." Brock hung his hat on one of the empty hooks by the back door holding an array of hats and jackets.

"We both are, thanks," she said. "Do you want me to help you, or do you want to explore on your own?" She asked.

He shooed her toward the door. "You go relax." He wanted to play in the kitchen.

"I won't argue."

Brock removed things out of a bag. "Hey, I have a question for you. Do you ever see Mort Riggs in town?"

She frowned. "No, not for a while. One time, he was hanging around outside my salon for a few hours, standing there watching."

Brock's hands stilled. "When? Why didn't you tell me?"

"It was back last fall. I never saw him again. I was hoping he'd left town."

"Well, I saw him at the Food Mart this afternoon. He gives me the creeps." Brock stopped what he was doing. "Keep an eye out and promise me you'll tell me if you see him again."

Gianna's eyes went soft. "I will, Brock, I promise." She left, and he started on the soup.

Almost an hour later, she wandered back in. "I'm so hungry. Do I smell homemade bread?" Her eyes lit up. "Is this Barb's?" She swatted his arm playfully.

Brock nodded and laughed. "I didn't have time to do yeast."

"Yeast isn't even in my vocabulary." She came next to him over the soup pot and inhaled deeply. "Mmm. Anything I can do?"

"Dump the salad into a bowl?" he said.

"You've discovered the extent of my culinary talent." They both laughed. She pulled a bottle of salad dressing out of the fridge and pointed to the table by the bay window. "Let's eat here. Paisley and I never use the dining room." She set the table with some pretty placemats and lit a big, round candle with three wicks. Brock dished up the food.

"I'll bring the girls," Gianna said. When they returned, he was happy to see Paisley moving well and looking more like herself.

When they all sat at the table, a lump rose in his throat. Brock was sure he was reacting to the aromas, candlelight,

246

and the beautiful setting. But as his gaze rested on Gianna and the girls, it was them. Simply them.

"Could I pray tonight?" Piper asked, her eyes bright.

Whew. Brock's throat was clogged with emotion. "Sure," he managed to say.

"Hold hands," she commanded, latching onto Brock's hand. He reached out to Gianna, and a jolt of electricity shot up his arm when she placed her soft, elegant hand in his.

"Dear God," Piper prayed, "thank you so much for taking care of Paisley when she was sick. Please help her to heal. Thank you for all of us being friends and kind of a family. And thank you for helping Daddy to not burn the soup tonight. Amen."

Brock let out a breath and returned Gianna's quick squeeze. "All right, who's ready for the best creamy chicken noodle soup in all of Big Sky Country?"

"And Barb's bread," Gianna added. They filled their bowls and plates and commenced eating.

Gianna managed to look delicate as she shoveled several spoonfuls into her mouth. She'd been as hungry as she'd claimed. Brock was surprised when she leaned over and grabbed his arm. "Brock, this is *fantastic.*"

His face warmed. "Really? You don't have to give me false praise."

She shook her head and dipped a piece of bread into her soup. "I'm not. This soup is delicious."

"Everything is so good," Paisley agreed.

"I told you," Piper said smugly. She looked at Brock. "I told Paisley you're the best cook in the world." Brock grabbed Piper's hand and kissed it.

They enjoyed the rest of the meal, and Sammy hovered close to the table, looking for a handout. Brock smiled. "She's grown since Christmas."

"Can we show Daddy her trick?" Piper asked.

"Sure," Gianna said. Her grin was a mile wide.

"Get him. Get him, Sammy." Paisley commanded.

The little dog came over to Brock and stopped at his feet, bared her teeth, and barked furiously. If she was loud earlier, her volume had now doubled, maybe even tripled. She alternated between barks and scary growls and looked truly ferocious.

The girls giggled hysterically. "Laughing hurts," Paisley said. She could barely speak. She took a deep breath. "Sammy, stop."

It was instantly, blessedly quiet.

They all laughed. Brock bent and scratched Sammy's ears. "You're an amazing guard dog, Sammy."

He and Piper helped Gianna clean the kitchen. "Wanna go back to your room now, Paisley?" Piper asked.

"Sure," Paisley said.

"I'll help you." She wrapped her arm around Paisley and led her away. Sammy trailed behind them.

Brock crossed his arms and smiled at the retreating figures. "I'm not sure Paisley needs a nurse."

Gianna returned the smile as she wiped the counter. "Your girl is really special."

Brock nodded. "I agree. After I told her she could pray tonight, I was afraid she'd say something outlandish." They both laughed, and he handed Gianna the placemats. "I didn't have a chance to tell you, the last time you and Paisley left the A-frame, Piper came back in with her chin dragging on the ground. I asked her what was wrong, and she said, 'joy and happiness just drove down the road.'"

Gianna laughed. "Which one was I? Joy or happiness?"

Brock leaned against the counter, and without even thinking, the words tumbled out of his mouth. "Joy, Gianna.

You're definitely ... joy." Brock's heart tripped. He'd nearly said *my joy.*

Her lips formed an *O*, and she blinked.

Too much. "Gianna—I'm sorry," he said. "I wasn't trying to—"

To his surprise, she reached out and squeezed his hand. "You say the most amazing things sometimes." Their gazes met and held for several seconds. She swallowed and shook her head, and the spell was broken. "I'll put the coffee on."

"I'm sorry I didn't bring dessert," he said.

"No worries. I ate enough sugary things at the hospital."

They chatted while the coffee brewed, then carried their mugs into the living room. Gianna flipped a switch and the gas fireplace roared to life. Brock settled into one end of the soft leather couch, Gianna into the other.

Brock hoped he could look around Greg's office tonight and wanted to wait for the right moment to broach the subject. "Until I brought you and Paisley here the other day, I kind of had the impression you didn't want me in your home."

Gianna looked at her mug, then took a sip. "You were right, I didn't, but I'm not sure why. I guess—it still feels like mine and Greg's." She raised her gaze to meet his.

"I thought so. Gianna, you and I are friends. You've only been widowed a few months. You still have a lot of healing to do."

She nodded and looked down. "But I—" She sighed and met his gaze again. "I'm drawn to you, Brock. You make me feel things I'm not sure I ever experienced during the whole time of my marriage."

Brock wanted to jump up and do a fist pump but managed to make a casual shrug. "The timing's not right." He wanted to add something like, *but I have all the time in the world,* but refrained. He must continue to trust God's timing.

Gianna nodded. "Sometimes I still expect Greg to come through the kitchen door with Chinese takeout or to walk into his office and see him working there." She twisted the hem of her shirt between her fingers. "Although I never walked in. He kept the door closed when he was working and insisted I knock."

Brock tilted his head at her. "Did you feel excluded?"

She shrugged. "He said he needed total privacy to concentrate."

Maybe this was Brock's opening. He set his mug down and leaned forward, tenting his hands in front of him. "I wanted to ask if you would let me look around Greg's office. I—I thought there might be something there." Brock avoided using the word *hidden.*

"Sure, no problem." She stood and held out her hand. "You want a refill?"

"Thanks." He handed her the mug. She came right back, and he followed her past the stairs down a hallway to a set of double doors.

Gianna had her hands full with the mugs. "Go ahead."

Brock opened the doors and reached for the light switch. The large room was pretty much what he expected. Oversized wood and leather furniture, an executive desk and matching credenza, built-in bookcases, lots of shelves holding knick-knacks, framed pictures of Harper with various people Brock guessed were local celebrities, a putting green, a sitting area with a couch, table, and two upholstered chairs. And one whole wall of windows with a spectacular view of the backyard.

"This is nice," he said. Gianna nodded. He took a sip of his coffee and set the mug on a coaster. His eyes roved to the wall beside the double doors where three rifles rested on racks.

"Are those real? I mean, are they decorations?"

Gianna's face registered surprise. "No, they're the real deal." She pointed to a shelf up high. "Ammunition is there, out of Paisley's reach."

"Did Greg ever use them? Was he a hunter?"

She shook her head. "They're for protection or if a bear or other animal comes in the yard. Not to shoot them, but to scare them away."

It was Brock's turn to look surprised. "What if Greg wasn't here?"

She crossed her arms and laughed. "That's pretty sexist, Hennessey. But I guess a California surfer boy wouldn't have a clue."

Brock rolled his eyes. "I've never surfed in my life. You can shoot with those?"

"Sure can. Every Montana girl knows how to protect her turf."

He smiled. "I stand corrected."

"Where did you want to start looking?"

"Ah, the desk, I guess."

Gianna sat in one of the chairs. "Go ahead."

He walked behind the desk and perused it. "OK if I sit?"

"Brock, it's not a problem, you being in Greg's space."

He pulled out the leather executive chair and sat, trying to imagine Harper here. One by one, he pulled out the desk drawers, checking for false bottoms. Nothing. He knelt on the floor and rummaged under the desk. Next, he inspected the credenza.

"What are you looking for?"

He pursed his lips. "Well, sometimes people have a hidden compartment or something, but I'm not seeing anything." He'd built quite a few of those compartments into executive homes.

Brock roamed around the room next, his feet sinking into the plush carpet. He stood in front of the first set of bookcases, hands on hips. Then he ran his hands over the books.

Gianna giggled. "Are you looking for a latch to open the bookcase leading into a secret room?"

Brock smiled. "Maybe." Something occurred to him. "You said you have a safe in the bedroom, right?"

"Yes," she said. "Mostly for my jewelry and some of his cufflinks and our passports and some other documents, the deed to the house. I've already looked through the safe. There's nothing there connected to the business."

Brock rubbed a hand over his jaw, deep in thought. "Do you know if he has another safe in here somewhere?" He'd already been looking for any imperfections in the carpet to indicate the presence of a floor safe.

Gianna frowned. "No, I don't think so." Then she shook her head decisively. "No, I'm sure there isn't."

Brock stood in front of an ornate mirror attached to the wall. He ran his fingers around the edge and did the same thing with two framed landscape paintings. Maybe he was on the wrong train of thought.

He stepped to the last bookcase and ran his hands over the books. Halfway up, he stopped. Something was odd. He ran a finger over a volume with a cloth cover, *Treasure Island*. Wait. The surface was smooth—a photograph of textured cloth. A decoy. Brock reached over the top of it, and discovered a round, raised button on the back.

Bingo.

"Hey, look at this." Gianna rose and came to his side. He pushed the button, and above them, the entire shelf of books glided up and along the underside of the shelf above, like a garage door raising. They weren't even real books, only a façade an inch deep.

And there, on a false front wall, was a built-in safe with a numeric pad.

"Oh, my goodness," Gianna breathed.

Brock shook his head. "We're not home free yet. Any idea what the combination might be?"

Gianna exhaled. "The upstairs one is our anniversary, 12/31."

Now he understood Gianna's reluctance to spend New Year's Eve with him.

Brock punched the numbers in. A soft *pop* punctured the silence, and the safe door fell open. He quirked an eyebrow at her. "They always tell us not to use the obvious and not to use the same combination or password on multiple devices."

The safe was deep, and Brock couldn't see all the way in. "Do you have a stepstool?

"Yes." She ran over to a closet and produced one.

Brock peered into the safe's interior. He handed a laptop to Gianna. "Ever seen this?"

"No." She set the computer on the desk.

Next came a large, thick accordion file.

"Anything else?" Gianna asked.

Brock felt around in the safe, then weighed his next words. "There are stacks of cash."

Her face blanched. "Cash?"

He nodded. "A lot of it, as far as I can tell."

Gianna gasped. "Do you think it's the missing money from our account?"

Brock looked at her. "I have no idea. I think we should leave the money for now." He stepped down and took the accordion file from her and set it on the floor. Then he rubbed her arms. "Are you OK?"

She ran a hand over her face. "Yeah, I'm—" Then she crumbled. "No, I'm not," she whispered.

Brock drew her into his arms and rubbed circles on her back. She clasped her hands behind his waist. She wasn't crying and might even be a little bit in shock. She needed to be held.

And Brock was glad to be the one to hold her.

Gianna pulled away, sat on the couch, and covered her mouth with both hands. "I don't think I can do this."

Brock rested his hands on his hips. "We can put everything back, lock it up, and deal with it tomorrow, or over the weekend."

She didn't say anything for a few seconds. Then she looked at him. "I won't sleep a wink until I have answers." The file was at least four inches thick. "And who knows if we can even access the laptop?"

Brock squatted in front of her and took her hands. "The girls will be fine upstairs. Paisley has something Piper can sleep in, right? She can roll up the pant legs." He was happy when that elicited a weak smile. "We'll sort through all this together if we're up all night." He looked at his watch. "We have about eleven hours until I need to take Piper to school."

She nodded and gave him a tremulous smile. "I'll go put the girls to bed and put more coffee on."

While she was away, Brock sat at Harper's desk, no longer uncomfortable with doing so, and dug in.

Twenty minutes later, Gianna returned. "Find anything yet? I'm ready to search all night to get the answers." She set two mugs on the desk and pulled a chair next to Brock.

"Thanks." He took a swig of coffee and held up a small ledger. "This was in the front of the accordion file. The first page contained the password to the laptop. That was the first domino. Once that fell, the rest followed. None of the files were password protected."

"I guess Greg thought his hidden safe was secure enough," Gianna said.

"Greg had been working for Bellmont the last eight years," Brock said. "Bellmont installed him in Canadian Meadows to buy up all the properties around his next targeted acquisition, Diamond Valley Lake. The property management business was a front."

Gianna's eyes widened. "A front?"

Brock nodded. "Everything was organized into folders." He handed one to her, and they spent the next few minutes reading.

Brock grunted. "As best I can tell, Greg used the cash to pay property owners off, and paid people like Mort Riggs to engage in various acts to force the owners out. Bellmont was pushing to begin construction on the Diamond Valley resort, their biggest project to date. He'd already sunk a lot of money into it. I think he was growing desperate."

Gianna opened a folder and held up a credit card. "Here's the card Greg used. The statements from the past year are all here. His business trips were to all the other resorts owned by Bellmont."

Cell phone records confirmed a separate phone used by Greg and paid for by Bellmont. The only phone recovered from the accident scene was Greg's personal one, and Brock and Gianna agreed this separate phone was at the bottom of the ravine, smashed to bits. They didn't need it, anyway.

Brock leafed through another folder. "Here's everything proving Greg hired me. The emails between us, and the two calls to my former California cell number from his cell paid for by Bellmont."

Gianna leaned over and squeezed his hand. "I believed you a long time ago. You know that, right?" Her lavender-blue eyes had never looked more beautiful.

"That means everything to me, Gianna."

The air hung between them. Brock wondered if it was the time to declare his feelings for her, but something held him back. He cleared his throat. "What else do you have?"

She removed her hand. "Umm ... look at these emails. They paid off a bunch of officials for expedited permits, and bribed or blackmailed others to provide materials at discounted prices."

Brock took a moment to scan the documents, then let out a low whistle. "They had dirt on everyone. This was how they did business in all their other locations."

Brock pointed to the laptop. "Let's find out what's here." He let out a soft gasp. "A file named *Hennessey*."

Gianna scooted close and read along as he opened multiple documents. He loved the feel of her arm pressed against his, and her fresh, floral scent swirling around them.

Moments later, after reading transcriptions of texts sent between Bellmont and Greg, Brock sat back in his chair and took another drink of coffee. "I always wondered why they hired me, why they thought I would want to join their ranks. I had never come close to breaking a law. I had no idea who would have recommended they reach out to me with an offer. But here it is."

Gianna laid her hand on his arm as he read Greg's words to Bellmont: *We need a Boy Scout to be the project manager—the public face of the project. Riggs has a contact who knows the perfect guy, someone in California named Hennessey. His old lady is in jail, so if he gets suspicious or starts to stray from the mission, we can use that to keep him in line, threaten to go public or better yet, manufacture something that puts him in cahoots with her."*

Brock hung his head. Carson Bellmont was a greedy, evil, vindictive man, and Brock was glad he'd never had to work for or with him.

Gianna's face went white. "Greg was leading a double life the entire time we were married," she whispered. "I can't believe I didn't know, that I trusted him so completely." She covered her mouth, and tears spilled down her cheeks.

Brock rose from the desk, led her over to the couch, and drew her into his arms. Her entire life with Greg Harper had been built on a foundation of sand, which now washed away. Brock wanted so much to take all the pain away, but he was powerless. All he could do was hold her as her life unraveled.

After she calmed down, she tapped a large damp spot on his chest. "I'm sorry. You must think I'm weak for crying."

He shook his head. "I think you're incredibly strong. Crying isn't always a sign of weakness. It's a God-given outlet for overwhelming emotions. It shows you're human. You love deeply and grieve deeply." He drew back and gazed at her. "Besides, what are friends for, if not to provide a shoulder to cry on?"

She bit her lower lip. "Yes, friends. I can't—Brock, I—"

He placed a gentle finger on her lips. "Hey, you don't have to explain anything. I am your friend." He stated the words gently but firmly. "No pressure, I promise."

Her eyes softened. She sat forward and put her hands on her knees. "What next? Do we have enough to go to the police?"

Brock rubbed a hand over his jaw. "We still don't have anything to tie Greg or Bellmont to Stanley Dole. We have proof of intent to commit crimes, I think, but not enough to stick. The minute we turn anything over to the police, they'll take over the entire investigation. Are you willing to give up control yet?"

As he anticipated, she shook her head vigorously. "No. This was my husband, my life. There are still too many unanswered questions. I still don't know who murdered Greg, or why. I want to find out the answers, all of them, and then I promise I'll bring in the law." She stared at him. "Are you with me?"

For life. "You bet."

CHAPTER 24

Gianna worked alongside Brock until she couldn't keep her eyes open one more minute. She fell asleep on the couch about four o'clock.

A few minutes after seven, Brock shook her awake. "I'm taking Piper to school in a little while."

Gianna yawned. She was physically and emotionally depleted. "Did you sleep?" He seemed to have endless energy.

"I'm fine."

She sat up to make room for him. "Did you find anything else?"

Brock sat next to her and folded his hands in front of him, then looked at her earnestly. "Have you ever heard of a company called the Lansing Corporation?"

Gianna shook her head. "No, I don't think so. Lansing?" she asked.

He nodded. "As in Michigan."

She gasped. "Greg grew up there, I'm not sure where. Perhaps near Lansing."

Brock handed her a bank book. "This is one of Lansing's accounts. All of the money from your joint account is there, except for a cash withdrawal for five thousand."

Gianna flipped it open. The proof was there in black and white. As soon as she sorted things out with the authorities, she could have immediate access to the money from their joint account. Her shoulders sagged with relief. The funds would provide until she received the insurance payout and all of Greg's property management mess was untangled.

Suddenly, something jumped off the page.

She gazed at Brock. "The five thousand dollar withdrawal was made the day before Greg died."

He nodded solemnly and reached for her hand. "I found a notation in Greg's handwriting: *5K to take care of SD.*"

Gianna's heart skipped a beat. "This is the connection," she whispered.

"Yeah." He rubbed his thumb over her knuckles.

Gianna frowned. "Where did the cash in the safe come from, and why wouldn't he use this money?"

Brock shrugged. "I have no idea."

She couldn't believe it. "We can go to the police now."

"Yes. I'll take Piper to school and then—well, I can do whatever you want. If you want to go alone, I'll be glad to stay here with Paisley."

She stood, grabbed his hands, and pulled him to his feet. "What if you bring Piper out here after school? I'll have Van close the shop early and come stay with them. You and I can go together." She looked at him. "Will you go with me?"

He leaned down and kissed her forehead. "Absolutely. Always."

After Brock left, Gianna brewed some coffee and went outside to her favorite spot on the back patio. Usually the stunning view soothed her, but not this time.

Her whole life with Greg Harper had been a sham. He wasn't anything he purported to be. Gianna's hand shook as she picked up her mug. She'd been so young and foolish when she met him. She had ignored the red flags and convinced herself after they were married and settled into life in Canadian Meadows, he would step up and be a father to Paisley. They would find a church to attend together. He might even change his mind about not wanting more children. Gianna would have the family she had always dreamed of.

But none of those things happened. Gianna spent eight years living a split existence, one being Greg's wife and the other being Paisley's mother. She had deep roots in the community as a local business owner, active school parent, and church member. Meanwhile, he was working to ruin one of the most beautiful, natural, and untouched areas of northwestern Montana and worse, to disrupt and destroy people's lives. Folks who hadn't done anything except to live peacefully on their own land.

He wasn't the man she thought she'd married. She had been a loving and faithful wife, but the man she'd fallen in love with didn't exist. He had been a façade. Now, everything made sense. Gianna didn't owe Greg anything. She was no longer bound to him legally or morally. She looked around at the beautiful scenery and her home of eight years. They no longer moved her. She was ready to leave.

This was God's answer ... in his perfect time.

Gianna recalled a recent sermon about God's timing always being perfect. Greg's death broke Gianna's heart. She never would have guessed she might be ready to move on with someone else in a few short months. But our ways are not God's ways, and our thoughts not his. The circumstances and timing of Brock and Piper's arrival in

Canadian Meadows could only have been orchestrated by him.

Her mind rewound to the day she met Brock and moved frame by frame through the months. His firm but polite insistence from the beginning regarding his moral and honest character. His painstaking and professional work ethic caring for her properties. His contentment with a simple life not focused on material goods and wealth. His willingness to help her unravel the mystery of Greg's death. His outstanding character as a man, father, and friend. His fierce protectiveness over his daughter, and his tender care for her daughter. His gorgeous sparkling brown eyes and ready smile. His easygoing demeanor and gentle touch. His strong and steady presence every single day. His patience and willingness to let her work things out on her own timetable. His commitment to their friendship. His devotion to God evidenced by how he prayed and the way he treated people and conducted himself.

The nightmare was almost over, and Gianna couldn't wait to spend more time with Brock, to learn more about the man he was, to deepen their friendship. To share coffee and muffins with him and introduce him to more of her native state, where she hoped he would make his home.

Gianna stared at the rings circling the fourth finger of her left hand. Filled with peace and contentment, she slowly twisted them off and set them on the patio table.

It was time to take the next step with Brock.

Paisley played on the front porch while Gianna cleaned up from lunch. Rain was moving in, and she kept her eye on the sky from the kitchen window.

A horn honked, and Gianna recognized Brock's truck. Why was he here so soon? Had he taken Piper out of school early? No matter. Her heart erupted into mad flutters. She couldn't wait to talk to him, to tell him everything she'd discovered, to open the door on a new chapter of hers and Paisley's life. She hoped Brock and Piper would join them.

"Piper's here," Paisley shouted. Gianna checked herself in the mirror and went outside. Piper climbed out of the truck, and Paisley greeted her.

Piper's eyes were red and her chin quivered. Brock alighted and leaned against the door, shoulders slumped. His usual smile was absent and his eyes were downcast.

Gianna walked down the steps and approached him. "Brock, what's wrong?"

"You're leaving?" Paisley wailed. She put her arms around her shorter friend.

Gianna's heart thudded. What? "Brock? No."

His lips were a tight line. "Cass is on her way here with her brother." Gianna could barely hear him. "My PI who was supposed to be watching them slipped up."

Gianna was incredulous. "How? How did they track you here? You've been so careful."

His eyes flashed under the brim of his hat. "I have no idea. But they left California day before yesterday, so they could be here any minute."

Her mind was reeling. "Brock, you don't have to go, you can—"

"Yes, I do," he snapped. Then his eyes softened. "You know why."

"But—let's call the sheriff—"

"And say what? It's not against the law for someone to drive to Montana." He reached in the truck and handed her a folder of papers. "My friend Tim's contact info is in here, e-mail and cell. He knows all about you. Call him if you need him. And go talk with the detective."

"I—I can't face him alone."

Brock brushed a lock of hair off her face. "Yes, you can, Gianna. You're stronger than you think. I believe in you."

Her whole body trembled. "You can't take off without a plan. Do you know where you're going?"

Brock glanced at the girls, who were oblivious to their parents.

"Where?" Gianna pressed.

He shook his head. "If you don't know, you can't offer any information if pressed."

He was right. Her heart plummeted. Wherever could Brock be headed? He didn't know this part of the country at all. He wouldn't go into Canada, would he? She recalled his overnight hunting trip with Tack and Ben and gave a little gasp. "Tack's cabin."

Brock ignored her. "Piper, we have to go," he said firmly. The girls joined their parents.

Piper's cheeks were wet, and she wrapped her arms around Gianna's middle. "G-goodbye, Mrs. Harper."

Gianna thought her heart would break in two. She stroked the girl's copper hair and placed a gentle kiss on top of her head. "Goodbye, Piper."

Brock held his arms out for Paisley, and she went into them. "'Bye, Mr. Hennessey. T-thank you for taking care of me when I was sick." Brock's jaw clenched as he cradled the girl.

He let go of Paisley and helped Piper into the truck. The girl's soft sobs broke Gianna's heart. Brock's hand rested on the handle, and he stared at the ground.

Her pulse sped up. "Brock, wait. I have something for you. Don't leave."

Gianna took Paisley by the hand and pulled her up the sidewalk and onto the porch. "Wait here."

Gianna dashed through the house onto the patio, then ran back out front to where Brock stood halfway between his truck and the house. She stopped in front of him and grabbed his hand, laying her rings in his palm. "Take these. Sell them if you need to."

Shock registered on his face.

Their gazes met and held.

The only sound was the wind picking up.

Brock's chocolate eyes softened. He opened his arms, and she leaned into his strength. He held her so tightly, and Gianna never wanted to let go. A misty rain fell, but she didn't care. The Stetson formed a canopy over their heads, wrapping them in a dark cocoon. Gianna didn't know how she would let him go. She wanted to tell him she loved him, but now wasn't the time.

He slipped away, millimeter by millimeter, moved his hands to cradle her face, and looked deep into her eyes.

"I'll be back," he whispered. "I promise."

Gianna and Paisley stood on the porch together and watched the truck drive away. Paisley was inconsolable. "P-Piper is my sister."

"I know," Gianna whispered.

Paisley looked at her mother with soulful eyes, and her voice shook. "We wanted us to be a f-family. We wanted you and Mr. Hennessey to get m-married."

Gianna closed her eyes and rested her chin on Paisley's head. She didn't want to lift Paisley's hopes by telling her about Brock's promise to return. Gianna herself didn't know what to think. Would he and Piper go on the run forever?

How could the terrible situation with Piper's mother ever be resolved?

The rain fell harder, symbolically washing away their chance at happiness. She and Paisley stood rocking back and forth for several minutes.

"Can I take Sammy and go into my clubhouse?"

Gianna nodded and handed Paisley an umbrella from the stand by the door. She gave her daughter one more hug and kissed her head before releasing her.

Gianna stood on the porch for a long time, staring out over the countryside. Her world was not just broken, but shattered now. She couldn't imagine hers and Paisley's life without Brock and Piper. Her mind raced. What could she do? Brock was right. Calling the sheriff wouldn't accomplish anything.

Trust my timing, the still, small voice whispered across her heart.

Gianna sent a text to Van telling her their plans had changed, and she didn't need to come out to the house.

Her friend replied with a thumbs-up emoji.

Suddenly, the noise of a muffler split the peace. Gianna stepped out onto the porch. A rusted tan truck roared up the street and flew into her driveway. Her heart thundered when she recognized the driver. What was Mort Riggs doing here?

He jumped out of the truck and slammed the door.

Gianna's heart hammered. What should she do? She'd left her phone in the kitchen. Even if she called the sheriff, he wouldn't arrive for at least fifteen minutes. *God, help me. Show me what to do.*

Riggs spat a stream of tobacco juice into her flowerbed. "Hello, Miz Harper, you and I have business to discuss," he snarled.

Her mind raced. If she could—

"Your boyfriend and his brat are gone, and you and I are partners." His watery eyes swam with evil. "Soon he'll be dead, and the brat will be on her way back to California."

Dear God, what was he talking about? Ice raced through Gianna's veins, and she strained to pull her scattered thoughts into place. Brock's voice whispered in her ear. *You're stronger than you think. I believe in you.* The path was crystal clear. Could she do this? Only with God's help. She sent up a desperate prayer and forced herself to speak civilly when all she wanted to do was scratch his eyes out. "Let's go into my husband's office and talk, as partners."

Riggs's face transformed. He grinned, showing broken, yellow-brown teeth. "Well, well, Miz Harper. That's more like it."

Gianna prayed she was doing the right thing and breathed a prayer of thanks Paisley was out in her clubhouse. She opened the screen door and stepped back. Riggs entered and turned left. He'd been here before. Gianna led him down the hallway to the doorway into the office and sent up another prayer. She motioned for Riggs to precede her.

The moment she pulled the door closed behind them, he turned. Gianna threw all her weight forward and lifted her knee as hard and as fast as she could. The air left him as he crumpled to the floor, letting out a grunt.

Gianna locked the door, grabbed her favorite shotgun from the rack, and reached up for the ammunition. She loaded the weapon in a flash, all the years of practice paying off, then poked Riggs. "Get up," she ordered.

He wheezed. "Lady, I can't even—"

"I said GET UP," she screamed. Releasing her heightened emotions was cleansing.

Riggs half-crawled next to a chair and crumpled over. After a few moments, he tried to stand.

Gianna cocked the gun. "Go ahead, try it," she said, her voice filled with ice. Riggs glared at her and slumped back down. She walked over to him. Taking aim, she kicked him squarely in the groin. He let out a keening howl.

Gianna was certain he would be incapacitated for several minutes. Still holding the shotgun, she tore into the kitchen, grabbed her phone, the duct tape, and scissors. When she arrived back in the office, he lay still. She set the gun out of his reach and bound his hands and feet, winding the tape as tightly as possible. She didn't care if she cut off his circulation. Then she dragged him over to the couch and lashed his feet to one of the sturdy wooden legs with more tape. He stirred and moaned.

For extra insurance, Gianna went to the closet and pulled out several weighty items, including Greg's golf clubs, and set them on the couch in case Riggs tried to crawl away.

She sat in one of the upholstered chairs, laying the gun across her lap. "All right, Mr. Riggs, *now* you and I will discuss business." She pushed some buttons on her phone and opened a program. "So there's no misunderstanding, I am recording this conversation."

Riggs didn't say anything. He bathed her with a hateful glare. Sweat beaded his forehead.

"All right," Gianna said, "You mentioned my boyfriend would be dead soon, and his daughter would be on her way back to California. No one—not even me—knows where they are. Care to explain?"

Riggs let off a stream of profanity. Gianna pointed the gun at his knee, and his eyes glittered black.

"You think I won't?"

He swallowed. "Do you know how easy I can put a tracker on someone's vehicle?"

Gianna crossed her arms. "You're not doing a very good job of tracking them if you're lying on my floor, tied up."

Riggs sneered at her. "Hey, I stick the tracker on and collect my fee. I don't know what happens after."

Oh God, who else could be after them?

She concentrated on keeping her voice calm and casual. "Who hired you?"

Riggs called her a vile name. Gianna stood and kicked him in the ribs. Riggs screamed with pain.

She sat again and waited, calm covering her, even though her heart still hammered. "I'll ask you again, who hired you?"

Riggs swore. "You're so stupid. Your husband brought Hennessey here for the resort project. Mr. Clean from California," he sneered. "We knew his old lady was in prison for killing his kid, so we kept tabs on her in case she might come in handy. Everything would have been fine if Harper hadn't screwed up with Dole."

Dole. Gianna's heart thundered. Here was further evidence of the connection.

Riggs's eyes glazed over with hatred. "Dole was the last holdout. All Harper had to do was get Dole to sign on the dotted line. He went to his cabin that night. But Dole fought back. Harper shoved him and the old man hit his head on the fireplace and died."

Gianna's terror grew with every syllable coming out of Riggs's mouth. *Greg killed a man.* "Tell me what happened to Greg."

Riggs glared at her and clamped his lips together.

Gianna lifted the gun and cocked it. "I can shoot you in the knee, or somewhere else. Your choice."

Riggs closed his eyes. "Harper called me in a panic. He was such a wuss. He never wanted to do any of the dirty work. We tossed Dole's cabin, and I kicked in the front door to fake a robbery. We found over forty thousand in cash under his mattress and in boxes under his bed. Harper wanted to split the money, but I didn't."

Gianna stared at him. "Then what?"

Riggs seemed to forget he was being recorded, or perhaps he no longer cared. "I knocked him out, put him in his car, and drove to the top of the hill. I poured some of Dole's whiskey on him and put it in neutral. I didn't want to leave him at Dole's cabin so he could be traced back to Bellmont and me."

Gianna had all she needed on tape to put Riggs away and implicate Bellmont. She was also sure Riggs would make a deal to give up Bellmont. They were both history.

The unanswered question was, who was after Brock and Piper? Gianna stood and towered over Riggs with the gun. "Who's after Brock?"

"His old lady and her brother. Our contact in California was lazy and didn't know she'd been released. I was notified yesterday and offered to help them track down Mr. Clean." He bared his ugly teeth. "For a fee."

Gianna wanted to shoot Riggs right there and then. Instead, she tore off a length of duct tape and covered his mouth, adding two additional pieces for security. His empty, evil eyes didn't move her one bit. Then she checked his binds, grabbed her phone and turned off the recording program.

Without a backwards glance, Gianna grabbed a box of ammunition and marched out of the room, still carrying the gun. She slammed the door closed and phoned the sheriff.

After she identified herself to the dispatcher, she issued terse instructions. "Tell Sheriff Tinsley Mort Riggs is tied up in my late husband's office here at my home. The front door code is 25451. I have him on tape saying Greg killed Stanley Dole, and Riggs killed Greg. Plus, I have documents, a laptop, and proof of other crimes implicating Carson Bellmont."

"Where are you right now, Mrs. Harper? Are you safe?" the dispatcher asked.

Gianna ignored the question. "I'll come into town later to make a statement." She disconnected the call.

Then she ran into the kitchen and grabbed Sammy's crate, a bottle of water, a plastic bowl, and some food. She strode out on the deck where she saw Paisley through the window of her playhouse and sagged with relief. She thanked God for keeping her daughter there.

"Paisley," she shouted. "Come quickly. We need to go." The girl ran up to the deck, Sammy trailing behind her. "Put Sammy in her crate." Gianna grabbed Paisley's hands and looked her square in the eye. "Paisley, I need you to do everything exactly as I tell you."

Paisley nodded solemnly. "Where are we going, Momma?"

"To save our family."

CHAPTER 25

Brock would never forget the look in Gianna's beautiful eyes when she laid her wedding rings in his palm. He had almost professed his love for her and wanted to kiss her more than he wanted his next breath. But in his heart, he knew the timing was wrong. Holding her had to be enough, for now. Their first kiss would happen in the right place, at the right time.

But had she ever felt incredible in his arms.

Brock clenched his jaw and pressed his foot as the winding road gained altitude. Piper had almost cried herself out, but she was still sniffling.

"D-daddy, Paisley is my sister. I want Mrs. Harper to be my mom, and Paisley wants you to be her dad. We want us to be a family."

He checked his rearview mirror for the thousandth time, and her blotchy, red face caused a dull ache in his chest. "I know, Pipe," he said quietly. "I want us to be a family too, more than anything in the world."

"Then why did we have to l-leeeeeave?" she wailed.

Brock bit back his frustration. "I need to—clear something up. And then I hope we can go back. Please, Piper, don't cry." What Brock needed to do now was take her to a secluded, safe place. Then he would call Tack and lay out the whole story and see what their legal avenues were to keep Piper's mother away from her.

And if there were no legal options, Brock would keep driving north into Canada. He had passports for both him and Piper now. He'd already decided on this course of action, even if he had to delay pursuing a relationship with Gianna—for the short-term, or, God help him, longer. His priority was keeping Piper safe, away from Cass. Brock had already lost one child. He wouldn't lose another.

Brock looked out both windows. The scenery was breathtaking, and under different circumstances, he'd appreciate it. He looked at the directions he'd scribbled on a card during his last phone conversation with Tack less than two hours ago when he left Canadian Meadows. He'd come here with them before, but he wasn't driving and hadn't been paying attention. Soon, he spied the landmark he was looking for. The turnoff should be in about another three miles.

"Are we almost there?" Piper asked. "I have to go to the bathroom, but I don't want to go in the woods."

Brock couldn't help but smile. "No worries, little one. We'll be there soon."

He found the turnoff and drove almost another mile before seeing the dirt drive, which was well hidden. This gave him a small measure of relief. He drove for another half mile through trees before coming into a small clearing. The cabin was weathered but well-constructed. Nothing on the exterior attracted attention, another good sign. Tack had assured him they would be safe here.

He pulled the truck up the driveway, parked, and helped Piper out. An overwhelming rush of love for his little daughter washed over him, and he knelt in front of her. "Hey, kiddo," he whispered, and wrapped his arms around her. He buried his nose in her hair and inhaled. "I love you, Piper Lee. Even if it's only you and me, we're gonna be OK, I promise. God has always taken care of us, and he won't stop now."

She pulled back, wiped her eyes, and nodded.

Brock held her hand as they walked up the wooden planks terraced into the steep incline to the front porch running the entire width of the front of the cabin. Brock found the hidden box with the keypad per Tack's instructions and entered the code. He stepped to the door and depressed the latch.

If the outside of the cabin was unremarkable, the inside was the opposite.

"Wow," Piper breathed.

Brock smiled. Yes, the interior of the cabin was beautiful, all rock and cedar, small but expertly constructed. A lot of tender loving care had gone into it. A stone fireplace and a galley kitchen sat to one side. Two doors on one wall led to bedrooms with another in between to the bathroom. An exterior door to the back had a chain and a lock on the knob but no keypad.

Piper had already found the bathroom and come out. She opened the door to one bedroom, then the other.

"Which one do you want?" Brock asked.

She looked uncharacteristically uncertain. "I want to sleep with you."

"You choose our room and I'll bring our things in."

When he came back in with their bags, Piper was in the bedroom on the left with a pretty blue and yellow quilt and curtains Tack told him Barb had made.

Brock and Piper worked together to unpack and organize. Then he brought in a box of kitchen items, food, and a cooler, which he put away in the small kitchen.

It was early evening, and Piper wanted to watch a movie on the little DVD player Paisley had left at the house, since they didn't have a computer. Gianna wouldn't mind he had borrowed the player. Piper went into the bedroom, lay on the bed, and put on her headphones. Brock closed the door.

The air in the cabin was cool but not cold. The temperature would fall when night arrived, so Brock built a fire. He was thinking about what to feed Piper for dinner when he saw a movement outside the back-door window. The hairs on the back of his neck stood straight up. Brock looked out, and his worst nightmare came to life.

Cass and her brother, Leo, were climbing out of a battered sedan.

Dear God, how did they find us here? His pulse thundered in his ears. He dashed to the bedroom door, opened it, pushed in the round knob to engage the lock, and pulled it shut, all within about a second. Hopefully, Piper was into her movie and didn't see or hear anything. *God, make her eyes not see and her ears not hear.*

Brock sent a stream of prayers to God for protection. He planted himself within easy reach of the bedroom door, just to the side. If they made any attempt to gain entry, they would have to come through him.

The back doorknob rattled, and even though the door was locked and the chain engaged, neither would hold. With a loud crash, the door shuddered, and the flimsy chain held for a second until a foot finished the job. Cass burst into the room, followed by her brother, who held a pistol.

"Where's my daughter?" she spat, without preamble.

Cass was petite like Piper and rail thin. Her strawberry blonde hair was dull and matted. Dark circles surrounded her eyes. She was either drunk, high, or both. Brock had no doubt he could subdue her.

Leo stood behind her, dirty and unkempt. Brock had a good six inches and fifty pounds on him on a good day, and this was not a good day for Leo. He was a crackhead and more emaciated than Brock had ever seen him.

But he had a gun. Brock scanned the room, trying to compute how he could disarm Leo. If he could obtain the weapon, he would shoot clean through both of them to protect Piper.

"I want my daughter," Cass said.

"You gave up your parent card when you killed your son and nearly killed your daughter." Brock bit the words out.

Cass pouted. "Everyone deserves a second chance," she whined.

Brock's heart turned to stone. Ignoring Leo, he walked right to her, towering over her. "What about TJ's second chance?" he roared. He wanted to slap her but fisted his hands at his side.

She stepped back. "But I promise I'll be a good mother to Piper," she pleaded. She was pathetic. "You know I always loved Piper. She was perfect."

Brock's insides churned. Yes, Cass adored Piper but hadn't connected with their son. Cass also had a short fuse and didn't have much use for either child if they cried or fussed. He glanced at Leo again, wondering if he should take his chances and charge him.

"Piper Lee?" Cass called. "Mommy's here." Bile rose in Brock's throat. Her eyes darted around. Thank God Piper was wearing her headphones. *Please, God, don't let her hear anything.*

Brock caught a movement over Cass and Leo's shoulders. He couldn't believe his eyes. The front door opened to reveal Gianna, feet planted apart, holding a shotgun.

Cass's empty eyes spewed vitriol at Brock. "I am leaving here with my daughter."

"Over my dead body," Gianna announced in the clearest, coldest voice Brock had ever heard. Leo and Cass whirled around to face her.

Brock's blood turned to ice in his veins. Leo now pointed his gun at Gianna. Her weapon trumped his, but his eyes were glazed, and Brock didn't trust his mental stability for one second. Could he make a grab for Leo's gun? What if Cass threw herself at him? What if the gun went off? *God, make a way. Bring us through in one piece.*

Paisley's voice came from behind Gianna. "Get him, Sammy," she shouted. The little dog tore into the room, barking furiously, and went straight for Leo, who screamed. His hands flew up, and the gun clattered to the floor. Brock picked up the pistol and covered Cass, while Gianna came into the room and aimed at Leo, bracing the shotgun on her hip. She stormed over to Cass, grabbed her by the arm, and threw her on the couch. Brock pushed Leo next to her.

Cass and Leo screamed, and Sammy still barked and growled ferociously. Gianna shouted over her shoulder, "Paisley, throw the duct tape in here. Stay on the porch."

Cass stood and found the business end of the shotgun stuck in her stomach. "You want to try?" Gianna said with a lift of her eyebrow. "I will happily shoot you dead." Cass received the message. She sat and broke into dramatic wails.

The roll of duct tape sailed into the room and across the floor. Brock made short work of binding both Leo's and Cass's hands together behind their backs. Then he bound their feet together individually and then to one another. He kicked Leo's gun away. "Should I tape their mouths too?"

Gianna rolled her eyes. "Yes, please." She still held the shotgun on them. She looked at the little dog. "Sammy, stop."

Paisley called out, "Come, Sammy. Good girl."

Brock finished taping and grabbed the blanket off the back of the couch, then covered the pair. He didn't want to look at their ugly faces for one more second. He ran to the door and opened his arms to Paisley, who hugged him fiercely.

Brock pulled back and searched her eyes for signs of trauma. After all, her mother was holding a gun. "Are you OK, honey?"

Paisley nodded and grinned. "Isn't my mom awesome?"

Brock threw back his head and laughed. "She sure is." He grabbed Paisley's hand and walked to the door of the bedroom where Piper was and pounded on it. "Open up, Piper."

A second later, her face appeared in the opening, and Brock made sure to block the crack as much as he could with his body. Piper looked at him with confusion. "What's going on?"

Brock couldn't believe she hadn't heard a thing, and his heart swelled with thankfulness. The God who shut the lions' mouths and stood with the three Hebrew men in the fiery furnace had shielded his daughter from harm.

"Paisley," Piper cried. The two fell into one another's arms.

"Girls, stay in the bedroom and lock the door," Brock said. Sammy scooted into the room and they closed the door.

He turned back to Gianna. She looked like a fierce lioness and was unbelievably beautiful.

Brock could barely draw a breath. *This is what it feels like to be in love.* He wanted to tell her so much and to ask so many questions, but now was not the time. He ran a hand through his hair. "Now what? I don't think either of us have cell service here." He supposed Gianna could go for help and take the girls with her.

He couldn't believe how cool and calm she was. "I called Tack before I left home. He should be here any minute. He also contacted the local sheriff."

Brock was about to haul Gianna into his arms and kiss her senseless, when Tack, Barb, and Lark burst through the open front door. Tack was holding a shotgun too.

They took in the scene, and Tack took Gianna's gun so Barb and Lark could lavish hugs on her. Brock brought them up to speed on what had occurred at the cabin. "I called the sheriff right before we lost service," Tack said. "They won't be far behind."

Tack stood sentinel even though Cass and Leo were immobilized. Barb glanced at the shrouded pair on the couch and took Gianna's arm. "Let's go out on the porch."

"If it's all the same to you, I'm not letting Gianna out of my sight," Brock said. In two strides, she was in his arms, where she belonged. For now, holding her was enough.

Barb gave him a watery smile. "Of course," she said. She looked around. "Where are the girls?"

"In the blue and yellow bedroom," Brock replied. "I told them to stay in there. I don't want them out here until those two—" he tilted his head at the couch, "are away from here."

"I'll go stay with them," Lark said. She crossed to the door, knocked, identified herself, then slipped in.

Brock continued to hold Gianna and would have been content to stay there, but soon three sheriff's deputies came through the door. They took statements from Brock, then Gianna, and left with their prisoners, taking Leo's vehicle with them. Brock turned his and Gianna's backs to them as they passed and hoped with all his heart he would never lay eyes on the two of them again.

Gianna's shoulders sagged. She almost sat on the couch, then grimaced. "No, I can't," she murmured. Brock took her hand and knocked on the bedroom door. "Hey, open up. We're all clear." Lark answered, and he and Gianna entered. The girls huddled on the bed.

Brock reached for Piper. "It's over. We don't need to run anymore." He put his arms around her and kissed her head. "I'll explain later."

Paisley rose and joined her mother in the doorway.

"Can we go home to Canadian Meadows?" Piper asked, her eyes wide with hope.

"Yes," Brock answered.

"And live happily ever after?" Piper said.

"I sure hope so," Brock said, looking at Gianna. He pulled Piper off the bed. "Come on, let's go."

The four of them went back into the living room, where the Garritsens waited. Barb stood in front of the open refrigerator. "Is anyone hungry?" she asked. "I could put something together." Dear Barb, always caring for everyone around her.

Brock exchanged a look with Gianna. "I don't think we could eat a thing right now, Barb, but thanks. There's fruit and crackers in the truck." He wanted to take his family home, not to the Harper's house, but to the A-frame, where he and Gianna had shared several meals, sat in front of the fireplace, and gazed at the stars on the deck. Where they'd already made memories.

Barb and Lark gathered the cushions from the couch. "I'll take these to the cleaners," Barb muttered. Lark and the girls helped her pack some other items she wanted to take back to Canadian Meadows. Brock went into the bedroom and scooped up his and Piper's things, and he and Tack took everything out to the vehicles.

When they turned back toward the cabin, the girls, Sammy, and Lark sat on the front porch. Barb and Gianna stood in the doorway, arm-in-arm. Tack motioned to them to come to the vehicles, out of the girls' hearing, and slung his arm over Gianna's shoulder, towering over her. "According to Sheriff Tinsley, they found Mort Riggs bound and tied up in the office at your house."

Brock's chin almost hit the ground.

Gianna colored slightly. "Yes." She held up her phone. "I have him on tape confessing to Greg's murder, and implicating Greg in Stanley Dole's murder."

What? Brock's mind reeled.

She looked at him. "Cass and her brother paid Riggs to put a tracker on your truck. He said they were planning to kill you and take Piper back to California. That's all on here too."

Brock looked at Tack, his heart soaring. "They'll charge them with attempted murder and kidnapping."

Tack held his hand out for the phone. "How about I take this to the sheriff?

Something else occurred to Brock. "How did Sheriff Tinsley know about Riggs being at your house?" he asked Gianna.

"I called and told him to come and pick Riggs up." she said calmly.

Brock, Barb, and Tack all grinned at one another.

Tack shook his head. "I can tell you something, little lady, I always want you in my corner." He kissed the top of Gianna's head, looked at Brock and smiled, "I'd tell you to take care of her, but I think she's already proven herself."

Brock stared at Gianna. "I'm hoping we can take care of each other."

Tack grinned. "Sounds like a good plan." He stepped to Brock, grabbed his hand and pulled him into a quick hug. "I'm looking forward to having you as a permanent fixture in Canadian Meadows." He exchanged a glance with Barb. "I think my wife has big plans for you."

Barb laughed and squeezed Tack's arm. Then she hugged Brock. "I'm so thankful everything turned out well. I was praying up a storm the whole way here."

"Thanks, Barb." Brock was so grateful for this family. "I—I can't tell you how much I appreciate everything you've done for Piper and me. I treasure your friendship." His throat closed up.

"Where are your car keys, Gianna?" Tack asked.

She looked a little startled, reached in her jeans pocket and held them up. Tack nodded toward the porch. "Lark can drive your car home, if you want to ride with Brock and the girls."

Gianna handed the keys over. "Definitely," she said.

"Where should we drop it?" Barb asked.

Brock spoke. "The A-frame on Lake Helena Road." He looked at Gianna.

"*Most* definitely." This time, her full, soft lips turned up in a smile full of promise.

"Come on, girls, let's go home," Brock called to them. They ran down the porch steps and a flurry of hugs ensued before the Garritsens returned to the cabin to secure everything.

Once Piper and Paisley settled into the backseat, Brock paused before opening Gianna's door. He turned his back to the girls, leaned in close and lowered his voice so the words would stay between them. "Before we leave, I need to say something. You, standing in the doorway, holding the shotgun, is the sexiest thing I've ever seen in my life. And we're going to have a talk about that sometime."

Gianna licked her lips and went a little pink, and Brock almost groaned out loud. She rested one hand on his chest, where Brock swore his skin burned. With her other hand, she touched the brim of his Stetson. "We can also talk about how sexy you look in this hat," she said with a teasing grin.

Once they left the twisting roads out for the highway, Brock leaned over and took her hand. She laced her fingers with his, and his pulse skittered. He drew her hand to his lips and kissed it.

Gianna leaned back and closed her eyes. but he had to concentrate to keep his gaze on the road. As he drove, a plan formed in his mind, but he needed some assurance. Brock didn't want to run ahead of God's timing. *Give me a sign, Lord?* He was familiar with the Biblical concept of laying out a fleece and asking God for confirmation.

He glanced over at Gianna. "OK if we make a quick stop on the way home?"

She squeezed his hand and turned her lavender-blue gaze on him. "I'll go anywhere with you, Brock." His chest swelled.

The girls chattered in the backseat and ate their fruit and crackers. When they pulled off the highway, Paisley looked out the window. "We're at Sapphire Falls." She and Piper cheered.

The parking area was empty. They exited the truck and began the short hike to the falls. The sunset painted the sky with a wash of oranges, pinks, and purples. The girls skipped ahead, while Brock and Gianna followed, hand-in-hand.

When they topped the rise and stepped onto the plateau, Brock held his breath before he looked up.

The girls squealed. "Look, the falls are blue." They bounded over to the pools.

The display was gorgeous, even magical. Brock's heart pounded.

This was God's sign.

Gianna stepped close to Brock, and he put his arms around her. Neither one of them spoke. It was as if they were on holy ground.

"Daddy, come look," Piper called out.

"The water is even prettier close up, Momma," Paisley shouted.

Gianna stepped away and turned when Brock didn't follow. "Are you OK?"

He fought for composure and nodded. "I need a minute. You go on."

She frowned slightly. "You sure?"

Peace settled on his shoulders, and he gave her a gentle smile. "I'm sure. I'll be right there."

She turned and jogged over to the girls. Brock stood rooted to the spot and stared, loving the way she moved. The girls met her and held out their hands, and she grabbed on to each of them, running the rest of the way with them, her lyrical laughter mixing with theirs on the breeze. They walked the length of the stream, looking at the falls, pointing and exclaiming.

And then on the wind, Brock heard a voice.

There she is.

Brock tingled. God spoke to him, answering a prayer Brock had never even prayed. There she was—the mother of his child. Not the one who gave birth to Piper but the one who would carry out the sacred role every moment for the rest of her days. The one who was willing to defend his daughter's life with her own.

The one who loved Piper as much as Brock did.

Gianna stood between the girls, her arms wrapped around them. "Come and look, Brock," she called.

He blinked away tears, then lifted his praise to God as he trotted toward them. *Oh, Lord,* his heart sang with gratitude, *this is my family, the one you've given me to cherish forever. Thank you for letting everything unfold in your perfect time.* He wanted to gather them into his arms and pray but didn't think his voice would hold up, his heart was so full. When they were back at the A-frame, he would kneel with his family and close the day with prayer, the way he hoped they would for thousands of nights to come.

He slowed as he approached them, where they stood together in a little half circle. "I...I have something to say." Ignoring their quizzical expressions, Brock lowered himself to one knee. Their faces took on looks of anticipation. Piper bounced on her toes. Paisley clasped her hands together as if in prayer. Gianna's eyes shone.

Brock looked at each of them, and rested his gaze on Paisley. He reached out and took her hand in both of his.

"Paisley Laura, you are a beautiful young lady, inside and out. Any man would be proud to have you for his daughter." Paisley's eyes widened, and when Brock glanced over at Piper, her mouth hung open. He couldn't hold back a smile. "I love you, Paisley. Would you please be my daughter?"

Paisley couldn't speak. She wrapped her arms around his neck and nodded.

Brock ran a hand over her shiny brown curls and gave her a gentle smile. "I'll adopt you, you'll call me Dad, and your name will be Hennessey." The sweet girl was so overcome with emotion, all she could do was nod.

Piper looked at Gianna. "Does this mean you'll be my mom?" Her voice squeaked at the end.

Gianna drew Piper into her arms and kissed the top of her head. "I would love to be your mom."

Brock stood, and Piper threw her arms around him in a fierce hug. "I didn't know you could be so amazing, Daddy. But you're not finished yet," she scolded, flipping her gaze toward Gianna.

Brock looked at Paisley. "Would you please help quiet your sister?"

Paisley grinned. "Sure, Dad." A bubble of joy burst in his chest. He would always remember this moment, the first time in her life Paisley called anyone *Dad*. She walked over and stood behind Piper, looped her arms over her shoulders, and Piper reached up and latched onto her hands.

Brock took a deep breath and stepped closer to Gianna until the toes of his boots nudged against hers. He reached for her hands. For all her bravery, her fingers were cold now. Brock cradled them in both of his and rubbed warmth into them.

Droplets of sapphire lights bounced off Gianna's raven hair, and she'd never been more beautiful. She stared into his eyes. "If you didn't already own my heart, Brock David Hennessey, proposing to my daughter would have sealed the deal." Joy dripped from every syllable.

Brock wrapped his arms around her. His smile was so wide he thought his face might split open. He took a breath and cleared his throat. "If you're going to be Piper's mom, and I'm going to be Paisley's dad, you and I should come to an agreement." He couldn't believe he was about to propose to a woman he'd never even kissed. But they would be fine. Their souls were already knit together, and the emotional connection was complete. All the kisses and everything following would be incredible.

"What did you have in mind?" Her blue-lavender eyes danced and Brock's heart about burst.

"Oh, are we playing twenty questions now?" He swallowed a laugh. His mind raced. He couldn't wait to be with Gianna alone tonight, after the girls had gone to bed. Outside on the deck. Moonlight. Starlight. Every inch of her slender, curvy body pressed against his. Long, deep kisses and whispered promises.

He lifted his hands to cradle her face. "May I bring you coffee in bed every morning for the rest of our lives?"

"Yes. May I always kiss you goodnight?"

"Yes. I love you, Gianna, and I want to build a life with you and our daughters. Will you marry me?" He should kneel again, but he couldn't bear to let her go. Later, when he had a ring, he would.

The girls jumped and squealed. He wouldn't be surprised if one of them fainted. But right now, Brock wouldn't break his gaze from Gianna's for a million dollars. The girls could take care of each other. That's what sisters did.

Gianna's eyes glistened, and she nodded. "Yes, I will marry you. I love you so much, Brock."

Brock couldn't wait one more second. He rained kisses on her wet cheeks, made his way to her mouth, pulled her close, and settled in. *Home.*

"We'll be sisters for real, Paisley."

"I know, I can't believe it. Sisters ever after."

Dramatic sigh. "Our bridesmaid dresses can be red. Red's my favorite color."

"You can't wear red. It'll clash with your hair. I look great in red. Green is your best color."

Retching sound. "I don't like green. And we can't wear Christmas colors in June."

"Who said anything about June? We haven't talked about a date yet." Now Paisley sounded like the schemer.

Gianna's lips smiled under his. Brock let up a bit but kept sipping from her sweetness. These G-rated kisses were OK. And one of the best things he could do for his children was to show them how much he loved their mother.

"June will be perfect." He knew Piper's calculating tone.

"We can wait till Christmas." Paisley wasn't giving an inch.

Piper stomped her foot. "Maybe you and I can wait, but I don't think they can."

Brock and Gianna collapsed in fits of laughter. He was long overdue to have *the talk* with his daughter. He was relieved Gianna would be there to help.

He took a step back and lifted his arms. "Bring it in, girls."

They stood in front of him and Gianna, encased in their arms, staring at the fading blue lights of the falls. The four of them, a real family.

Brock turned the girls around and looked between them. "Someday, you'll both be married and plan your own weddings."

"Blech, not me," Piper mumbled.

"And I will love walking you down the aisle. But this wedding is your mother's and mine. We'll include you in some of the decisions, but we'll have the final say." He grinned. "Understand?"

Paisley nodded. "Yes, Dad." Brock grinned.

"Whatever," Piper said in a sing-song voice.

"Piper."

The corners of her mouth lifted in a prim smile. "Yes, Daddy." She gazed at Gianna. "And Mommy."

Gianna clapped a hand on her chest. "I love being called Momma and Mommy."

Brock kissed each of the girls on the head. "Let's go home."

Once they reached the edge of the plateau, Brock and Gianna stopped and watched the girls skip and jump down the steps, hand-in-hand. Their laughter floated into the night air, and when they reached the bottom, they stopped, faced one another, and launched into their sister dance. Their joyous faces glowed in the waning light.

Brock leaned his head against Gianna's. "Our daughters," he whispered.

She lavished him with a blissful smile. "Yes, our daughters."

Brock turned her in his arms and pulled her flush against him. She was an absolute perfect fit. He treated himself to one long, deep kiss.

When they drew apart, he gazed into her eyes. No more twenty questions, for now. He had the answers. He cradled her face in his hands, as if she were the most precious thing in the world to him. Because she was.

"You're the woman I delight in, the one whose soul sings with mine."

"You're the man God gave me at exactly the right time. I love you, Brock."

"I love you, Gianna." He kissed her again. "Short engagement?"

"Yes. Long honeymoon?"

He threw back his head and laughed. "Definitely yes."

Piper's voice rang out. "Hey, Mommy and Daddy, could we move along here?"

"You're so impatient, Piper." Paisley's voice was tinged with annoyance.

"But I'm ready to start our new life as a family."

Brock took Gianna's hand and together, they took the first step. "So are we."

Epilogue

New Year's Eve

Gianna smiled and squeezed Brock's hand as the technician, who had introduced herself as Patti, lifted the ultrasound probe and wiped the surface with a towel.

Patti looked at them. "I have everything I need. To confirm, you don't want to know the gender now?"

Brock nodded. "If you could write the answer and put the slip in an envelope, we'll share the news with our daughters tonight."

"Sure thing." Patti smiled and turned off the machine. "You can get dressed now, Mrs. Hennessey."

Gianna's chest still fluttered when someone called her Mrs. Hennessey.

Brock helped her sit up.

Before Patti opened the door, she turned and looked at both of them. "I wanted to ask, do you own Hennessey Homes, by chance?"

Gianna smiled. "My amazing husband does. The company was his brainchild."

Brock looked a little sheepish. He never enjoyed the limelight.

Patti's eyes sparkled. "My nephew recently received a grant to move into one of your tiny houses." She swallowed.

"He's a veteran and has had some rough times, but this has made a difference." She stepped forward and gripped Brock's hand. "He never thought he would own a home. You've given him a piece of the American dream. Thank you so much."

Brock glanced at Gianna, and his Adam's apple bobbed. "You're welcome, Patti. I'm happy for your nephew."

The woman left the room.

Gianna opened her arms, and Brock embraced her. "See?" she said. "God is blessing your business."

"He is," Brock agreed. "Todd Kingston's coming on board part time. Things are taking off."

"I'm so proud of you," Gianna whispered. Emotion clogged her throat. "You've earned a good reputation and are already part of the community in a way Greg never was in eight years. I'm so thankful to be your wife."

Brock gave her a quick kiss. "And I'm thankful to be your husband. I'll wait for you outside."

As she dressed, Gianna thanked God for bringing Brock into her life at the perfect time. Their marriage was a true partnership. Brock was her best friend and soulmate, and their life was filled with love and centered on their family. He took Paisley on a date night twice a month, and Gianna had a mother/daughter night with Piper. After their wedding, they'd spent the first four months in the cozy A-frame, then moved into the house on Autumn Hill—the only one of Greg's properties they'd kept. After the estate settled and the property management business was dissolved, Gianna and Brock were able to buy the home outright.

Once they were in the car, Brock pulled Gianna into his arms and kissed her passionately.

"Mmm ... what did I do to deserve such a delicious kiss?"

"Nothing. I adore you." His eyes sparkled. He laid a

gentle hand on her abdomen. "You're OK with everything now?"

"Yes," she said, placing her hand on his. She stared into his eyes. "I would love to give you a son," she whispered.

Brock leaned in and kissed her again, softly. "Whatever God gives us, girl or boy, is fine as long as the baby is healthy." He leaned his forehead against hers, and she nodded.

The new addition would arrive right after their first wedding anniversary. The pregnancy had come sooner than they'd expected, and at first, Gianna had mixed emotions. She and Brock were still getting to know one another, and she cherished their private moments. She feared the demands of a newborn would encroach on their time.

Brock, however, had been ecstatic. "You know, the minute the baby is born, Paisley and Piper will swoop in and raise it," he joked. "You and I will still have plenty of time together."

Brock and Gianna drove home and made their final preparations for New Year's Eve. Tack and Barb had invited them to come over tonight to play games, and, of course, eat. At Brock's request, Barb agreed to make her special enchiladas.

According to Barb, she and Tack wouldn't have any grandchildren of their own anytime soon, so Brock and Gianna had appointed them honorary grandparents of Paisley, Piper, and the new baby. They wanted to open the envelope with the girls before they left and then share the happy news with their dear friends who had become family.

The time had come. They gathered in the living room, Brock and Gianna on the couch, the girls on the carpet at their feet.

Brock lavished Gianna with a loving smile and held up the envelope. "Since Mom is the one doing all the work, I think she should be the first one to see the news." The girls held hands and nodded, their faces etched with anticipation.

Gianna took a breath and reached for the envelope. Her heart skittered in her chest. Whatever was inside would change their family's life forever. She opened the sealed flap, drew out and unfolded the slip, and held it up for each of them to see.

Girl.

Paisley and Piper leapt up and screamed and jumped, holding onto one another. Brock leaned over and kissed Gianna tenderly. "I hope she has your gorgeous eyes."

Gianna's heart thrummed with joy. They were having a daughter. They had made a deal with the girls. She and Brock would select the first name and let the girls choose the middle. They had all agreed the initials *P.L.* would be a wonderful tradition to continue, linking the three children together.

Piper waved her hands around. "OK, Mom and Dad, we have the perfect name," she said.

Paisley nodded. "It's so amazing, you're gonna love it."

"You mean the perfect middle name," Brock said. He squeezed Gianna's hand, and they exchanged glances. "We've kind of settled on a first name."

Piper shook her head. Her long braids swung with each shake. "No, trust us, you're gonna love this." She looked at her sister and held out her arms in a dramatic pose. "Hit it, Pase."

Paisley took a deep breath. "Pippa." she announced with a flourish.

"*P-i-p* for me," Piper said.

"And *p-a* for me," Paisley concluded. They grabbed onto one another's hands and grinned. "Well?" Their brown eyes glimmered with hope.

Brock stared at Gianna and neither of them said anything for a few seconds. "Pippa," Brock said. He gazed at her, and she knew what he was thinking.

"Pippa." Gianna smiled.

"Perfect," they said in unison.

The girls broke into their sister dance.

Brock helped Gianna to her feet, and they joined in, laughing and clapping. They finished with a group high-five and jubilant shout. "Sisters ever after!"

Author's Note

I hope you enjoyed *Sisters Ever After*. This story has a special place in my heart. The premise is autobiographical, but from there, it's completely fictional.

I am Piper, the little, short redhead.

Paisley and Piper, 1964   Piper and Paisley, 2019

"Paisley" and I met when we were tots. Her widowed dad was my father's work colleague and best friend. My dad died suddenly when I was nine and she was ten, and at some later point, we decided our parents needed to marry so we could be sisters.

They were *nothing* like Brock and Gianna, and we've had a good laugh over that. By the time we became young teens, we realized they weren't a good romantic match and gave up our clumsy efforts to throw them together. They remained good friends but neither one ever married again.

I'm not sure why I reversed the roles and wrote Piper with a dad and Paisley with a mom. Honestly, as the story poured out, it simply happened. I wonder if my heart wanted to experience a relationship with a dad.

Even though our parents never married, we're still sisters of the heart.

P.S. Sammy the dog is real.

About the Author

Erin S. Quint has been writing fiction for almost a decade and is an active member of ACFW (American Christian Fiction Writers). She has published seven books in various formats, one of which was an ACFW 2021 Carol Award finalist. She has four children and four grandchildren and is recently retired, traveling the country with her dog in a camper, looking for inspiration for her next books.

Sign up for Erin's newsletter and learn about all her books at www.esqwrites.com

If you enjoyed this book, please leave a review on Amazon, Goodreads, Barnes & Noble, and Bookbub.

Coming in 2024

Book 2 of the Canadian Meadows Series

In From the Storm.

Vanessa Kingston is engaged to the son of the likely next president of the United States. Her life is about to change in ways she never imagined, and preparing for her upcoming fairytale wedding is a welcome distraction, leaving little time to reflect on her first love and past mistake. Then, one phone call uncovers the secret Vanessa thought she had completely hidden, one that threatens to destroy all her future hopes and dreams.

Since a shattering betrayal from his wife several years ago, Ben Garritsen has been alone. His longtime career is deeply fulfilling, but otherwise his life is empty. He has never forgotten the woman who first held his heart. Now, a life-threatening situation brings the past to light, and Ben is once again betrayed and faced with more pain and heartache that can never be undone.

When Ben and Vanessa meet and the truth is revealed, old and new hurts surface, but they must put aside the past and work together for a greater purpose. Against all odds, they find themselves at a place of healing, but another crisis destroys any hope for reconciliation. Will they ever find their way back to the love they lost, but both desperately want?

Set against the stunning backdrop of northwestern Montana, *In From the Storm* is the second book in the Canadian Meadows series, a tale of lost love, lost hope, and the healing grace of forgiveness.